AFTER DEATH

JACQUELINE E SMITH

Wind Trail Publishing

After Death

Wind Trail Publishing
PO Box 830851
Richardson, TX 75083-0851
www.WindTrailPublishing.com

First Paperback Edition, October 2015

ISBN-13: 978-0-9896734-6-4
ISBN-10: 0989673464

Library of Congress Cataloguing-in-Publication Data
Smith, Jacqueline E.
After Death / Jacqueline E. Smith
Library of Congress Control Number: 2015950632

Cover Design by Wind Trail Publishing

Printed in the United States of America.

For the dreamers and the entertainers. Also for my friends. Hannah, Jessica, Kat, Rachel, I don't know where I'd be or what I'd do without you.

Chapter 1

In the five months that Michael Sinclair had been dating Kate Avery, he'd learned a lot about women.

For one thing, there actually were shoes that did not go with certain outfits. For another, women went to the bathroom in groups, not by chance, but to talk. They loved dessert, especially cake, and preferred sweat pants to just about everything. They were also really into men with good dental hygiene.

"Trust me, nice teeth are important," Kate had told him. "If a guy has bad teeth, I'm not going to stick around long enough to find out if he has a good personality. Bad teeth will automatically disqualify you from the dating game."

Michael had found that particularly interesting. Having ghosts frequently hanging around and crashing their dates didn't bother her at all, but a few weeks without flossing? Apparently that was a deal-breaker.

He'd also learned that in the world of women, nothing was simple. Everything was open to interpretation. How, he wasn't sure. But apparently, a simple text message like **Yes** or **OK** could mean anything from "You're the most wonderful person in the world and I have no idea what I did to deserve you" to "I'm really mad and I'm going to break up with you."

1

And Michael had always thought that seeing ghosts was stressful. Those wandering spirits were nothing compared to whatever women had going through their heads at all odd hours of the day. That was why, when Kate had asked him if he wanted to go grocery shopping with her that Saturday morning, he'd prepared himself for long hours of self-doubt and anxious deliberation.

Normally, he knew, she wouldn't have asked him, but her grandparents were in town for the weekend. Her parents were hosting a small family get-together and Kate had volunteered to make dessert. She also wanted to take the night as an opportunity to formally introduce Michael as her boyfriend. That meant everything had to be perfect.

The good news was that Kate's father, Rex Avery, seemed to like him pretty okay. He'd believed Kate when she told him that Michael could talk to the dead. He also understood how much they had been through together and how they'd saved each other on more than one occasion and he appreciated that.

As far as Terri Avery was concerned, however, her daughter wouldn't have needed saving had she not been with Michael in the first place. And as much as Michael hated to admit it, she kind of had a point. If Michael and Kate had never met, she never would have been exposed to a crazed woman wielding a gun in a summer field or a forlorn ghost, so desperate to find his long lost love that he possessed her and threatened worse.

On top of all of that, Michael was going into his seventh month of unemployment. He'd managed to find work through temp agencies, but it was barely enough to survive on. It was difficult nowadays for him to get interviews, because as soon as potential employers did any sort of research on him whatsoever, they always ended up finding out about the ghosts, after which, they'd assume he was either crazy or a liability. Lousy as it was, he understood. He probably wouldn't hire a guy who ran around saying that he could see ghosts if the roles were reversed. Unfortunately, they weren't, and he was the one stuck without a job.

But at least he had the ghosts to keep him company.

All joking aside, Michael had come to realize that as much as he wanted a stable job for himself and for the income it provided, he wanted it even more for Kate. She deserved to be with a guy who was gainfully employed. He knew she didn't hold his circumstances against him and that she'd still love him even if he wasn't working at all, but more than anything, he wanted to be worthy of her love. That, and he desperately wanted her parents' approval.

It was for all those reasons that he was more than willing to stand by Kate as she valiantly strove to select the appropriate frosting for her homemade cupcakes.

"Do you think I should buy the fat-free chocolate fudge? Or do you think they'd prefer the buttercream?" Kate asked Michael, examining her choices. He didn't want to bring her down, but she probably would have been better off asking him about small particles in the ozone layer, or some other obscure factoid that he knew absolutely nothing about.

"You know your family better than I do," he told her. "Which do you like better?"

"Well, you know chocolate is my favorite, but there's definitely something special about buttercream icing. I can't deny that."

"Okay. Then which one is more expensive?" Michael asked.

"The chocolate, but it's also better for you."

"That probably means it doesn't taste as good."

"But maybe I could add in some chocolate chips or sprinkles."

"Which would make the chocolate fudge more expensive and less good for you," Michael summed up.

Kate considered what he said.

"I think I'm going to get the chocolate fudge. And sprinkles."

And that was that.

~*~

3

Upon arriving home at the Riverview Apartment complex, Michael helped Kate carry her groceries up the stairs. For an outing that had originally started as a quest for cupcake ingredients, they certainly had come home with a lot of bags. Of course, Kate had also bought milk, toilet paper, microwave meals, and then there was the fruit: mangos, grapes, and broccoli stalks for the newest member of the Avery family, Marlon Brando, the Green-Cheeked Conure.

Michael had never liked birds, so he hadn't been particularly thrilled when Kate adopted the six-month-old conure from the local animal shelter. He hadn't met many conures, but at least with Marlon Brando, the feeling seemed to be mutual. The bird, ridiculous as it sounded, apparently had decided that Kate belonged to him and he didn't like sharing her affection with anyone, especially someone who never fed him.

As usual, the moment Marlon Brando saw Kate, he began doing his little welcome-home-dance, bobbing his head up and down, picking at the side of the cage with his beak, and squawking those ungodly chirps and squeals of delight that he reserved only for his human.

"Hi, baby!" Kate greeted him with just as much enthusiasm. She opened up his cage and immediately, he climbed out onto her hand and up her arm to her shoulder. "How's my pretty boy? I got you some treats! You want some mango? You love mango."

The first time Brink had ever witnessed the phenomenon of Kate conversing with her bird, he'd pointed at them and said, "You know, that's how crazy you look when you talk to invisible people in public."

Kate, of course, hadn't heard him, but as it turned out, the bird had. As soon as Marlon Brando set eyes on Brink, he went absolutely ballistic, piercing the air and everyone's ears with horrible, aggressive screeches, and trying so desperately to attack Brink that he half flew, half tumbled off of Kate's shoulder and onto the floor. The little demon bird then proceeded to charge Brink, while Michael, in what would certainly be remembered as

4

one of the lowest points of his life, fled the scene and barricaded himself in the bathroom.

Really, was it any wonder he wasn't a fan of Marlon Brando?

As though summoned by Michael's thoughts, Brink materialized inside the apartment that Kate shared with her brother, Gavin.

"Hello lovebirds, actual bird," he nodded at Marlon Brando, who was suddenly shrieking like the Grim Reaper himself had just appeared, demanding his foul, feathery soul.

"Brink?" Kate asked, upon witnessing her conure's despair.

"Yep," Michael and Brink answered together.

"Tell her I said hello," Brink said.

"He says hello," Michael had to yell to be heard above Marlon Brando's fit.

"Brink, you know I love you, but you scare my bird," Kate shouted back.

"I scare *it*? That thing tried to kill me! Again!" Brink insisted. Michael couldn't help it. He laughed.

"Are you boys making fun of my baby?" Kate asked, kneeling down in front of Marlon Brando's cage to placate the poor, paranoid conure with a small slice of mango.

"Never," Michael assured her.

"Yeah, right," she grinned at him over her shoulder. "Okay. Do you think I should make the cupcakes now so they'll be cool by the time we actually leave tonight? Or do you think I should wait until later so they'll still be warm and fresh?"

"Has either of you figured out yet that it doesn't actually matter what *you* say? She just uses you to bounce ideas off of and then does whatever the hell she wants anyway," Brink remarked.

"Um..." Michael's non-response was actually intended for Brink, but it kind of worked for Kate, too.

"You know what? I'm just going to go ahead and make them now. That way, later, when I have to shower and change and get ready, I won't be rushed," Kate said.

5

"Good thinking," Michael said. That was probably what he would have suggested too, had he actually been given time to weigh all the options.

"Would you like to help?" Kate asked, rising to her feet and wiping her hands off on her jeans. Meanwhile, Marlon Brando, who'd calmed down considerably, climbed through the open door of his cage, around the side, and up to the top. It was his favorite spot in the house, lording over all the people (living and dead) that he hated.

"Sure," Michael replied, trying not to dwell on the idea of the attack bird loose in the living room.

"Okay, if you would, dig around in the drawers until you find my measuring spoons," Kate told him. "Oh no, wait! On second thought, could you maybe rinse out a bowl?"

"Absolutely," Michael said. Two steps into the kitchen, however, and Kate threw her hands up as if to stop him from moving another muscle.

"Sorry, wait! Hold up! I actually think there's a clean bowl in the dishwasher. Let me check." And with that, she rushed passed him to the other side of the kitchen.

Brink cast Michael a sidelong glance and asked, "Having fun yet?"

Michael ignored him. He had known Kate long enough to know that when she was nervous about something, her anxiety presented itself in mile-a-minute chatter and a near whiplash-inducing case of indecisiveness.

After retrieving the clean bowl from the dishwasher, Kate clambered around the kitchen for her measuring cups, stirring spoons, and cupcake liners. Finally, she stood up, pushed the frazzled, stray hairs away from her face, and looked at Michael.

"You know, Sweetie, I love you so much, but I think it might be easier if I just do this myself. Would you mind?" she asked.

"I would not mind at all. In fact, I was just thinking the exact same thing."

"Okay, good." Kate rose up and kissed him on the cheek. "You can definitely wash the dishes after I'm done if you want, though."

"Actually, I think I'll pass on that too, but thanks," Michael teased, even though he would absolutely help her clean up if she asked. She knew it, too.

"We probably won't even have time to clean up before we have to start getting ready for dinner tonight. That's okay. I can make Gavin do it tomorrow."

"You can make Gavin do what tomorrow?" Gavin asked, emerging from his bedroom unshaven and still in his pajamas.

"Clean up the kitchen."

"Hell no you won't. You were the one who volunteered to make cupcakes. You get to clean it up," Gavin muttered, running a hand through his messy hair and turning on the coffeemaker.

"What are you doing? Get out of my kitchen," Kate ordered.

"Relax, oh crazed sister of Cuckoo Land, I'm just making coffee."

"Well, I need to make cupcakes so move."

"Kate." Gavin stood directly in front of her and grabbed her by the shoulders. "Do you remember that time when we were kids and I accidentally sat on you and knocked all the air out of your lungs? That's about to happen again, only this time, it won't be an accident."

"Fine." Kate crossed her arms. "Though you should know that you didn't actually knock the air out of my lungs. You forced my diaphragm to spasm and freeze up, thus making it very difficult for me to breathe. That's what knocking the wind out of someone actually is."

"Wow, I am so glad I know that," her brother deadpanned. As if in agreement, Marlon Brando the Conure whistled from the perch atop his cage. Gavin scowled. "That bird is stupid."

"He is not stupid! Are you, baby?" Kate asked her conure.

"It doesn't even talk! If you're going to get an annoying bird, at least get one that can learn to curse," Gavin said.

7

"But I like *him*. He's a good boy."

"He's a pest."

Michael would never admit it to Kate, but he was with Gavin on that one. His relationship with Kate had been perfect until that stupid bird came along. For the most part, it still was pretty perfect, except for when Marlon Brando was around. If Michael even so much as tried to wrap his arm around her, the little conure went off like a fire alarm, squawking and pecking at his hand.

Michael had occasionally wondered if he'd have to deal with another man seeking Kate's attention. He just never thought that man would be a bird.

"*You're* a pest. Get out of the kitchen," Kate ordered.

"Sis. Do you not see the empty coffee mug in my hand? Be patient," Gavin asked.

"I shouldn't have to be patient. I was here first."

"If you really want to play that card, then technically, *I* was here first. Like, two and a half years before you."

"We get it. You're old. Hurry up."

"Michael, does she ever treat you like this?" Gavin asked. "Bossing you around and being mean to you all the time?"

"I don't have to be mean to him because he's wonderful," Kate told him before batting her eyelashes back at Michael. He grinned sheepishly in response while both Gavin and Brink pretended to throw up.

"Ugh. Happy couples. Gross," Brink groaned. "If I had a working stomach, I'd be so nauseated right now."

"And that is my real incentive to get out of the kitchen," Gavin commented, grabbing his mug, now full of steaming hot coffee, and making his way back to his bedroom. Once he was gone, Michael looked at Kate.

"We're not *that* bad, are we?" he asked her.

Kate smiled and took his hands in hers. "Of course we're not."

"No," Brink remarked from the sidelines. "You're worse."

8

Chapter 2

After the cupcakes had been frosted to perfection, Michael returned to his own apartment so that both he and Kate could shower and prepare for the evening. As always, Kate hated seeing him leave, even if only for a few short hours, but she also needed the time alone with her thoughts. She knew that this wasn't going to be the first time she'd introduced a serious boyfriend to her family. She must have brought Trevor home on more than one occasion. The problem was she couldn't remember all those times, so this was pretty much a new experience for her.

It wasn't that she was nervous about it. She was really excited to introduce Michael to her grandparents and to give her parents the opportunity to get to know him better. True, her mom hadn't been *thrilled* when Kate had announced that she wanted to bring Michael along as her dinner date, but she also understood how much he meant to her daughter.

Okay, so maybe she was a little nervous, but more for Michael's sake than for hers. She knew how much he wanted to make a good impression and she loved him for it, but she also wanted him to enjoy the evening and be able to relax and have a good time around her family. And of course, she wanted her family to love and adore him, too. They may not have realized it, but she planned on keeping him around for a while.

When seven o'clock finally rolled around, Kate and Gavin stopped by Michael's apartment. When he opened the door, Kate felt her heart skip a beat. Michael looked so handsome, nicer than she'd ever seen him. He was wearing dark slacks the color of charcoal and a fancy button-down shirt the color of a clear night sky. He was also holding a brand new bottle of what looked to be very fancy wine.

"Wow," she smiled. "You look amazing."

Michael grinned. "So do you."

Kate blushed. She'd tried to look pretty. She was wearing a springtime skirt and a shirt the color of the sun. She'd clipped her hair up into a loose bun and she'd applied a light touch of mascara and lip gloss.

"I look amazing, too," Gavin joked.

"Yes, Gav, you're a total stud," Kate humored him. She had to admit that her brother really had tried. Of course, he was the only one in jeans, but whatever.

When they arrived at the Avery house, Terri was waiting to embrace both of her children. Michael, she simply greeted with a polite, "Hello, again."

"Good evening, Mrs. Avery," Michael replied. Then, he held out the bottle of wine and said, "I um... I brought some Cabernet."

"Oh, thank you, dear. That's very thoughtful."

Kate would have preferred a little less rigidity and a little more sincerity in her mother's tone, but at least she was trying. She had hoped that with time, Terri Avery would warm up to Michael, but it simply hadn't happened yet.

Inside, Kate introduced Michael to her grandparents, June and Jack Weir, whom she and Gavin affectionately called Mimi and Pop. As her only granddaughter, Kate had always been especially close to Mimi. If there was anyone in the world she could count on to make Michael feel right at home, it was her grandmother.

Sure enough, June gushed, "Michael! It is so wonderful to finally meet you! Kate's told me so much, it feels like I already know you."

"It's nice to meet you too, Mrs. Weir," Michael replied.

"Oh Sweetheart, you can call me Mimi. All the kids do. And this is my husband, Pop."

"Good to meet you, Son. You sure seem to make our Kate happy," Pop said. He was a tall man with intelligent eyes and a surprisingly soft and gentle voice.

"She makes me happy. That's for sure," Michael said, grinning down at Kate.

"Now is it true what she's told us about the ghosts and the spirits?" Pop asked.

"Yes, sir. It is."

"Really? Because when she was little, she certainly would make up some strange stories. Once, she was sitting all by herself in the playroom we had for them back in our old house and she would not stop talking about this giant yellow rabbit that she'd made up named Russell."

"What?" Michael laughed.

"Oh my God, I remember that dumb rabbit," Gavin groaned. "She used to draw pictures of him and run around the house telling me that if I didn't do exactly what she said, she would command Russell to sneak into my bedroom and eat me."

"That is so bizarre," Kate said. Bizarre, twisted, creepy. Any of those adjectives would have been pretty accurate. She had to admit, she didn't remember Russell or what may have compelled her to create such a fantasy.

"Yeah, we thought so too," Gavin remarked.

"I'm surprised Mom and Dad didn't ship me off to the local cathedral for an exorcism."

"They thought about it, but there was all this paperwork involved..." her brother teased.

"Well, I may have made up a weird imaginary killer rabbit, but I promise, I'm not lying about the ghosts."

"Or the fact that you saw a UFO when you were five?" Gavin laughed.

"You what?" Michael asked Kate.

"It's a family joke," Gavin explained.

11

"It's not a joke! When I was five years old, we were all driving out in the middle of nowhere and I looked out the window and hovering over this gathering of trees was a weird, shiny rectangular aircraft. It had a lot of blinking different colored lights and was shaped kind of like a box, and I'm telling you, it looked like nothing I have ever seen before," Kate said.

"That *never* happened," Gavin insisted.

"It so happened. Besides, if I'd just made it up, then don't you think I could have embellished it a little? Made the story a bit better?"

"You were five years old. You barely knew how to use the toilet. No, I don't think you could have come up with anything better."

"Whatever. It totally happened." And she absolutely knew how to use the toilet when she was five.

"How does it feel, Michael?" Gavin asked. "Knowing you're dating a girl who is certifiably insane?"

"You know, that might explain *why* she's dating me, so to tell you the truth, I'm kind of okay with it," Michael said. At that, Pop threw his head back and laughed.

"I like this kid," he told Kate, wrapping an arm around her shoulders. "Accepts you just the way you are, doesn't he? Quirks and all."

"Thank you, Pop," Kate grinned. "I like him, too."

Once the family had dispersed, Kate took Michael's hand and looked up at him.

"Well, you've won the grandparents over," she said.

"I like them, too. By the way, did they have a dog? A pug?" Michael asked.

"Yeah, his name was Buddy. Why?"

"He keeps running around and jumping up your grandpa's leg."

"You mean he's here?" she asked.

"Yeah. He's barking at your grandma right now. I don't think he realizes that he doesn't need food anymore."

"That is just like him. He was the cutest dog ever but he wasn't very bright. But oh my God, he was so sweet. He died when I was fifteen, but even in his last days, he still tried to play fetch with Pop. They'll be happy to know he's still around." She smiled. Then she said, "I'm so glad you came tonight."

"I am, too," Michael replied. But there was a slight catch in his voice, a hint of hesitancy.

"What is it?" Kate asked.

"Nothing, just... There's another one."

"Another what? A ghost?" she asked before realizing just how dumb that question was. What else would he be talking about? A banana peel?

Michael nodded. "Just outside that window," he answered, indicating the large living-room window just on the other side of her parents' piano. "She looks like she wants to come in, but she doesn't understand that she can."

"Does she look angry?"

"Not angry. Agitated. Like she has something heavy on her mind."

"I imagine death has that effect," Kate remarked. "I wonder if she's someone we know?"

"I don't think she is," Michael said, speaking in hushed tones, careful not to be overheard. "She doesn't seem to recognize any of you. She's probably just a drifter. Or maybe someone who used to live here before your family."

Even though she'd known about Michael's gift for almost eight months, there were still times she found herself overwhelmed by the idea of what he experienced on a day-to-day basis. For most people, ghost stories were a spooky escape, a glimpse into a world that they probably didn't want to imagine. To the average passerby, a ghost story was all about clinking chains and doors creaking open by themselves. It was easy to forget that the real ghost stories had little to do with that cinematic nonsense, but everything to do with the human experience: life, love, loss, faith, redemption.

13

The woman that Michael saw standing outside the window had a past. She had memories. She probably had family still living. Kate didn't even know if the woman realized she had died. Michael had explained to her that while most understood and accepted what had happened to them, some remained unaware - or perhaps in denial - for months, even years. Sterling Hall, the ghost they'd encountered the previous October, had existed in a state of willful ignorance for over a century. The idea of death, it turned out, was difficult to overcome, even after one had already died.

"Do you think you should go talk to her?" Kate asked.

"I don't want to ruin the evening," Michael said.

"You wouldn't. You'd be helping someone."

Michael stared at her with soft, dark eyes. "How is it you can always see the good in everything?"

"I can't. I just know how she feels," Kate reminded him. It was true. After all, the very first time they had met, she had been a ghost herself. She'd never forget the comfort she felt in his acknowledgement, or even simply in his presence.

"Okay," Michael finally said. "I'll go see if she's alright."

~*~

He didn't want to admit it as he stepped out onto the front porch and made his way around to the side of the house where the frantic young woman was still staring in through the window, but Michael had a bad feeling. Granted, bad feelings often accompanied encounters with spirits, but this was a particularly nasty one.

The spirit didn't notice him approaching. She kept her pale, weary face pressed up against the glass, in between her bony hands.

Not wanting to startle her, Michael cleared his throat. When she didn't respond, he decided to speak up.

"Um... Hi," he said.

Still nothing.

"Excuse me? Miss?" he tried again, taking a few steps closer to her, careful not to trample any flowers.

14

Finally she turned to look at him. Her light blue eyes were wide and sunken in, surrounded by dark circles, and her long blonde hair hung freely down her back. She wore a ragged white dress and her feet were bare. Michael couldn't begin to wonder what had happened to her, or why she was so attached to the Averys' house.

All he did know was that the moment she laid eyes on him, she began to panic. Her breath came in short, labored gasps, and she seemed to be trembling.

"Hi," Michael greeted her again. "I know... you're probably not used to people seeing you. I just wanted to make sure that - "

"Stay away!" the girl cried shrilly, backing away from him.

"What?"

"Back! Back!" she screeched, lashing out at him.

Michael stumbled backwards, holding up his hands.

"I just want to talk to you," he told her.

"You can't talk to me! You're a devil! A *devil*! Back!" she screamed again. Her anger and fear electrified the air, resulting in a power surge throughout the entire neighborhood. Lights in every house flickered, as did the streetlights.

Every instinct told Michael to run back inside to Kate, to leave the mad ghost on her own, as she so very clearly wished to be, but for some stupid reason, he stayed steadfast in his place.

"Listen, I'm not trying to hurt you. I just wanted to see if you were alright. If you need any help!"

Instead of screaming again, the girl covered her ears with her hands, bowed her head down, and began to mutter, "*No, I said I can't see past the shadows. You'll have to hide. You'll have to hide. Take him out to the back and dig. I said dig! I heard you, I heard you...*"

As her murmurs intensified, Michael felt the electricity spike again. This time, he heeded his gut and sprinted back toward the front door. He made it inside just as the power began to flicker again.

"What's happening?" Kate asked him.

But before he could answer her, the electricity gave one final surge, and with a loud zap, the entire house went dark.

It wasn't the worst thing that could have happened. True, Michael would have preferred not to have been responsible for a neighborhood-wide power outage the night he was supposed to be meeting his girlfriend's family, but things certainly weren't as horrible as they could have been.

Kate, however, was still a little shaken.

"What in the world was that?" she asked him. "Did she do this?"

"Yeah," he said.

"But why?"

"I couldn't say," Michael replied honestly. Then a movement out of the corner of his eye drew his attention back to the dark living room. "Wait a minute," he said, stepping in front of Kate.

"What is it?"

Michael didn't respond. Instead, he watched silently as the ghost of the madwoman glided swiftly through the window and into the house. She passed by as though she didn't even see Michael or Kate standing there.

"Michael, what's going on?" Kate whispered.

"We need to go check on your family," he told her.

Together, they hurried into the kitchen, where Gavin was showing off the flashlight feature on his smart phone. Terri seemed slightly agitated, but the rest of the family appeared no worse for the wear.

"Well, this is fun, isn't it?" Gavin asked them.

"Is everyone alright?" Kate asked.

"We're fine, Pumpkin," Rex assured her. "Are you alright?"

Michael wasn't sure if she ever answered him or not. The ghost had appeared in the corner, still mumbling to herself. As she inched her way along the outline of the room, she dragged her hand across the countertop.

Please don't do anything rash. Please just leave. Please, please leave this family alone, Michael prayed. Too bad he couldn't communicate with her telepathically. It would have been nice to have psychic powers that were actually useful.

"Who do they think they are, silver and silver. No, you know you can't touch. How dare you? You know you'll regret it..."

Then, all of a sudden, she fell silent and stared down at the pots full of vegetables and rice on the stove. After a mere moment's hesitation, she began to swat at them, as though she were trying to push them off the counter and onto the floor. They didn't move.

With each effort, she became more and more agitated, and as her frustration grew, the temperature in the room began to drop.

Unfortunately, he wasn't the only one who noticed.

"Well, it feels like the air conditioner is still working. It's freezing in here," Pop commented.

"You know, Pop, sometimes that means there's a ghost present," Gavin told him, even though the smile in his tone indicated that he did not believe that was the case here.

"Why is that, I wonder?" Pop asked.

"Dad, please," Terri murmured. "I'd like to try and salvage what's left of this evening. The last thing I need is - "

But before she could get the words out, the ghost girl gave an electrifying screech that brought a crystal pitcher full of iced tea toppling off the kitchen table and shattering to the ground into a thousand shards, shimmering in the faint glow of dusk pouring in from the windows.

Terri screamed. Mimi gasped. Rex and Gavin both cried out in alarm. Kate, meanwhile, clutched Michael's arm, the same way a frightened child might cling to her favorite toy.

"Was that her?" she asked him.

"Yeah," he replied shortly, keeping his eyes locked on the girl, who stared, transfixed, at the pool of tea and ice and lemon, mixed in with the broken pieces of what had once been the pitcher.

17

As he spoke, the girl's head snapped up and she looked at him, her pale eyes frantic and alert and terrified.

"*You did this! You did this!*" she shrieked.

Then, with one final burst of energy, the ghost vanished.

Chapter 3

"If it makes you feel any better, that was not the worst family dinner we've ever had," Gavin told Michael during the drive back to the Riverview apartment complex.

"Unfortunately, that is true," Kate remarked. "There was one time our crazy aunt made our cousin so angry that he threw keys and toothpaste at her. Then he stormed out and ended up running over Gavin's bike with his car and Gavin cried."

"I didn't cry. I was fifteen years old."

"Whatever. You totally cried."

Michael appreciated Kate and Gavin's attempts to cheer him up, but he couldn't ignore the little voice in the back of his head that kept reminding him of just how much of an idiot he was. Besides, regardless of what they told him, it was difficult for him to imagine anything worse than what had happened back at the Averys' house.

Even after the ghost had vanished, the power still didn't return to the block, so the family ate their dinner by candlelight. It would have been nice, except for the fact that one of the candles that Terri burned ended up setting off allergies that Michael didn't even know he had, thus reducing him to a sniffling, wheezing mess of a dinner guest. Then, when Gavin offered to fetch Michael some Benadryl, he accidentally wandered barefoot right through the spot where the pitcher had shattered and ended up with a stray shard of glass embedded in his bare foot.

Thankfully, the wound wasn't deep enough to need stitches, but Michael still felt like the entire ordeal was his fault.

"So that ghost tonight. You have no idea who she was?" Gavin asked.

"No," Michael replied.

"What was she doing hanging around our house?"

"She was just a straggler."

"A straggler? What does that mean? She wanders around from house to house wreaking havoc and causing power outages?"

"It usually only happens if they're provoked."

"Okay, so what did you do to provoke her?"

"It was my fault," Kate interjected before Michael could answer. "He told me that she was there, so I told him to go out and talk to her. I thought he could help her."

Gavin snickered. "Guess she didn't want his help."

"Apparently not," Michael agreed.

"So, that just happens? Ghosts pass by with no rhyme or reason?"

"Sometimes," Michael answered. "They're usually the ones with no memories. It's rare, but it happens. The shock of death, the trauma, it can be too much for them."

"Like Sterling Hall," Kate said. She was right. The man who had constructed the lavish Stanton Hall Manor in Maine, the very place they had investigated with Luke and the *Cemetery Tours* crew mere months before, had withered away and passed in such a state of wretchedness that he hadn't realized he was dead for over a century. Or if he had realized it, he hadn't been able to accept it.

"But she's gone now? She's not going to come back and haunt Mom and Dad, is she?"

"I don't think so," Michael said. Truthfully, there was no way of being sure. He hoped, for everyone's sake, that the girl was long gone. But if he'd learned anything in his twenty-eight years, it was that the dead were even less predictable than the living.

That wasn't always a good thing. In fact, it rarely was.

When they arrived back home, Gavin bade them goodnight while Kate lingered back on the landing with Michael.

"I need you to tell me you're not beating yourself up over this," Kate said.

"I'm not," Michael replied a little too quickly. Kate caught it.

"I'm serious. Nothing that happened tonight was your fault. This is all on me."

"Kate, no. If it wasn't my fault, then it definitely wasn't your fault. You couldn't have known all that would happen."

"Neither could you."

He decided to believe that was true.

"I just wanted tonight to be perfect for you," he told her. He knew how badly she'd wanted it to be perfect. He wished he knew how to make that happen for her. She deserved perfect.

But instead of lying to him and assuring him that the evening *had* been perfect, regardless of every ghostly mishap, Kate wrapped her arms around his shoulders and pulled him down into a sweet, gentle kiss.

"You know what?" she whispered. "There is no such thing as perfect. But even if there was, I would pick you over perfection any day."

Somehow, she always knew exactly what to say to him. Just when he thought she might be better off without someone like him, that it might be selfish to hold on to her despite her best interests, she reminded him of every reason he'd fallen in love with her in the first place. Her spirit. Her smile. Her ability to see the good in every situation. And best of all, she loved him, too.

He looked down at her beautiful face and smiled.

"You mean you don't think I'm perfect?" he teased.

"Why would you want to be perfect? Perfect is boring," she told him. Then she said, "I think I probably owe you an apology also, for being so neurotic this morning. I put a lot of pressure on you with all the baking and the icing and... I realize now that none of that was important."

"You were nervous," Michael said.

"I was a train wreck," she corrected him. "I want my family to love you. Not just for me, but for you. I want you to feel like they're your family too. I want you to feel welcome and accepted. And I guess I thought cupcakes were the way to go."

Michael couldn't help it. He laughed.

"So what you're saying is the cupcakes were a bribe to get your family to like me," he grinned.

"No!" Now it was Kate's turn to laugh. "Oh my God, no! The cupcakes were a symbol, a representation of my love for you." Now it was just getting ridiculous. Neither of them could keep a straight face. "I don't know what the cupcakes were for. Maybe a sacrificial offering to the relationship gods in the hope that everyone would get along like the ending to a cheesy Lifetime movie."

"Well, maybe the relationship gods demand something a bit more personal than cupcakes. Like your soul."

"Or at least a little bit of blood," Kate added.

"Ew."

"Okay, okay, I'm sorry. Changing the subject," Kate promised him, wrapping her arms back around his neck. "Thank you for being there tonight."

"Anything for you," he murmured, pressing his lips to her forehead.

"I love you, Michael Sinclair."

"I love you, too, Kate."

~*~

After a very long goodnight, Michael meandered back into his own apartment with a goofy grin on his face. Brink appeared immediately.

"Well. Someone had himself a pleasant evening," the teenage ghost smirked. And for a split second, Michael really had almost forgotten about how unpleasant it had actually been.

"The later part was good," Michael told him, flopping down onto his old, tattered couch that Kate had threatened to launch off the balcony at least a dozen times.

"Uh-oh. Dinner with the in-laws didn't go so well?" Brink asked, taking his usual spot atop the coffee table.

"We had an unexpected guest." Michael told him briefly about the woman and the havoc she'd wreaked on the Avery household. Brink, meanwhile, hooted with laughter.

"I bet Rex and Terri just love having you around," he remarked.

"By the way, they're not my in-laws yet." Michael wasn't sure why he felt compelled to remind Brink of that.

"They might as well be." When Michael didn't respond, Brink asked, "What? You don't think you and Kate will get married?"

"It's not that. I just... haven't really thought that far ahead."

"Really?" Brink's eyebrows shot up toward his early-90s, swoopy hairdo. The look on his face almost made Michael feel ashamed of his confession.

"Yeah. I mean, we've only been dating five months. It's only been a little more than a year since Trevor died..."

"You still feel guilty about that?"

"Not guilty. Just... I don't know. I know she doesn't remember, but it still feels wrong somehow. Rushed. Just because she doesn't remember doesn't mean it didn't happen."

"I understand," Brink said, crossing his long legs. Then after a brief moment, he asked, "So, what's going to happen? You know, if you guys do get married?"

Michael wasn't sure where his friend was going with that.

"Well, I guess we'll go to a church. She'll wear a white dress. We'll eat cake - "

"No, Einstein. I meant... what will happen to us? I'm guessing you won't really want a roommate anymore..."

Oh.

Michael didn't know how to respond. The truth was he hadn't really thought that far ahead. Had he considered the possibility that he might marry Kate? Of course. He'd even browsed the internet for engagement rings. But he hadn't considered how different life would be for all of them after he and Kate were married.

"Brink, I think Kate would be the first to tell you that you're welcome to haunt us as long as you want," Michael told him.

"You really think so?"

"Yeah. We'll probably want some privacy every now and then, but I don't think either one of us would ever want you gone."

"Aw. You mean it?" Brink smiled.

"Yeah, I do. You're family."

"Dude, you're going to make me cry." Brink told him. "If I could hug you, man, you wouldn't be able to breathe right now."

Michael laughed, but their conversation had reminded him of something else that had been on his mind recently.

"Hey Brink, can I ask you a question?"

"Of course, bro. Anything."

Michael paused, unsure of how to broach a potentially sensitive subject. Finally he said, "All this talk of family, it makes me wonder. Why haven't you ever asked me to go talk to your family?"

Brink had died in a skateboarding accident at the age of eighteen. The accident occurred in the parking lot of his high school, incidentally the same high school that Michael would attend more than a decade later. That was how they'd met. Brink had stuck around to keep an eye on his siblings, the youngest of whom happened to be a senior when Michael was a freshman.

Yet, despite the many opportunities, Brink had never asked Michael to contact his family.

In answer to Michael's question, Brink simply shrugged. "I don't know."

He was lying. Michael had known him too long. Brink was nothing if not totally transparent (metaphorically, not the way ghosts were often imagined). His expressive blue eyes gave him away almost immediately.

"Yes, you do. Come on, you can tell me."

Brink sighed. "Do you remember what it was like for your mom when your brother died?"

Of course he did. How could he forget? Jonathan's death had left their mother devastated. There's no grief, no pain, no sorrow more profound than that of a mother who has lost her child. It was like a part of her had died, too. There was no way to console her, nothing that could be said or done to lessen her grief. Michael had grieved too, for the loss of his brother, but not the way his mother, Dianne, had.

"Yes."

"Okay, now imagine that, but knowing that you were the cause of it."

It took a moment for Michael to absorb what his friend was saying. He knew how Brink had died, but in all the years they'd been friends, he'd never really opened up about it, and Michael had never asked. A person's death was personal, and Michael had always figured that if Brink had wanted to talk about it, he would.

Now, Michael finally understood why he hadn't.

"Brink... You're not saying that you feel *guilty* for dying, are you?"

"Dude, I wasn't wearing a helmet! It was totally my fault! Do you know how many times she begged me to wear my helmet? She even bought me a brand new one for my birthday. I promised her over and over that I would wear it, but I never did because, get this, *I wanted to look cool*. I lied to her and I betrayed her just because I thought that helmet made me look stupid. If I'd just listened to her, I'd still be alive. If I'd listened to her, I never would have had to put her or any of my family through that."

25

Michael didn't know what to think. All these years, Brink had taken such a nonchalant approach to his death and afterlife, like it was just a thing that had happened, no big deal.

Before he could think of something to say, Brink continued, "I'll never forget going home that day. I still hadn't figured it out yet, that I'd actually died. I just thought, 'Oh, if I don't get home soon, Mom's going to freak.' Then when I got home, the house was still. I mean, absolutely silent. I knew something was wrong then. I noticed my dad talking to my brother and sister in the backyard. He was telling them something serious. Penny started to cry. Ike didn't seem to understand.

"Then, I heard someone crying upstairs. I ran up to see what was wrong, and I found my mom, curled up on my bed, clutching my pillow. I started yelling then, begging her to tell me what was going on, but she didn't respond at all. She couldn't hear me. I raced down to the backyard to ask my dad what was wrong, but by then, he and my brother and sister were huddled together, sobbing. I called to them over and over, but they never heard me..." Brink trailed off, sounding so pained that Michael reached out to comfort him before remembering that his friend couldn't feel a friendly hand on his shoulder.

"Maybe if you could talk to them, maybe some of that would go away."

"I'm just not sure I'm ready for that," Brink admitted. "Every time I think about it, I go back to that day, and it's just so much easier for me to... not. You know?"

Michael did know, unfortunately. He'd been taking the path of least resistance all his life, ignoring the ghosts who had turned out to be a very huge part of who he was and who he'd become.

"Well you know, if you ever change your mind..."

"I know. Thanks," Brink grinned. "You know, I've never told you, but I don't think I could do it."

"Do what?" Michael asked.

"This. This counseling the dead all the time. Let's face it, we're kind of a depressing bunch."

"It's not something I would have chosen, but you know, for the first time, I don't think I'd give it back. I wouldn't change anything. Because without it, I wouldn't have Kate. I wouldn't have you," Michael said.

"Aw, man. You love me. You really do." Brink waved a hand in front of his face, mimicking a pageant winner. Michael rolled his eyes, but smiled nevertheless.

"Don't let it go to your head," he advised.

"Oh, it is way too late for that."

And then, just as suddenly as he'd appeared, Brink was gone.

Chapter 4

As it turned out, the phantom fiasco at the Averys' was only the beginning of what was quickly turning out to be one of the worst weeks Michael could remember. On Monday, he was turned down for not one, not two, but three different jobs.

Then he got involved in a minor fender bender when a girl accidentally backed into his car, knocking out one of his headlights. It wouldn't have been that bad, except when he got out to exchange insurance information, the girl recognized him and got so scared that she actually screamed, jumped back in her car, and sped away. Michael was dumbfounded. What, did she think he was going to sic a ghost on her?

As if that wasn't enough, he'd also spilled his breakfast onto his only pair of clean pants, stepped in gum, and ended up with a terrible haircut that made him look about twelve years old.

Yeah. It was definitely one of those Murphy's Law kind of weeks.

Thankfully, Kate seemed to like his new haircut. Or if she didn't, she at least had the decency to lie about it.

Upon hearing about his very bad week, she'd decided that he needed a fun date night in. So on Wednesday night, she came over dressed in purple and blue plaid pajamas, carrying a mountain of pillows, sheets, and blankets, and announced that they were going to build a fort. She'd also brought over a selection of what she claimed to be "the best pity-party movies ever" and had already ordered a pizza to be delivered to his apartment.

"Are you doing okay?" she asked, greeting him with a quick kiss. She also ruffled his now way-too-short hair.

"Better now that you're here."

"That was cheesy," she told him.

"But it's true."

"You're lucky you're cute, you know that?" she teased. "Oh! Before I forget," she said, reaching into her backpack full of movies, "This accidentally ended up in my mailbox this afternoon." She pulled out a large black envelope, addressed to him in extravagant silver ink calligraphy.

"The return address is in Oklahoma," Michael observed. "Do we know anyone in Oklahoma?"

"I have a lot of cousins up there," Kate replied. "But I don't think any of them know calligraphy."

Curious, Michael tore open the envelope. Inside, he found a letter, handwritten in crimson ink.

Greetings Mr. Sinclair,

Welcome to the Circus. I am your Ringmaster, Alfred Van Dalen. It is with honor and greatest pleasure that I invite you to the grand debut of Cirque Somniatis, The Circus of Dreams. Here, we strive to unlock your hidden desires and unleash your innermost fantasies. Experience the magic, the mystery, and the truth of the realm beyond our waking world.

Enclosed, you will find three complimentary weekend passes as well as a map of the grounds and packet of information detailing your stay, should you choose to accept our offer. I hope you will enjoy your journey with us.

Yours Most Sincerely,
Alfred Van Dalen

"Who is this?" Michael wondered aloud as Kate wrapped her arms around his waist and read the letter over his shoulder.

"I guess we can consult the almighty Google," she said.

"Do you think this is real?" Michael asked her.

"I hope so. I've never been to a circus."

"You haven't?" Michael asked her.

"Nope. Gavin has a clown phobia so our parents never took us. By the way, feel free to use that against him, just don't tell him I told you."

"So I'm guessing he probably doesn't want the extra ticket..." Michael trailed off.

"Probably not, no," Kate agreed. Then she asked, "Wait a minute. Are we seriously considering this?"

Michael didn't know how to answer her. For one thing, he had no idea who this Alfred Van Dalen character was or why he was reaching out to him. For another, it could very well just be junk mail that went out to everyone with certain numbers in their address. But even if it was real, he wasn't sure he even wanted to go.

He had been to a circus only once before, when he was seven years old. His older brother, Jonathan, was ten, almost eleven. He'd been having a lot of problems at school, even more so than usual, and their mother, Diane, was just about at her wit's end. She'd thought, or at least hoped, that a trip to the circus might lift everyone's spirits.

The trip turned out to be a disaster. Jonathan, overwhelmed by a combination of the crowds and the high energy of the circus itself, began to panic almost immediately and within thirty minutes had completely shut down. Michael, too young to understand what was going on with his brother at the time, had taken that to mean that something about the circus, maybe clowns or acrobats, was scary and that he needed to be scared of it too. Not knowing what else to do, he began crying and begging their mother to take them home.

"I don't know," Michael finally answered Kate. "There's a lot that we need to think about. Whether or not this is real or just another mail hoax. Where we would stay if it does turn out to be real. Your job. My lack of job..."

"Well, I have some vacation time saved up, so we don't have to worry about that. As for everything else... I don't know. I think we should go," Kate said.

"Really?" Michael asked, though he didn't know why he was surprised. Kate was adventurous, always up for new experiences. She wasn't afraid to take chances. That was something Michael loved and admired most about her.

Then again, it also scared the hell out of him.

"Really. When was the last time we went somewhere new?" Kate asked.

"Last October. We went to Maine. You got possessed."

"Oh, what are the chances of *that* happening twice in the same year?"

"Technically, it's not the same year," Michael reminded her.

"Shut up. You know what I mean. My point is this might be a really great opportunity for us to get away for a little while. You're having a terrible week, right? This might be just the thing to cheer you up," Kate said.

"I want to go!" Brink appeared out of nowhere, nearly giving Michael a heart attack.

"Son of a - Brink, I've told you not to do that!"

Kate flinched, clearly surprised by Michael's outburst, but he could also tell that she was trying not to laugh.

"Sorry, compadre. Whoa. Nice hair. Who cut it for you? A sheep shearer?" Brink grinned. Michael glared at him. The ghost was unfazed. "What, too soon for jokes? Okay, I get it. So, where are we going?"

"You don't know where we're going? You just said you wanted to go."

"True, but I'm up for going pretty much anywhere that isn't here. I've been haunting this popsicle stand long enough. So have you, for that matter."

"What does that mean?" Michael wanted to know.

"It means I have more of a life than you do, and that's kind of sad," Brink remarked.

31

Michael wanted to contradict him, but as much as he hated to admit it, Brink may have had a point. While Michael was happier than he had ever been in his life, he was also, well, a little boring. That disastrous dinner at the Averys' was the most exciting thing to happen to him in months. Brink was right. That *was* sad.

"Alright," he consented. "I'll go look up Cirque... What's it called?"

"Cirque Somniatis. And there's no need," Kate informed him. "I've already pulled it up on my phone."

"Okay," Michael said, nervously running his hands together. He wasn't sure why he was feeling anxious. "What's the verdict?"

"It seems like a real thing. Alfred Van Dalen, owner and ringmaster, has been building this Circus of Dreams for years. It looks like this opening weekend is going to be a pretty huge event."

"There's something that's still bothering me, though," Michael said.

"What's that?" Kate asked.

"I have no association with the circus business or anything remotely close to it. I'm not a celebrity. I'm not known for anything... except the ghosts."

As soon as the words were out, he knew Kate understood where he was going.

"You think this place is haunted," she said.

"Why else would anyone want me there?"

"Because you're fun at parties and have really pretty eyes?" Kate offered playfully. Then she said, "You know, there is the possibility that they drew names from surrounding cities out of a hat. I mean, they're opening in Hugo, Oklahoma and from what I can tell, it is a very small town. This could have absolutely nothing to do with ghosts."

Michael supposed that could be true, but free weekend passes? He doubted the Cirque Somniatis, or any other circus for that matter, sent those out at random.

"Maybe," he replied.

Kate must have sensed his uncertainty, because she took both of his hands and said, "Look, if you don't want to go, we don't have to go."

"It's not that I don't want to go. It just doesn't make any sense to me."

"Well, you know, there's no rule that says we have to stay the whole weekend. We could drive up Thursday evening, attend the opening on Friday afternoon, and if there's anything weird or suspicious, we can leave."

"She makes a solid case," Brink chimed in.

Michael considered it. He guessed there really wasn't any harm. Worst case scenario, it turned out to be a rip-off or a set-up, and they wasted a few hours on the road and a night in a motel. On the other hand, it could end up being the best weekend of his life. In this situation, there seemed to be little to lose and a lot to gain.

God, that was a first.

"Thursday, you said?" Michael asked.

Brink threw his fist up into the air and whooped. "Yes! We're going to the circus. We're going to the circus," the teenage ghost chanted and danced a weird little jig.

Kate, meanwhile, wrapped her arms around Michael's neck.

"Are you sure about this?" she asked.

"Yeah, I am," he assured her.

Kate smiled again before pressing her lips to his.

"This is going to be amazing. I can feel it," she said. "Now there's just one thing left to figure out."

"What's that?" Michael asked, his head still spinning from her kiss. Five months together and he still hadn't built up a tolerance to her touch.

"Who gets the extra ticket?"

"Well, Gavin's definitely out. I know my mom doesn't care for the circus much either. You could ask Val if you wanted," Michael told her.

"She's not really the outdoorsy-circus type," Kate told him. "What about Luke?"

"Luke?"

"Yeah! His birthday is later this month. He'd probably have a blast! It would be the most awesome birthday weekend ever!"

"Would he have time for something like this? I mean, we don't even know if he's in town."

"He is. Or at least, he will be later this week," Kate said. The look on Michael's face must have asked the question for him, because she explained, "He texted me the other day and asked if we wanted to hang out sometime after he got back."

"What did you tell him?"

"I said of course we would! Why wouldn't we?"

"I don't know. He hasn't really talked to us in a while."

"No, he hasn't talked to you because you're terrible at texting and you never write people back. But we text here and there. Besides, you know how busy he is. They were just in Italy last month filming on this old island where a bunch of people died of the plague."

"Gee, that sounds like fun," Michael muttered.

"You know, I think it would really mean a lot to him if you asked him to go," Kate told him.

"Why?" Michael couldn't help but wonder.

"Because I think he really respects you and looks up to you. You've been through a lot together. You're not going to believe me, but you're one of the few real friends he has."

That really caught Michael off guard.

"But he's so popular. He has all those fans. Everyone loves him."

"True, but celebrity comes at a price. Sometimes it's hard to trust everyone around you, because you can't be sure that they like you for you or what they think you can do for them. It's a weird world to be in, and I think Luke really appreciates genuine people when he meets them."

Even though her words made sense, Michael was having a difficult time processing them. He'd always sort of been under the impression that Luke thought he was doing Michael a favor by keeping in touch and inviting him along on his adventures. He'd never once considered that maybe Luke was reaching out to him because he needed a friend.

"You really think that?" Michael asked.

"What?"

"That I'm one of Luke's only friends?"

"Yeah, I do."

"Why?"

Kate wrapped an arm around Michael's torso and hugged him gently.

"Because he told me."

Chapter 5

Luke Rainer was in desperate need of a vacation. He'd been working non-stop for the past five months, with only a few days off for Christmas and New Year's, and several of their investigations had been particularly draining.

Ratings for *Cemetery Tours* had begun to slide, not enough to pull them off the air, but enough for their executive producers to voice their concern that the popular ghost hunting show might be losing its edge. Hoping to prove to his fans and his producers that he was more than a one trick pony, Luke had begun pushing previously set limits on investigations. Instead of taking a break when he felt his energy diminishing, he forced his mind and body to power on. He antagonized spirits he knew might be dangerous. His actions had also caused some tension amongst his team. JT and Peter usually had his back, but he and Gail had been stepping on each other's nerves more than ever. She'd even come close to quitting a few weeks back, after their investigation of Alcatraz. She said Luke had become too obsessed. He told her she didn't care enough. It was one big mess.

Thankfully, JT had been able to talk her out of leaving the team, though that was probably more for his sake than Luke's. JT still hadn't confessed his hopeless crush on Gail, but there were times Luke wished that he would. Maybe if she knew how JT felt about her then she'd stop screwing around with every other loser to pick her up at a club.

As much as Luke would have loved to blame the prematurely graying strands of hair he'd found in his comb on distracted coworkers and dwindling ratings, he knew they were only half the cause. The other half taunted him from the television screen every Friday evening in the form of Chance McDermott, lead investigator of the SyFy Channel's newest series, *Grave Crusaders*. Already being hailed by critics as "the next big paranormal hit" and "the new and improved *Cemetery Tours*," *Grave Crusaders* and its narcissistic, cheeky, pain-in-the-ass host had been taking primetime by storm in recent weeks. And unfortunately, they didn't show signs of slowing down any time soon.

Long story short, when Mikey had called him out of the blue and asked if he wanted to go to the circus with him and Kate that weekend, Luke didn't hesitate to accept the invitation. He hadn't been to a circus since he was a kid, but he'd always wanted to go back. The sights, the sounds, the acrobats and illusionists, everything about the circus had seemed magical, especially to a young boy who already believed in things that others couldn't hope to explain. He couldn't wait to experience all that again as an adult.

Not to mention this particular circus, the Cirque Somniatis, was set smack-dab in the middle of Hugo, Oklahoma, known to the rest of the nation as Circus City, USA. A small town, located in Choctaw County, just nine miles north of the Texas border, Hugo had been the wintering home of traveling circuses since the 1930s. There was even a cemetery, Showmen's Rest, where countless circus performers had been laid to rest. With so much history and so many passionate artists buried there, Luke had been itching to investigate Hugo for years.

But that wasn't why he was going. He was going to relax and to spend time with his friends. If they just so happened to stumble across a ghost or two while they were there, then so be it.

On that thought, he'd better take his equipment. Just in case.

~*~

When Thursday evening rolled around, Luke loaded up his weekend luggage into the back of his mom's Lexus (there was no way he would be able to fit two extra people plus their overnight stuff in his beloved Ferrari) and drove over to the Riverview Apartment complex. Since Mikey and Kate were providing the tickets, he'd offered to drive. It was the least he could do. Besides, he was willing to bet that Mikey drove like a grandma.

Kate had texted him during the drive that they were both waiting for him up in Mikey's apartment, so after Luke pulled in to one of the visitor's parking spots, he sprinted up the stairs and knocked on the door numbered 1723. Kate was the one who answered.

"Luke!" she grinned and threw her arms around him.

"Hello, Beautiful," he greeted her fondly. From the moment he'd met her, there was just something that he liked about Kate Avery. It was true, she had a natural elegance and beauty, but his admiration for her went far beyond her looks. She was very genuine and he respected her for that. Unfortunately, he hadn't been able to see her or Mikey since the day they'd come home from Maine last October. "I think it's been too long."

"I think it has, too," she agreed. "I'm so glad you could come this weekend."

"Oh, I wasn't about to pass on a free trip to the circus! Not to mention spending time with my third favorite couple in the world."

"Third favorite?" Kate raised a playful eyebrow and crossed her arms over her chest.

"Well, yeah. My parents are my first favorite. Ed and Lorraine Warren are a close second, though."

"Fair enough," Kate conceded. "Come on in. Michael's just getting the rest of his toiletries together."

"Toiletries?" Luke smirked.

"Yeah, you know. Toothbrush, razors, deodorant - "

"Kate, sweetheart, this might be hard for you to accept, but Mikey and I are men. And men do not have 'toiletries,'" Luke informed her, following her into Mikey's living room.

"Oh, really?" she asked. "Then what, pray tell, do you have?"

"I don't know. But whatever it is, we don't call it 'toiletries.'"

"I think I just walked in on a really weird conversation," Mikey announced, appearing in the doorway of his bedroom and dragging a gray rolling suitcase behind him.

"Hey, there he is!" Luke smiled upon seeing his friend. "You look good, man. I like the haircut."

"Really?" Mikey asked.

"He hates it," Kate muttered to Luke.

"Nah, really. It makes you look cool, young, and hip. You know, as opposed to what you actually are," Luke teased.

"Ha, that's funny," Mikey pretended to be miffed, but Luke knew him well enough to know that his friend had a terribly dry sense of humor. So dry, in fact, that it was often hard to tell when he was actually joking. But this time, he was fairly certain that he was.

"Age happens to the best of us, my friend," Luke continued to tease.

"You know, last time I checked, you were five years older than I am," Mikey reminded Luke.

"This is true. But I look *fantastic*, so the years really have no effect on me."

That is, until that twenty-something, lowlife, paranormal plebeian showed up and declared himself the "younger, hotter Luke Rainer." But Luke *really* didn't want to talk about him. In fact, all he wanted to do was pretend he'd never heard of Chance McDermott or his lawsuit-waiting-to-happen SyFy series.

"You're both beautiful examples of the male specimen. Now let's lock up and hit the road!" Kate demanded.

"Yes, ma'am!" Luke saluted her and grabbed her bags. Mikey, in turn, grabbed his own bags and together, the three of them headed to the front door.

"Brink, we talked about this last night. I already said you could come," Mikey said out of the blue. "Yes, there will probably be monkeys... No, you're not allowed to scare them."

"Do you want to ask?" Luke muttered to Kate.

"Not really," Kate replied.

Once they were on the road, Luke turned up the radio and rolled the windows down. It was a gorgeous, clear night, he was with two of his best friends in the world, and they were about to embark on a fantastic adventure. True, it would have been nice if he had someone sitting in the backseat to give *him* a nice shoulder massage like the one Kate was giving Mikey, but whatever. As long as he didn't have to put up with too much ooey-gooey romantic grossness from the happy couple, it was going to be a great weekend.

"Hey Kate, what's going to happen to Marlon Brando while we're gone?" Michael asked.

Okay. That was an odd question.

"Marlon Brandon? The actor?" Luke asked.

"My conure," Kate explained from the back seat. "And I dropped him off at my parents' earlier this afternoon. There was no way I was leaving him alone with Gavin. He'd probably shoot him with a crossbow and make it look like an accident."

"That's gruesome," Luke remarked. "I want to meet your bird. If he lives through the weekend."

"Oh, he will. My mom loves animals," Kate assured him.

Mikey, on the other hand, tried to suppress a grimace. Luke could see it even out of the corner of his eye.

"What's with that face, Mikey?" Luke asked.

"He doesn't like my bird," Kate answered him.

"I like him, we just... don't get along very well." Mikey tried to vindicate himself.

"He gets jealous," Kate said.

"Who? Mikey or the bird?" Luke asked.

40

"Both," Kate laughed.

"So, what have you been up to, Luke?" Mikey asked, clearly trying to steer the conversation away from him and his rivalry with Marlon Brando.

"Filming. Talking to ghosts. You know, the usual," Luke replied. He told them all about their trips to Italy and Alcatraz, minus, of course, all the stupid drama that had befallen his team members. If there was one thing that Luke couldn't stand it was unnecessary drama. That was probably why he went out of his way to avoid relationships. Maybe if he could find a woman like Kate, he'd make more of an effort. Unfortunately, he only seemed to attract the psycho drama-mongers.

Perhaps it was his strong personality.

Of course, he'd had a shot with Kate once, but he'd known even then that she and Mikey had a thing for one another. He probably knew it before either one of them. Besides, even if he'd decided to pursue Kate afterward, in the end, she was always going to end up with Mikey. That was just how it was supposed to be. And Luke was fine with that.

Though she could have offered to give him a shoulder massage, too. He was driving, after all. It would have been the polite thing to do.

On that thought...

"So, where are we staying anyway?" Nothing against Hugo, Oklahoma, but he was willing to bet there weren't many five-star resorts there.

"We're actually staying on the grounds, which is kind of neat," Kate replied, glancing through a packet that Luke guessed had been enclosed with the tickets. "It says that their luxury guest condos are reserved for VIPs and guests of the Ringmaster. Sounds intriguing."

"The Ringmaster?" Luke asked. He wasn't about to admit it to his friends, but this Circus of Dreams was beginning to sound a bit creepy.

He loved it.

"Yeah. Alfred Van Dalen. He's the one who sent Michael the invitation," Kate said.

"And how much research have you done on this Alfred Van Dalen?" Which probably wasn't even the guy's real name. And if it was, well, that was a tough break. He couldn't imagine the torture the poor guy had been forced to endure as a kid.

"There's actually not a whole lot to find, which means that Van Dalen is more than likely not his real name," Mikey answered.

"I wonder who else he's invited?" Kate asked. "Maybe we'll get to meet someone really famous!"

"More famous than *moi*?" Luke gasped.

"No, that would be unthinkable!" Kate graciously catered to his admittedly large ego.

Luke had to admit, however, he had wondered the same thing. Was there a supernatural element to this Cirque Somniatis? It would certainly explain why this Alfred Van Dalen had gone out of his way to make Mikey a guest of honor. But why hadn't the *Cemetery Tours* crew been invited? He liked to think that they were pretty easy to reach. In the age of social media, anyone could send them a tweet, a Facebook message, an email...

Not that it was a big deal, really. There were a hundred reasons why he and the rest of the crew hadn't made the VIP list. Maybe the ghosts were a secret thing and having a world famous paranormal investigating team present would be too conspicuous. Or maybe Van Dalen thought that he wouldn't be able to reach them so he hadn't even tried.

Whatever the reason, Luke promised himself that he wasn't going to dwell. Just because the last couple of weeks had been nothing short of craptacular, it didn't mean that the universe was conspiring against him.

It was going to be a great weekend. He was going to make sure of it.

Chapter 6

The fairgrounds were dark when Kate, Michael, and Luke arrived in Hugo, Oklahoma two and a half hours later. It was a calm, clear night and a few early crickets had already begun to sing. It was an open and peaceful atmosphere, if not more than a little haunting.

The condominiums were set up almost like a small-town neighborhood, with old-fashioned lamp posts and even driveways in which to park your car. In the distance, Kate could make out the shape of a Ferris wheel and the shadowy silhouettes of circus tents against the backdrop of the starry sky.

"So, is there a concierge desk where we check in or what?" Luke asked.

"I called ahead to tell them I wanted to reserve two condos, and the lady said she'd have our keys waiting for us and that we could pick them up any time before ten PM," Michael said.

"Did you get her name?" Kate asked, slinging her overnight bag over her shoulder.

"I think it was Cindy Grout? Does that sound right?" he asked the empty space next to him. Kate had been around long enough now to know that he was consulting Brink. "Yeah, Cindy Grout."

Luke wrinkled up his nose. "Sounds like gout."

"Luke!" Kate snapped.

43

"What? It's a gross word!"

As it turned out, Cindy Grout's office was located at the opposite end of the makeshift neighborhood. The building itself looked a lot like the rest of the condos, but much smaller. Clearly, it was not intended for long-term habitation, though if she needed to sleep there, Kate was willing to bet that she could. There may have even been room for a small refrigerator.

Inside, the office looked very much like the lobby of a small hotel, with a Persian rug on the floor and a vacant one-person reception desk.

Never one to shy away from the task at hand, Luke rang the bell on the desk. When no one appeared, he rang again.

"I'm coming, I'm coming!" A woman's voice from the back called out. "I'm just waiting for a commercial!"

Kate glanced up at Michael, who shrugged, and then up at Luke, who raised an eyebrow and said, "Sounds like my grandma."

Sure enough, the woman who appeared looked like a grandma, with short, thin, sand-colored hair, a floral-print blouse, and plum-colored reading glasses that she probably wore all the time. Kate also noticed a large cross made entirely of amethysts dangling around her neck.

"Hello, children. How may I help you?" she asked.

"Hi," Michael greeted her. "I'm Michael Sinclair. I called a few days ago to reserve two condominiums?"

"Oh yes, of course. You're one of Alfie's guests. Now, let's see what we've got here for you..." The woman, whom Kate could only assume was Cindy Grout, rummaged through some files on her desk and then began to dig through one of the drawers beneath her desk. "Most of you aren't scheduled to arrive until tomorrow. But I guess you wanted to beat the crowd."

"Yes, Ma'am," Michael replied awkwardly.

Kate smiled. He was kind of adorable.

"Right, here you are. Two condos for Sinclair, Rainer, and Avery," she said, glancing over the paperwork. Then, her cool eyes shifted upward and landed on Kate. "You're not Mrs. Sinclair?" she asked.

"Oh... Uh... No..." Kate knew she probably could have lied and gotten away with it, but being put on the spot like that unfortunately turned her into a compulsive truth-teller.

"Then I'm *assuming* this extra condo is for you." She spoke with the air of a teacher who'd just caught her kids sneaking cookies from the snack cupboard.

"Yes, absolutely," Kate assured her.

"I'm serious, young lady," Mrs. Grout warned. "You don't want to lead either of these men into temptation."

By that point, she was so embarrassed, she could feel her entire face flushing furiously. She couldn't bring herself to even look at Michael. Luke, on the other hand, was giggling so hard that Kate half-expected him to keel over.

"No, definitely not. That is the last thing I want." Even to her own ears, the words sounded stiff, but Kate hoped that if she kept on agreeing with her, the older woman would let the whole thing drop. "Temptation is bad."

"Yes it is. In my younger years, I led several young men into temptation. It is a dark road, Missy. You remember that."

"I will. Thank you. Now may I *please* have my key?" It wasn't going to get any worse. It couldn't. Even *Michael* was laughing and he was supposed to be on her side! That was how Kate knew she had hit rock bottom.

Rock bottom in Hugo, Oklahoma. If she were a guy and five years younger, she could have started up an indie punk band.

Thankfully, Cindy Grout's humiliating lecture ended there and she handed Kate a small envelope containing two keys on a ring. She passed an identical envelope along to Michael.

After bidding the older woman a very awkward goodnight, Michael, Luke, and Kate stepped out into the cool night air, where Michael and Luke immediately burst into a new round of laughter. Kate, however, remained bitterly unamused.

"What the hell was that?!" she demanded.

"The funniest three minutes of my life, that's what," Luke replied, wiping tears from his eyes.

"I'm sorry, Kate," Michael tried to apologize, but he was still just as tickled as Luke. "I'm sorry. That was totally uncalled for."

"Uh huh," Kate crossed her arms and stared at him. It wasn't that she was actually mad at him. But she didn't necessarily want to let him off the hook that easily either.

"I love you," he told her.

"Me too. I love you too, Kate," Luke chimed in.

"And I love the two of you. You know that." She stood up on her tip-toes and gave Michael a swift kiss. Then she said, "Well, I'll see you in the morning."

"Wait, what?" Michael reached out to stop her. "Where are you going?"

"I'm going to go find my condo. I wouldn't want to be responsible for 'leading you into temptation,'" she replied lightly, mimicking Cindy Grout. "Goodnight boys."

Then, with a final smirk, she hoisted her bag up onto her shoulder and set out in search of her weekend accommodations.

~*~

Michael stood dumbfounded in the glow of old-fashioned street lamps and waning moon, watching Kate's blonde hair swish and sway across her retreating back.

"What just happened?" he asked, echoing her sentiments from moments earlier.

"Well, I'm not much of an expert on relationships, but it looks like you and I are roomies this weekend," Luke replied.

"Oh, this will be fun," Brink remarked with a wicked grin.

"Is she mad at me?" Michael asked.

"Yes," Brink chimed in.

"No," Luke answered simultaneously. "I don't think she's mad. She's just punishing you. Now me, personally, I think we're going to have a great weekend."

Michael truly did not know how to respond to that. Kate was just messing with him, right? She wasn't actually going to let

46

him spend an entire weekend rooming with Luke. Not that Luke wasn't one of his best friends or that he wasn't grateful for everything - well, most everything - that he'd done for them. But rooming with him? Sharing a *bathroom* with him? Michael wasn't sure he could handle that.

"Do you think I should grovel?" he asked Luke.

"Yes," Brink repeated.

"Nope. Wouldn't do you any good. Trust me," Luke advised. "Look, I know you think this is going to be torture and it probably will be. I'm going to actually have to sleep with shorts on now - " Michael scrunched up his nose and glared at Luke. That was way too much information. " - But it might also be a really good chance for us to bond! I could give you a few pointers about dealing with women and in return, you could summon up some ghosts and help me record some killer new audio evidence. What do you say?"

Honestly? Michael wanted to say he thought Luke was crazy. He didn't need Luke to give him advice on women. He was the one in an actual, committed relationship. As far as he knew, Luke had never dated anyone longer than a few weeks. And the ghost thing? How many times did he have to remind Luke that ghosts didn't just magically appear whenever Michael called them. In fact, they usually showed up in the moments he least wanted them.

Although he did have Brink with them that weekend. He'd probably be willing to sit down and answer some questions for Luke. It might be kind of cool and -

Oh, no. Something was terribly, terribly wrong. All his life, Michael had tried to distance himself from the paranormal. He valued the ordinary and never sought to stick his nose in places it didn't belong. But now Luke had him thinking that it might be cool to participate in one of his ridiculous EVP sessions. And he actually knew what an EVP session was! That was the worst part!

What was happening to him?

"Sure, Luke. That sounds like fun," he finally replied.

Luke's face lit up, and Michael found himself thinking back to the conversation he'd had with Kate about Luke considering him to be one of his only real friends. For some reason, that memory left him feeling incredibly guilty. If he was one of Luke's only friends, he hadn't been a very good one. He'd spent the better part of their relationship making a mockery of Luke's fascination with ghosts and the supernatural. He met Luke's enthusiasm with dry wit and cynicism. He barely attempted to stay in touch when Luke was away. Some friend.

Maybe this weekend would be good for both of them. An opportunity to learn and grow, as his mother would put it.

"Perfect! Now, let's go find our new home away from home, shall we?"

It didn't take them very long to find the condo that Cindy Grout had assigned to them. Outside, it really didn't look like much, but inside, Michael was pleasantly surprised to find, it was pretty nice. Complete with a small kitchen nook, lush red carpeting, and gold accent pieces (he'd learned the term from Kate), it was a fit setting for a traveling circus performer. Or a student at a wizarding academy.

Unfortunately, there was only one bed.

"I can sleep on the floor if need be," Michael offered.

"Nonsense. Back when we were first starting out, JT and I shared beds a lot smaller than this one. Besides, sleeping on the ground can't be good for your joints. I wouldn't want you to hurt your back or anything. You know, since you're getting so old."

"Again with the age jokes. I am not as old as you!"

"I know. But it's still funny," Luke grinned. Then, he tossed his luggage onto the floor next to the bed and kicked off his shoes. "If you don't mind, I think I'm gonna take a shower. It's been a long day. Hell, it's been a long couple of weeks."

It was just a comment, but something in Luke's tone caught Michael's attention. It wasn't like the famous Ghost Prince of Primetime to express anything remotely resembling vulnerability.

"Everything okay?" Michael asked him.

"Oh, yeah. Just been busy, that's all," Luke replied. Then, he grabbed some clothes and a small black bag out of his suitcase and disappeared into the bathroom.

The moment the door shut, Brink remarked, "He's lying."

"Why do you think that?" Michael wondered.

"I can read people, and Luke Rainer is easier to read than most. Something has definitely got his goat."

"Good to know that phrase is around," Michael remarked. "What do you think's bothering him?"

"Hard to say," Brink answered, resting his hands on his hips and staring at the bathroom door.

"I thought you just said that he was easy to read."

"It's easy to tell that something's bothering him. I'd have to be a mind reader to know what that something is. But hey, we're at the circus! Chances are there's at least one psychic running around here. And when I say psychic, I mean like a real one. Not a poser like you who can only talk to dead people and do absolutely nothing else."

"Thanks, man," Michael quipped.

"Always happy to help," Brink replied with a quick grin. "On that note, would you mind turning on the TV? It has been a pretty long day and I could really go for some Breaking Bad."

"You mean you're not going to go wander? I thought that's what you did at night."

"No way. It's creepy out there. What if I ran into a clown? In the dark?"

"Yes, I'm sure that would be very traumatic for you," Michael deadpanned. Of course he would be haunted by the only ghost in the world who was afraid of the dark.

"I'm glad you understand that. Now then. TV?" Brink asked.

Michael sighed. It was official. Every person he knew, both living and dead, was some kind of crazy.

Regardless, he didn't want to keep the Master of all Things Plaid waiting, so he knelt down in front of the bedroom's entertainment center and searched for a remote control to the television. As he did, he felt the age-old sensation of eyes on the back of his neck.

Really? Brink was so impatient for his *Breaking Bad* fix that Michael was getting the stare down?

Irritated, Michael turned to glare back at Brink, only to find his friend lounging across the Queen-sized bed, gazing up at the ceiling.

So was he imagining the feeling of being watched? He didn't think he was. Then again, he'd been watched by unseen eyes all his life. It was possible he'd grown so accustomed to it that he'd begun to feel it even when there was no one there.

Then, all of a sudden, there was someone there. Across the room, standing in front of the door, a young boy stood staring at Michael with wide brown eyes. Not wanting to startle the boy, Michael rose to his feet slowly.

"Hello," he offered.

But before the boy could respond, the bathroom door opened and Luke appeared in a cloud of steam.

"Alright, Mikey. Shower's all yours," he announced. Then he noticed Michael standing in the middle of the room, staring into the entry hall. "What's going on?"

Michael didn't know how to answer, so he turned his attention back to the ghost in the doorway, but he was met with empty air and a vacant space. The boy was gone.

Chapter 7

The next morning, after a complimentary breakfast courtesy of the still-elusive Alfred Van Dalen, Michael, Kate, and Luke finally ventured into the circus itself. It was opening day and the sights and sounds of festivity surrounded them in the forms of balloons, jugglers, music, and laughter. Most of the visitors seemed to be families with kids, but Michael saw a few couples interspersed in the crowd as well.

"Wow. This is a lot bigger deal than I thought it would be," Luke remarked. "I feel like half the population of Oklahoma showed up."

Michael had to agree with him on that one. Hugo was a small town. People must have been pouring in from at least two or three surrounding counties for the grand opening of Cirque Somniatis.

At the gate, Michael, Kate, and Luke presented their complimentary tickets, and after receiving a stamp on the hand, they were welcomed into the circus itself. There was so much going on that Michael could barely take it all in. Vendor's booths and carts lined the makeshift pathway across the meadow, leading into the heart of the circus. To his left, a man wearing a glittering gold mask and a purple cape crafted animals and rockets and flowers and crowns out of balloons. Up ahead, two performers, dressed in a similar fashion but with the addition of

51

stilts, directed families toward the petting zoo. Everywhere he looked, there was something new to see.

"This is so amazing!" Kate exclaimed.

Before he could agree with her, Michael heard someone call his name.

"Michael! Michael Sinclair!"

He turned to see a woman whom he thought he recognized, but for some reason couldn't place. She was older, at least in her early fifties. She wore a long gypsy skirt, about a dozen gold necklaces, and had a purple scarf tied in her frizzy brown and gray hair.

"Rasia Leyland," Luke muttered.

"Oh my God! I've heard of her!" Kate said.

"Who is she?" Michael asked.

But the woman was too close for either Kate or Luke to answer without it seeming rude. She approached Michael like an old friend, arms outstretched to embrace him. After the world's most awkward hug, she kissed Michael on both cheeks while Kate and Luke snickered in the background. Now he knew how Kate felt last night.

"Oh, it is so nice to finally meet you in the physical plane," Rasia greeted him.

Michael had no idea what that meant.

"Yeah... um... You too."

"And this must be your lovely Kate." Rasia turned to Kate and took both of her hands in hers. "Must be? Listen to me. Of course you are. I know you very well."

"Really?" Kate asked. "How?"

"Your dreams, my dear. Your dreams."

Michael had been afraid that he might be the only one out of the loop, but the look on Kate's face told him that she was just as confused as he was. Perhaps even more so. The only one who didn't seem at all fazed by her extravagance was Luke.

"And Luke. Oh, my darling Luke Rainer," she threw her arms out once again.

"How are you, Rasia?" he asked, returning her embrace.

52

"I'm well, my dear. Very well. The spirit keeps me enlightened in all I do and say."

"Well, that's the best way to be," Luke said. "What brings you here to Hugo?"

"Why, I was invited for the grand opening! I see that young Michael Sinclair was as well. I am so glad he decided to bring you along."

"Did you hear that?" Michael asked Luke. "She called me young."

"Yes dear, your body is very young indeed, though I detect the soul dwelling within you to be quite old, perhaps ageless," Rasia announced.

"Oh. Um. Thank you." Was that the appropriate response to a declaration like that? Michael wasn't sure. But thanks to her hopefully accurate prediction, he'd finally remembered where he'd seen her face before. She'd been a guest on *The Sarah Stone Show* a few weeks back. Despite having been a guest on the show himself, Michael didn't usually make a habit of watching the late-night celebrity talk show, but he'd found himself unable to sleep one night due to the ghost of an older, heavyset gentleman stomping around his bedroom.

He didn't remember much of Rasia's interview because mercifully, he'd managed to fall asleep on the couch. He did, however, recall her introducing herself as a psychic medium who communicated with the dead, predicted the future, and traveled along something called "astral planes." She was talking with Sarah Stone about the new book she'd just written about her spiritual gifts.

"Tell me, have you met with Mr. Van Dalen yet?" Rasia asked.

"No. We actually just made it through the gate. Haven't seen much of anything yet," Luke replied.

"Well let me tell you, you are in for a treat. What an extraordinary young man. Such ambition! To achieved all of this at such a tender age. It's more than I dared to fathom in my twenties, I'll give you that."

"Great. Well, we'll look forward to meeting him," Luke said.

"Did he tell you why he invited us? You know, people like us?" Michael blurted out. Rasia gazed at him with wide, curious eyes.

"You mean you don't know?" Rasia asked. "Why my dear boy, it's because of Claire."

"Who's Claire?" Kate asked.

"Claire Tellers, the young acrobat who is said to haunt these grounds. She passed tragically during one of her performances several years back. In this, the grand opening of his Cirque Somniatis, Mr. Van Dalen seeks to communicate with Claire. As it turns out, she desires a relationship with him as well," Rasia explained.

"You mean you've already met her?" Michael asked.

"Yes. She is a sweet spirit. A little shy at first. But you'll like her. I know it. Oh..." Rasia suddenly placed a hand to her head and stared off into the distance, as though she were trying to fight off a dizzy spell.

"Are you okay?" Kate asked her.

"Yes, fine my dear, quite fine indeed. The real question here is are *you* alright?"

"Me?" Kate asked. "Yeah, I'm fine. I think."

"I wouldn't be so sure, dearest Kate. I'm told that you're struggling with a deep and profound inner sadness. You feel that you're missing something. Perhaps you still haven't fully recovered from the memory of a lost love?"

Michael felt the blood drain from his face as he watched Kate take an involuntary step backwards, her eyes wide with something that looked very much like shock. Could it be true? Was there a part of Kate that still longed for Trevor? There had to be. Losing a fiancé was a traumatic experience, one that was sure to stay with her even if, technically, she couldn't remember it. He'd known all along that she still loved Trevor, in one way or another. But he never thought that her love for him might be hurting her.

54

"And you, Luke," Rasia continued. "Before this weekend is over, you will be facing your most dreaded fears. And I'm afraid those fears may find you sooner rather than later."

"Oh, Rasia," Luke laughed. "I'm afraid you might be losing your touch, old gal. I'm Luke Rainer. I have no fears."

"None that you put on display, anyway." Rasia raised a knowing eyebrow.

Luke shoved his hands into his pockets and tried to laugh it off, but Michael couldn't help but notice he didn't look nearly as confident in his machismo as he had mere moments before.

What was going on? Was it possible that the woman standing before him was for real? He supposed it was. After all, he saw dead people. And he knew for a fact that he wasn't the only one. Emily Drake, the daughter of the woman who owned Stanton Hall Manor, possessed the same ability as he did. But as far as he knew, neither of them had ever been given the gift of foresight. Unfortunate, because that really would come in handy, you know, all the time.

"You always were a tease, Rasia," Luke said, addressing her as though she were his favorite aunt. "So how about Mikey? Do the spirits have any messages for him? Aside from the ones they already give him?"

Michael was ready to argue that he didn't have access to *those* kinds of spirits, the future-telling kind, but Rasia cut him off, saying, "It's hard to tell with the plethora of entities surrounding him. His aura is all but engulfed by a cloud of energy."

"Really?" *That* was good to know, especially considering how lousy he'd slept last night, being forced to share a bed with Luke, who turned out to be one of the worst tosser-turners on the face of the planet. But somehow, he got the feeling that wasn't the kind of energy she was talking about.

"Oh yes, my dear. Your particular set of gifts has opened you up to a whirlwind... of..." Suddenly, Rasia trailed off and the smile faded from her face. Her eyes drifted in and out of focus, as though she were seeing something beyond Michael, or perhaps something inside of him.

"Everything okay, Rasia?" Luke asked.

"No," she replied, her voice trembling. Then, she turned frantic amber eyes up at Michael. "You are in grave danger, Michael Sinclair."

Her words were so certain, her voice so deadly serious, that Michael felt his stomach drop. If she was just making all this up on the spot, she was doing a hell of a job.

"What are you talking about? What kind of danger?" Kate asked.

"I can't say. But I can tell you that your peril is imminent," Rasia replied, turning back to address Michael. "You need to leave. Leave this place. Immediately. Go home. Be safe." Then she shivered and, wrapping her lacy shawl tightly around her shoulders, said, "I'm sorry. I can say no more. I have to go."

And just as swiftly as she'd appeared, Rasia Leyland disappeared into the bustling crowd.

~*~

"So who exactly is she?" Michael asked once he, Kate, and Luke had passed through the first row of vendors and brightly colored street performers. They wandered to the outer rim of the festivities and took refuge on a bench at the edge of the surrounding woods.

"Rasia?" Luke asked, observing the patrons as they passed by. "A psychic. Or so, she claims to be."

"You didn't seem very skeptical earlier," Kate remarked.

"Neither did you," Luke countered.

Michael would never admit it, but he was grateful to Luke for pointing that out. He hadn't wanted to bring it up at the risk of sounding like what he was - a petty, jealous boyfriend - but he couldn't deny that he'd been writhing with curiosity to find out what was going on inside Kate's head. See, that was why it would have been helpful to be a real psychic.

"I was freaked out that she knew about Trevor, not because anything she said was accurate," Kate explained. "I'm not wallowing in depression or secretly longing for the life with him that I can't remember. But I..."

"What?" Michael asked, dreading her answer.

Kate took a deep breath and toyed with a leaf that had drifted down next to her on the bench. "Sometimes I do wonder just how much I had changed before... everything."

"What do you mean?"

"Back before the accident, I'd reached a point in my life where I was ready to get married and spend the rest of my life with someone. And for me now, it's really weird to think that that person... wasn't you," she admitted, smiling sheepishly at Michael. "I don't know. It's silly. But I did think it was weird that she kind of called me out on it."

"It's not silly. Rasia has a way of getting inside your head like that. She's good," Luke told her.

"Okay. So how did she get inside yours?" Kate asked. "What are you afraid of?"

"I said that she was good, not that she was right."

"So, you don't think she's legitimate?" Michael asked.

"What, you mean like does she really see into the future and talk to dead people and all that other stuff she boasts? Maybe. The thing about Rasia though, is she's one of those celebrity psychics who always has to have an audience."

"Sounds familiar," Michael quipped before he could stop himself.

"Excuse me, I did not seek the spotlight. The spotlight sought me," Luke told him. "But despite what you may think, Mikey, I do not always have to be the center of attention. In fact, most of the time, I prefer not to be. Rasia is different. She loves to have people ooh-ing and ahh-ing over her. She feeds on it. That's why I try to take everything she says with a grain of salt."

"You mean, you think everything she said was for show?" Kate asked.

"I think everything she said was meant to get exactly the reaction that she got out of you. You gave her credibility and power, and she loves that," Luke replied.

"So you don't think Michael's in danger?" Kate pressed on.

"I mean, he could eat too much cotton candy and go home with a tummy ache, but I highly doubt that even that will happen since I don't know anyone over the age of seven who actually indulges in cotton candy."

"Hey, I love cotton candy," Kate told him. She looked so offended that Michael had to bite his tongue to keep from laughing.

"The point is no, I don't think Mikey is in any danger," Luke said. "What do you think, Mikey? Do you feel frightened for your life here?"

"Honestly? No." And he didn't. Maybe he should have, especially considering the way Rasia had begged him to turn around and leave. But surrounded by the balloons and music and popcorn, not to mention the company of the woman he loved (okay, and Luke), he was actually feeling quite content. Which, admittedly, was odd for him, being the all-around pessimist that he was.

"There you have it," Luke announced as though his say-so settled the matter. "Rasia may be psychic. She might be right about most things. But she's not right about everything. And that is the only thing that she will never admit."

"Well, if it isn't Luke Rainer."

The new voice startled Michael and he glanced up to see a man, dressed in black jeans, a black sleeveless shirt, a black leather vest, and not one but three silver cross necklaces, sauntering toward them. He looked very out of place in such a bright, cheerful environment.

Beside him, Michael felt Luke go rigid. He was staring at the newcomer as though he'd just crawled straight out of the pits of hell itself. For all Michael knew, he could have. He certainly dressed the part. Well, minus the crosses.

"It's nice to finally meet the Haunted Heartthrob in person," the stranger continued. "You'll have to forgive me if I don't seem starstruck. I really am. Truly. And who might the rest of you be? Wait, don't tell me. Let me guess. The one and only Michael Sinclair, America's Medium. And you, Doll Face," he addressed Kate with a smarmy grin. "I bet you came all the way just to see me, didn't you?"

Kate looked stunned, speechless, like she had no idea how to respond to such condescension. Michael was right there with her. He liked to think he'd be able to stand up to any guy who talked to his girlfriend like that, but this particular guy looked very capable of punching him in the face. Or worse.

Luke, however, clearly felt no such qualms. He was on his feet in an instant, glaring at the man with a dark, furious expression that Michael had never seen on his friend's face before.

"Oh, you son of a bitch."

Chapter 8

For as long as Luke had been in her life, Kate had never known him to exhibit any kind of hostility or show any signs of hatred toward anyone or anything. Even in the face of death and danger, he managed to exude positive energy. But now, in the face of whoever this guy was, or thought he was, Luke seemed an entirely different person from the man she'd come to regard as one of her closest friends.

The stranger, meanwhile, grinned as if Luke had just given him the best compliment he could ever hope to receive. "Ah. So my reputation does precede me. I wasn't sure."

"Wait a minute, do you know him?" Kate asked Luke.

Before Luke could answer her, the young man cut in. "Please, if you'll allow me. I'm afraid my colleague here would distort your perception. My name is Chance McDermott, host and lead investigator of the SyFy Channel's newest series, *Grave Crusaders*. Airs every Friday night at eight. If I'm not mistaken, that's the same time that *Cemetery Tours* used to be scheduled. Isn't that right, Luke?"

By now, Luke was seething. His face had drained of any and all color and Kate could see his fists shaking. She honestly didn't blame him. This guy, Chance McDermott, was a jerk. Unfortunately, he was a very, very, very good-looking jerk, so it was no wonder he'd gotten his own television show. With light, striking eyes, rough stubble, and dark hair styled to perfection, he was clearly the type of guy who'd never had to work for anything in his entire life. Everything had just been handed to him.

Judging by the curious glances he kept throwing her way, he was also probably used to girls falling at his feet.

"Listen, you cheap, cheating, sociopathic lowlife," Luke growled. "I don't know what you think you're doing here, but we don't have time for you or whatever two-bit nonsense you're trying to stir up."

"Really? Because from where I'm standing, it looks like you're sitting around doing nothing. As for what I'm doing here, well I'll have to swear you to secrecy," McDermott smirked. It was all Kate could do to keep herself from smacking the smug look right off his stupid face. It was like he thought they should consider themselves lucky to be allowed in his presence. "My team and I are here, at the personal invitation of Alfred Van Dalen, to see the sights, take in some shows, and film the two-hour-length season finale of *Grave Crusaders*. Let me tell you, it is going to be one hell of an episode. According to Rasia Leyland, this place is crawling with ghosts. Did I mention that she's agreed to appear as a celebrity guest? You know, I'd ask you, but I think that might be a little awkward, seeing as how we were asked to come here while you and the *Cemetery Tours* gang were, you know, snubbed."

At that point, Kate and Michael were both on their feet and standing on either side of Luke. Kate didn't have to be any kind of psychic to know that Chance McDermott was one snarky comment away from being sucker-punched by Luke, so she grabbed hold of his elbow, if for no other reason than to keep him somewhat grounded.

"Now *you* Sinclair," Chance continued. "You, I'd happily welcome on the show. It's going to be a long weekend and we've got two hours to fill instead of just one. I know we could find a place for you. That goes for you as well, Princess," Chance grinned, eyeing Kate up and down. "I'm not sure if you've got any paranormal in you, but a little extra eye candy never hurt the

61

ratings. I could even give you a little behind-the-scenes action if you know what I mean."

The way he looked at her made Kate's skin crawl. Half of her wanted to attack him. The other half wanted to puke.

"That's enough!" Michael hissed, using a tone that Kate had never heard before. "Look, I have no idea who you are, but *no one* talks to her that way. You got it?"

"My bad, my bad," McDermott said, throwing his hands up in mock surrender. "Didn't know she was your squeeze. But you've got to admit, it's a mistake anyone could have made. She is way out of your league."

"Will you please leave?" Kate snapped.

"I'm just kidding, Cupcake," Chance tried to appease her. "Jeez, someone forgot to take her Midol this morning."

That did it. Kate was so angry she was beginning to feel light-headed. It wasn't often that she was rendered speechless, but she couldn't remember ever feeling such blind fury towards a person. The only thing she could think to do was to grab Michael's hand and walk away.

So that's what she did.

Granted, it wasn't a perfect plan. After all, they'd left Luke to fend for himself against Chance McDermott. But it was the best she could come up with on such short notice. Besides, if she hadn't gotten away, someone was going to end up throwing a punch. And it wasn't going to be one of the guys.

As it turned out, Luke wasn't far behind them. Thankfully, he was alone.

"Tell me he's not following us," Kate said to him as they once again found themselves lost in a sea of cheerful circus-goers.

"He's not. But I know that won't be the last we see of him this weekend. God, I hate that guy!" Luke snarled.

"Maybe Rasia was right," Michael remarked. "Maybe we *should* leave. Not for my benefit, but for yours."

"Hell no. I am not going to let that douchebag think he can run me off with a few asshole comments. No way. We're staying."

"Oh, good," Michael muttered dryly.

Kate had to admit, while she didn't like the idea of running into Chance McDermott again, she didn't want to leave. Even in spite of Rasia's warning to Michael about him being in grave danger, which honestly, she didn't buy. And she was usually the cautious, overprotective one. If she had truly thought that Michael's life was, in fact, at risk, then she would have been the first to suggest hightailing it out of there and back to Dallas. She got the feeling Michael didn't put much stock in Rasia's prediction either. At least, she hoped he didn't. If he did, then she was willing to bet that her prophecy concerning his well-being wasn't on the forefront of his mind.

Hoping to placate him, regardless of what was bothering him, Kate took his hand and laced her fingers through his. Then, she stood up on her tiptoes and kissed his cheek.

"It's still going to be an amazing weekend," she assured him.

"Yeah, speaking of ghosts," Luke butt in. Kate wondered if she should point out that no one had actually mentioned ghosts, but decided against it. "Mikey, have you seen any of those supposed spirits wandering around?"

"Not really, no. But it's so crowded that they might be hard to spot."

"Chance McDumbass says the place is crawling with them," Luke muttered, glancing around. "Or that's what Rasia told him."

"How certain are we that she's a legitimate psychic?" Kate asked.

"Well, she's world-famous. Had some pretty high-profile clients. Written at least four or five books, all bestsellers. If she's not legit, she pretty damn good at faking it," Luke replied.

"Earlier though, you said we should be taking her predictions with a grain of salt," Kate reminded him. "You said she wasn't always right."

"And she's not. But of all the celebrity psychics out there, she's the one I'm most inclined to believe in. Most of the time, anyway."

"How come?" Kate asked.

"She just seems more genuine, more personable. Like us, I really don't believe she's in it for the money or the fame. I think she's trying to give people a little bit of hope and help them make connections with the other side. *Chance McDermott*," he was so angry that he spat the name, "on the other hand, is the rancid source of all that is foul and rotten and evil in this horrible world that we live in. I've never met anyone so fake, and considering some of the girls I've dated, *that* is saying something."

"Your mom must be proud," Michael commented.

"Oh, great. Wit. Sarcasm. You know, Mikey, those are my favorite things in the whole wide world," Luke snapped.

"Boys..." Kate tried to imitate her mother's warning tone. It didn't sound quite as threatening to her ears, but it must have done the trick, because both Michael and Luke looked a little frightened. "Look, I know the guy's a jerk, but that's no reason for the two of you to start bickering."

"He started it," Luke muttered. Kate raised her eyebrows. "Sorry."

"Yeah, sorry," Michael echoed.

"Good. Now that that's settled, it's time to start enjoying ourselves. No more phony prophecies. No more Chance McDermott. We're going to have a lovely weekend. Got it?"

"Got it," Michael and Luke mumbled together. Their lack of enthusiasm didn't escape Kate for a second, but she chose to ignore it.

"Right then. I want to go see a show. I've heard there are all sorts: acrobatics, dance, magic, you name it." Kate made another pitiful attempt to boost the guys' spirits, but both seemed pretty set on pouting. Their dedication to their cloudy moods would have been impressive if it wasn't so annoying.

They were at the circus, for heaven's sake! How could anyone be miserable at the circus? The smell of caramel corn, the sound of bells, whistles, and laughter, the colorful costumes and tents... It should have been the perfect equation for happiness.

As they passed an entrance to one of the fun houses, Kate thought of one last trick that might put a smile on Michael's face. Luke, she'd determined, was a lost cause. But Michael might still be salvageable.

Wrapping her arms around his slender torso, she leaned in, and batted her eyelashes up at him. "I wonder if they have a Tunnel of Love?"

"Doubt it," he answered. "They'd probably have to build some kind of river or underground moat for that."

Well, that was it. Kate was out of ideas. As cute and sweet and moderately intelligent as he was, Michael could be very, *very* dense. Especially when it came to flirting. A little sad, considering she'd been his girlfriend for over five months now. But she loved him anyway.

Instead of dwelling on circumstances she couldn't change, Kate tried to turn her attention to the festivities surrounding her. The Cirque Somniatis almost reminded her of fairs and carnivals growing up, but it was far more elegant, more majestic, than the fairgrounds of her childhood. The colors were primarily those of gemstones: garnets and amethysts, with touches of sunlight and moonlight embellishments. It was like stepping through the door to Wonderland. Being there with Luke, and especially Michael, made it that much more magical.

Or it would have, if they weren't being so mopey.

"Come one, come all!
Heed fortune's call!
Inside a world of dreams come true,
Let wonder tempt and beckon you.
Come one, come all! Do not forego!
Step inside, enjoy the show!"

The man, dressed in a costume the color of night, complete with a staff and shimmering mask, stood outside one of the grander tents and announced the beginning of a performance. Exactly what performance that may be, Kate wasn't sure. But perhaps a bit of magic or dance or acrobatics was exactly what Luke and Michael needed to elevate their spirits.

She looked up at Michael. His eyes were narrowed and locked on something, or someone, in the distance.

"What do you see?" she asked him.

He responded with a swift shake of his head, as though her voice had snapped him out of a trance.

"Nothing," he replied. "At least... I don't know."

She resisted the urge to press him for answers. She knew that when he wanted to talk about it, he would. She also knew that if it were something important, he wouldn't be holding back.

"Do you boys want to go see the show?" she asked.

"We're here. Might as well," Luke replied, still morose as ever.

Kate sighed. It was going to be a long weekend.

Chapter 9

Michael could tell that Kate was trying her hardest to lighten the mood, and he loved her for it. He was hoping to forget about Rasia and Chance McDermott and the little boy from the night before and the fact that Kate may or may not still be subconsciously longing for Trevor, but with one continuously piling up on top of another, it was difficult. Not to mention the fact that his life was supposedly in grave danger. Probably due to some kind of mental breakdown.

How he'd made it to twenty-eight without any sort of psychological crisis was, quite frankly, a mystery and a miracle all in one.

He made an effort to at least look like he was having a good time, especially after Kate grabbed his hand and led him and Luke into the tent where dreams were supposedly made real. As soon as his eyes fell on Chance McDermott and two other men dressed in a similar fashion sitting smack dab in the middle of the audience, however, he realized that the so-called dream was probably going to end up being a night terror. Even worse, the Grave Crusaders had taken up three or four additional seats in front of them to set up their state-of-the-art cameras and filming equipment.

Kate noticed them too and muttered, "Oh no..." She glanced up at Luke. "We can leave if you want."

"No. I want to see what those scumbags are up to," Luke told her. "Maybe if we keep an eye on them, we can find out what they're really doing here this weekend."

"I thought they were filming their season finale," Michael said. Was he missing something? Were he, Kate, and Luke suddenly an undercover amateur detective agency sent to unmask the evil ghost-hunting villains at a circus?

He really, really hoped not.

"They might be. But there's something else going on. I can feel it," Luke insisted.

"How? Are you a psychic now, too?" Michael expected a sharp scolding from Kate, but as it turned out, she was too distracted by the man in the center ring to comment.

At first glance, he didn't stand out. At least, not compared to any of the other performers. But upon closer inspection, Michael began noticing tiny details that set him apart: the golden mask, the black velvet top hat, the air of authority...

Alfred Van Dalen.

It had to be him. After all, hadn't he introduced himself in his letter as the Ringmaster? The guy standing dead center in the middle of the Big Top, preparing to address the audience, looked as much like a Ringmaster as any Michael had ever seen.

"Greetings," the man announced. "I am delighted to welcome all of you to this, the debut of Cirque Somniatis, and what will surely become one of the most memorable and magical experiences of your lives. Now, let the fantasy begin!"

"What is this, the Hunger Games?" Luke muttered.

"You've read *The Hunger Games*?" Kate sounded impressed. She'd been trying to convince Michael to read the trilogy for ages.

"I spend a lot of time on airplanes," Luke reminded her.

Thankfully, this particular show turned out to be quite different from a teenage tournament to the death (Michael knew at least that much). It began with high-flying trapeze artists, dressed in white, leaping off platforms so high, the acrobats probably could have reached up and touched the tent's purple and white striped ceiling. As the artists tumbled through the air, sparks and small explosions lit up the open space surrounding them. While most of the audience seemed awed and enthralled by the pyrotechnics, Michael couldn't help but wonder if fire inside a tent was actually safe. Unwittingly, he once again thought back to Rasia's prediction regarding his safety. What if they were all in danger?

Before he could dwell further, he noticed another acrobat, also dressed in white, on the far side of the center ring. She looked somewhat lost and out of place, but nevertheless a part of the show. She danced to the music playing over the speaker, moving gracefully as if she were the only one who could hear it, as though the rest of her fellow acrobats didn't exist.

There was something very peaceful, almost magical, about the way she lifted her hands and curved her legs to the melody. Watching her, she seemed less like an acrobat and more like a breath of mist as she continued to dance across the ring.

Then, with a swift running start, she did something that Michael had never before witnessed. She leapt up off the ground and flew. Raising her arms again, she glided and twirled effortlessly through the air. She circled the tent as though on a trapeze before she descended back down to the ground.

Of course. She was a spirit. An exquisite, ethereal spirit, but a spirit nevertheless. No wonder no one else was watching her. He was the only one who could see her. And she was, without a doubt, one of the most beautiful girls he'd ever seen. Tall and lithe with big gray eyes and thick brown hair, she seemed the very embodiment of grace. She wore a white leotard, trimmed with gold, and a white, gossamer skirt tied around her waist. With a start, Michael realized she was the young acrobat girl that Rasia had talked about. If only he could remember her name...

"Whoa!" Kate's exclamation drew Michael's attention back to the live performers, now dancing across tightropes and juggling shimmering, sparkling hoops. "Did you see that?" Kate asked him.

"What? I mean, yeah!" But of course, he'd never been able to lie to her and get away with it. She turned to look at him.

"Is everything okay?" she asked. "Is Rasia here?"

"No. But that girl, the one she mentioned before, is," he replied.

"She is?" Kate asked. "Where?"

Not wanting to draw too much attention to himself or the spirit in the ring, Michael simply turned his gaze back to where she still danced. Kate followed his eyes, but then she looked over to where Chance McDermott and his lackeys were filming.

"I wonder if they know," she murmured.

"Know what?" Luke asked.

"Michael sees the ghost that Rasia told us about earlier."

"Claire?" Luke asked. Both Michael and Kate stared at him. "What? I listen."

"I guess that's more than can be said for either of us," Kate remarked.

"So is she the only one?" Luke asked.

"As far as I can tell..." Michael replied. But in such a crowded setting, it was difficult to be certain. She was definitely the only one flying around. As much as he hated to admit it, Michael was curious to know if McDermott and his crew had caught any of her dance on camera.

"We should go down and talk to her after the show. Tell her that under no circumstances is she, or anyone else, to make contact with the Grave Con-Artists. You might want to mention that to Brink, too," Luke said.

"Or maybe we could just stay out of it and not get involved at all," Michael said. "To me, that sounds like a great idea."

"Mikey, you were invited here for a reason. We have an opportunity here."

"To make sure that the Grave Crusaders don't get very good evidence for their season finale?"

"No!" Luke declared. "To vanquish evil in all its loathsome forms. Specifically, the form of Chance McDermott!"

After the show ended, McDermott and his crew packed up and left almost immediately. Michael couldn't help but notice, however, that all three stopped to greet fans and sign a few autographs on the way out of the tent. Were they really that popular? Michael had never heard of them before. But then, he'd seen girls go out of their way to stop Luke and ask him for his autograph, Kate being one of them.

He was so distracted watching the Grave Crusaders cater to their adoring fans that he didn't notice the man approaching until he was so close that Michael could see the whites of his masked eyes. The Ringmaster.

"Unless I am very much mistaken, I believe I am in the presence of Michael Sinclair." That was a weird way to say hello.

"Um, yeah," Michael replied. "Hi. Nice to meet you."

"The honor is mine, I assure you. I have been looking forward to meeting all of my esteemed guests, but none so much as you," the Ringmaster replied before sweeping his top hat off his head. "I am Alfred Van Dalen.

"Oh, hi. Thank you. Nice to finally meet you," Michael wasn't sure what else to say except that if this guy was thinking he was cooler than Rasia Leyland or Chance McDermott, then he was in for a huge disappointment. Maybe if he introduced his friends, it would draw the attention off of him. "Um, this is my girlfriend, Kate. And our good friend, Luke Rainer."

"Of course! Of *Cemetery Tours*. I'm delighted to have you here as well. I'm sure by now you've met our other celebrity guests."

"Yeah, we've run into them," Michael offered. "If you don't mind me asking, why are we all here? I mean, your circus is great and I'm really glad you invited us. It just doesn't really seem the place for this kind of crowd."

"I suppose it does seem a bit odd, doesn't it? But you see, I've known for some time that these grounds are haunted. I thought to myself, how extraordinary would it be to gather the world's most famous mediums and spirit chasers and host them as our guests? And what an honor for Cirque Somniatis and all who've worked so hard to make their dreams a reality."

To Michael, the words were sincere enough, but they were awfully vague. Van Dalen clearly knew how to spin a good yarn, but Michael couldn't help but feel he'd also avoided giving a straightforward answer.

"So why did you invite Chance McDermott?" Luke asked. Michael saw Kate throw him a dirty look, but Luke had absolutely no shame. "The *Cemetery Tours* crew would have been happy to come down for an episode."

"You'll have to forgive me, Mr. Rainer. I don't watch a lot of television, and when I asked, I was advised to invite the Grave Crusaders. I do hope there are no hard feelings." The way Van Dalen spoke in such a smooth, even tone, reminded Michael of a hypnotist. It was soothing, suggestive, and more than just a little creepy. Almost as though he'd read Michael's mind (and with so many psychics running around, Michael couldn't be sure he hadn't), Van Dalen withdrew a gold pocket watch and flipped it open. "Oh dear, look at the time. I'm afraid I must be off. It was a pleasure to meet all of you. I will see you again."

And just like that, he was gone.

"That was bizarre," Kate remarked.

"I liked the part where he didn't answer any of our questions," Luke said. "Something's definitely off about that guy."

"Maybe he's had a long day." Michael didn't know why he was suddenly jumping to Van Dalen's defense, especially since he thought the guy just as weird and suspicious as his friends did.

"I don't think so. There's obviously something wrong with him. I mean, choosing Chance McDermott over *Cemetery Tours*? What kind of world are we living in, anyway?"

Michael didn't respond. A new, graceful movement across the now empty center ring had caught his eye. It was the acrobat girl from earlier. She was still dancing, and try as he might, Michael couldn't tear his gaze away from her. He wasn't altogether certain that he wanted to. He wondered how long she'd spent perfecting her routine, not only in life, but in death as well. He imagined she'd passed several hours, days, perhaps even years, dancing for an audience that wasn't there.

Until now.

"Michael?" Kate asked, her voice once again snapping him out of his stupor. "Are you okay?"

But he wasn't the only one caught off guard by the sound. As soon as she spoke his name, the girl in the center ring stopped dancing and looked up, right into Michael's eyes.

It was a moment that Michael had experienced far too many times. That sudden connection with a spirit when they realized that someone, a living and breathing someone, could see them. She knew it then, and he knew that she knew. The strange part was, however, she didn't look surprised. Instead of wide eyes and a mouth agape, she simply smiled at him. The look on her face was soothing, serene. It was almost like she was sharing a secret with him.

Then she turned and kept on dancing.

Chapter 10

Something was rotten in the state of Oklahoma. Luke could sense it.

First, Chance McDermott and his legion of the undead (and not the cool kind) show up and act as though they own the place. Granted, he hadn't met McDermott's lackeys yet, but they had to be just as evil as their loathsome leader.

Then there was Rasia, stirring up drama and old emotions. Even though Luke knew she probably didn't mean to, it was still kind of irritating that she'd called him out on being afraid of something and then spouted out all that about Kate not being over a lost love. He knew Mikey was dwelling on it, even though he was certain there was nothing to dwell on.

Finally, their host, Alfred Van Dalen, was one of the creepiest dudes Luke had ever met. Running around in a mask and cape? Even if he was the master of the circus or whatever, he could have at least let people see his face during a conversation. And the way he talked? He sounded like a robot reciting lines. He'd managed to answer all of their questions without really telling them anything at all. Clever. Tricky. Suspicious.

"We've got to find out what's going on," Luke announced.

"What do you mean?" Kate asked through a mouthful of cotton candy.

"With all the kooks running around here."

"You mean like Michael?" Kate teased.

"What?" Mikey asked. He clearly hadn't been listening. In fact, he was being so quiet that Luke had almost forgotten he was there. It was like talking to a corpse.

No, that wasn't true. In Luke's experience, dead people were a lot chattier.

"We're trying to figure out what the deal is with this place," Luke explained.

"How can you be sure there even is a deal?" Kate asked, tearing off another piece of the pink, fluffy candy. "Why can't it just be that the guy running the circus wanted to generate a little publicity?"

"Because he didn't invite Bozo the Clown or Horton the Elephant. He specifically invited ghost-hunters and psychics and mediums. There's something here that he wants to know about or there's something here that he's hoping to get rid of. Either way, he has an ulterior motive. I can feel it."

"Well, until you figure out what that is, can't we just have some fun? Look, there's a Ferris wheel, there are tons of games, we could go see a magic show..." Kate rambled off a list of basically everything within her line of vision.

"Yeah, sounds fun," Mikey replied half-heartedly.

Kate frowned.

"Are you okay? You seem so distant," she said. "You're not still thinking about what Rasia said, are you?"

"No. Not really," he replied. "It's that girl."

"What girl?" Luke asked.

"The ghost from the acrobat show."

"What? Is she following us?" Luke asked.

"No, it's nothing like that. It was the way she looked at me. It was really strange."

"Don't ghosts usually look at you like you're really strange though? These are people who, never in their wildest dreams, expect to be seen again," Luke reminded him.

"That's the thing, though. She didn't look surprised at all. It was almost like she'd been expecting me," Mikey explained.

"Well, didn't Rasia mention something about having already met her?" Kate asked. "Maybe she saw her again and told her that she'd run into you."

"Yeah. Or maybe Van Dalen is concocting a more sinister plan than he'd like to let on and he's told all of the ghosts out here to be on high alert for a tall, gangly guy who just happens to make eye contact with them," Luke theorized. Mikey and Kate just stared at him. "What? It could happen. Do not tell me that neither of you thought there was something off about that dude."

"No, there definitely was," Kate acknowledged. "But then again, the guy runs a circus. You can't really expect him to be all that normal."

"I'm beginning to think that normal doesn't exist," Mikey remarked.

"Not for people like us, it doesn't," Luke said. "Which is why, at least for the time being, I don't think we can trust anybody."

"What?" Kate asked, somehow managing to look confused and annoyed at the same time. Women, it turned out, were incredibly efficient multi-taskers. "Luke. You know we all love you, right? But I think you are reading *way* too much into all of this. I think you're still really agitated over the whole Chance McDermott thing, and I don't blame you at all. The guy is a huge jerk. But this is a circus, and a really nice one. Alfred Van Dalen isn't some master schemer or secretly in cahoots with McDermott to bring you or Michael down."

"What about Rasia?" Luke asked. "What about her prediction that Mikey was in grave danger?"

"We've had this discussion twice already. You said yourself that she likes to shock people and that you don't actually believe that Michael is in any danger here."

"But that was *before* meeting that Van Dalen character and being confronted with the man who is making my professional life a living hell. No pun intended."

76

"Okay, maybe everything Rasia said was accurate to an extent, but why on Earth would anyone here be plotting to hurt Michael? Or any of us?" Kate asked.

"Oh, I don't know. Because they're *evil*?" Luke asked.

"If you think that, then why don't we just leave?" Mikey asked.

"We can't leave. They'll know that we're onto them," Luke insisted.

"You are making absolutely no sense at all," Mikey remarked, rubbing his forehead with the heels of his hands. "If you don't want to leave, and you don't think we can avoid them, then what do you suggest? We break out the magnifying glasses and deerstalker hats?"

"That's one option."

"You know Luke, the good news is if you ever decide to stop chasing ghosts, I can totally see you being one of those TV conspiracy theorists," Kate told him. "You could investigate Area 51, the Illuminati, the Denver International Airport..."

He knew Kate was making fun of him, but that actually wasn't a bad idea. He made a mental note to pitch it to his producers as soon as he got back to LA.

Still, he wasn't about to back down. Something foul was afoot at the Cirque Somniatis, and he intended to find out what that was.

~*~

After listening to Luke give a long-winded speech about destiny, responsibility, and Chance McDermott's plot to conquer mankind and ultimately, the universe, Kate was just about ready to throw in the towel. They hadn't even been in Hugo for twenty-four hours and already, everyone was miserable. Worst of all, Kate had no idea how to make things better.

Except, perhaps, to go home and pretend like none of this had ever happened. It wasn't like they'd actually had any sort of fun at all. And wasn't that the whole point of the weekend? To get away and have a good time?

When Kate had fantasized about her time at the circus with Michael and Luke, she'd envisioned laughter, rides, magic tricks. She thought she might buy Michael a funny balloon hat, or that he might win her a cute stuffed animal from a booth. Then, she imagined they might end the day with a romantic sunset ride on the Ferris wheel with Michael while Luke... well, she wasn't sure what she thought he might be doing. But she'd been certain that he would respect her desire to at least spend a little time alone with Michael.

She'd never admit it out loud, but she'd also been wondering if maybe Michael had been thinking about... well... a proposal. True, they'd only technically been dating for a few months, but she'd been in love with him for much longer, and she was pretty sure he felt the same. When he'd uncharacteristically agreed to make the trip to the circus for the weekend, she'd gotten her hopes up that maybe, just maybe, he'd been planning something more. She was pretty sure she'd been wrong. Or if he had been thinking about it, he wasn't anymore. Thanks to Rasia and her stupid prophecy, it was now probably the farthest thing from his mind.

But when she was being honest with herself, that wasn't what was really bothering her. As much as she loved Michael and truly believed that he was the one, she was in no rush to get engaged. He would propose when the time was right. She was certain of that.

She was more concerned that maybe she *was* still being affected by Trevor's love and loss. She wasn't the same person that she would have been had their car not swerved off the road that icy January evening. Was there a chance she might still grow into that person? Or had her course forever been altered by the sound of screeching tires and the impact of metal and glass? She didn't know, and truthfully, that terrified her.

Kate hadn't worked up the nerve to tell Michael, or even Gavin or their mother, but she'd been talking with her father about Trevor. Rex had told her how Trevor had first asked for his blessing and how he'd planned to propose to her after a night of dancing, right in the middle of the floor, in front of everyone. Instead, he ended up dropping to one knee on her front porch. It sounded intimate, personal, and oh so romantic.

It was nice, getting to know more about Trevor, and she would forever be grateful to her dad for answering her questions. Rex had been fond of Trevor, and Kate knew that he still missed him. However, talking about Trevor, their memories, everything she had lost, had left her scared to death that one morning, she might wake up and remember. What would that do to her? What would that do to Michael? She felt certain that she could live with a certain degree of heartache. But hurting him? Even the thought was unbearable.

Maybe Rasia's prediction was a sign that Kate needed to talk with Michael about all she'd been feeling lately. The only problem was she didn't know how to do that without making it sound like she was pressuring him. Or worse, having doubts.

The thing she wanted more than ever, she realized, staring at Michael's distracted face, was to be alone with him. She was glad they'd invited Luke along, but at the moment, he seemed hell bent on solving problems that didn't even exist, and it wasn't making anything fun. In fact, it was just giving her a headache. Unfortunately, she couldn't think of a tactful way to tell Luke to take a hike for a few hours.

Maybe tonight. She knew that she hadn't been under any real obligation to keep to her own condo, but she'd wanted to get him back for laughing. It had all been in good fun. Sort of. Hopefully she could make it up to him.

In the meantime, she was going to try to enjoy the circus. She just wished that the boys would lighten up and try to enjoy it too. Although she agreed that Alfred Van Dalen probably had an ulterior motive in inviting Michael to be a part of opening weekend, she sincerely doubted it was anything quite as sinister as what Luke had in mind. In fact, she was almost certain it was a publicity stunt. She suspected Rasia was in on it as well. As for Chance McDermott, the guy was arrogant, obnoxious, and a huge jerk, but he wasn't there to hurt anyone. He was there to do his job.

Unfortunately, as much as she longed to put everything that had happened behind them and simply savor what remained of their weekend, she had a terrible feeling the drama was far from over.

In fact, it probably hadn't even begun.

Chapter 11

By nightfall, Michael felt his mood beginning to lift considerably. It could have been because the day was almost over and they'd somehow managed to avoid Chance McDermott, Alfred Van Dalen, Rasia Leyland, and the acrobat girl. Or maybe he was just finally beginning to appreciate the escapist atmosphere of the circus. It really was remarkable, especially after all the lights on the rides and attractions came to life, illuminating the evening air with magnificent color. Or it could have been because of Kate.

A few hours earlier, after Luke had excused himself to take a phone call, Kate had wrapped her arms around Michael's shoulders and kissed his cheek, his neck, and finally his mouth. Then, she looked him in the eye and said, "I love you. You know that, right?"

"I know," he'd whispered back. "I love you, too."

And that was it.

Michael knew he shouldn't need her reassurance. He knew that she truly did love him. But hearing her say the words sent his heart, his very spirit, into a frenzy. Suddenly, he felt weightless and unburdened, as though whatever dark shadow had clouded his mind earlier had been vanquished, and all that remained was her light and her love.

Luke, on the other hand, wasn't quite so easily placated, but at least he'd taken a break from his ranting and raving to enjoy a corny dog and a world-class juggling act.

Now, watching the stars come out one by one across night's inky blue sky, Michael was finally beginning to feel at peace. Kate had been right all along. It was going to be a good weekend.

Then he saw her. The acrobat girl from the performance earlier. She was dancing and twirling her way around the carousel, which was lit up and full of children. Their shrieks of laughter didn't disrupt or dissuade her from her routine. As before, Michael felt himself slipping into some sort of trance. He couldn't explain it. He didn't want to watch her. And yet, he couldn't imagine tearing his eyes away.

Again, she turned and met his gaze with clear gray eyes, and again, she smiled that knowing smile.

What was she expecting? For him to go over and introduce himself? Or was it possible that, thanks to Rasia, she already knew who he was? If that was the case, then what exactly had Rasia told her about him? It was a shame Brink couldn't see or communicate with other ghosts. Michael could have sent him over to talk to her for him. Though that tactic seemed a bit juvenile...

Just then, someone began to scream. Michael turned just in time to see a red and white striped vendor cart hurtling directly toward them.

"Look out!" someone yelled.

There was no time to think. Acting purely on instinct, Michael dove out of the way, taking Kate with him as he fell. The cart then barreled through a line of innocent patrons, waiting for a turn in the bumper cars, and crashed into the wall of the ride, spilling pieces of glass and kernels of buttery popcorn flying onto the ground beside it.

Bystanders from left and ride began crowding around them, asking if they were alright and if they needed to call an ambulance. Michael ignored them and instead, turned all his attention to Kate.

"Are you okay?" he asked her.

"I think so," she replied, brushing her hair away from her face. "What happened?"

"Something must have hit that popcorn stand. Pity too. I hate to see good popcorn go to waste," Luke lamented.

Ignoring the throbbing pain under his right kneecap, Michael helped Kate to her feet as an unpleasantly familiar laugh rang through the evening air.

"Damn! I wish I'd gotten that on tape!" Chance McDermott announced, clapping his hands in mock applause.

Oh, great.

"Get lost, McDermott," Luke snapped. Then he turned to the small crowd of onlookers. "Go on, move along. Nothing to see here."

"Can you imagine? America's Medium avoids death by runaway popcorn cart, featured on the nation's favorite ghost hunting spectacular. That'd make one hell of a season finale, huh, Rainer?" Chance smirked.

"*You* did this." Luke sneered at McDermott.

"I beg your pardon?" Chance scoffed.

"You're up to something. I *know* you're up to something."

"And what could I possibly be up to, Luke? My crew and I are out here filming, minding our own business, totally innocent. If you ask me, you're the one who's acting suspicious," Chance crossed his arms and raised an eyebrow. "What do you think about that, Luke? Are you jealous that we were asked to film here and you weren't? Or is this all just a desperate cry for attention? You know honestly, I can't tell you which sounds more pathetic."

"Hey, Chance! Not to interrupt, but the EMF Detector is spiking!" One of Chance's crew members announced. He was a short, burly guy with spiky blue hair and a tattoo of a skull on his forearm.

"Well, what do you know? I get a good laugh *and* a ghost. Hey Sinclair, why didn't you say something? Oh, wait. I guess you were a little busy diving for your life," Chance snickered. "Seriously though, if you could be a pal and point us in the right direction. Maybe even introduce us? Surely you've spoken to her by now."

"I'm sorry, who?" Michael asked.

"Don't play dumb with me, Sinclair. That's Luke's area of expertise. I'm talking about Claire Tellers, the acrobat who died here on these grounds. According to Rasia Leyland, the girl has a bit of a thing for you, if you get my drift."

"What?" Michael knew he sounded like the world's biggest idiot, but at the moment, he was kind of feeling like it, too. "Chance, I have no idea what you're talking about. I haven't even met her yet."

"But you have seen her," Chance pressed.

"Yeah, I have. She..." Michael paused, silently debating whether or not he should even be speaking to Chance McDermott at all. "She was here earlier. Over by the carousel."

"But she *does* exist."

"Yes...?"

Chance threw his head back and heaved a sigh of relief. "Thank God. I was a little worried that Rasia Leyland was full of it."

"How do you know I'm not?" Michael asked.

"I guess I don't," Chance shrugged. "But you don't really strike me as a liar. And I am an excellent judge of character if I do say so myself."

Luke gave a rather loud snort of derision.

"Yeah, well, so am I," Michael responded, taking Kate's hand. "Come on. Let's get out of here."

"Gladly," she replied.

"Oh, wait a minute. She's with you? Like, *with* you, with you?" Chance asked. "Gotta hand it to you, Sinclair. You aim high. Especially for a guy with no ambitions." Michael ignored him. But Chance just wouldn't let it go. "Or maybe your girlfriend just has exceptionally low standards. That's a possibility."

At that, Michael felt all the blood draining from his face and his hands. It was like his body was physically preparing him for a brawl he'd never win. But at the moment, he didn't care if he ended up in the hospital with half his limbs missing. He was going to pulverize Chance McDermott.

Kate must have known, at least on some level, what he was feeling, because she grabbed him by the arm and hissed, "Michael, no. He's not worth it."

But Michael didn't have to worry. As though she'd been summoned by his thoughts, the acrobat girl reappeared, staring McDermott up and down. Michael watched as the cocky grin faded from McDermott's face, only to be replaced by a grimace of unease. Stumbling slightly, the ghost-hunter pressed a hand to his head and squeezed his eyes shut.

"Son of a - What are you *doing* to me?" Chance cried.

Michael had to admit he was wondering the same thing. He'd come into contact with enough angry spirits to know that their presence often caused headaches and fatigue, especially from those whose energy was already susceptible, but this girl seemed to be actively attacking Chance McDermott. Not that Michael could really blame her. In fact, he was tempted to encourage her to keep it up.

Once McDermott fell to his knees, however, Michael knew that he needed to put an end to it.

"Stop! That's enough!" He cried as the small audience from earlier began to congregate once more. Michael barely noticed them. His attention was focused entirely on the girl, who'd finally torn her eyes away from Chance and who now stared directly back at Michael.

"What is going on over here?" a man called out.

"Are you alright, Sir?" a woman asked Chance.

"Yeah. Yeah, I'm fine." He kept his voice weak, using a tone that suggested he wasn't actually fine at all, but putting on a brave face for the sake of those surrounding him. As he regained his composure, he glared and pointed at Michael. "You stay away from me."

"What is he talking about?" another woman wondered.

And just like that, the crowd turned their attention to Michael, who stood, dumbfounded and, as usual, at a total and complete loss for words. He imagined that this must be how all those magicians and acrobats felt being put in the spotlight. But instead of gazing at him with awe and wonder, this group stared at him with suspicion, unease, and, if he wasn't mistaken, a little fear.

"This guy is a freak," Chance warned the crowd. Then, with one last hostile glance at Michael, he turned and walked away. His cronies followed shortly thereafter.

As they retreated, the crowd began to murmur amongst themselves. Michael felt both Kate and Luke closing in on him, like they were trying to defend him from whatever people might be saying or thinking.

"I think it's time to head back to the condos," Luke remarked, his eyes shifting from one onlooker to the next.

Michael nodded. "I couldn't agree more."

~*~

Luke led the way back to the grounds' makeshift neighborhood while Kate and Michael lingered a few steps behind. He was talking loudly about Chance McDermott and how he was probably sitting alone in his condo, trying to figure out new ways to perpetuate discrimination and world hunger, but neither Michael nor Kate was really paying him any real attention.

Kate knew that the events of the evening had left Michael shaken, weary, and maybe even a little scared. She kept telling herself that it wasn't like that popcorn cart could have done any *real* damage, but the way it had seemed to target him... It was a little strange. Then there was Chance McDermott and his bizarre accusations. She knew what had happened had to have been the work of a spirit, but Michael had remained mum on the details. In fact, he'd been silent for the entire walk.

"You okay?" she asked him softly.

"Yeah," he replied half-heartedly. "It's just been a long day."

"I know," Kate told him, running her fingers through his hair and kissing him on the cheek. Then, without even thinking about how Luke was just a few meters in front of them, she turned his face toward hers and kissed his lips. Even if she didn't have words to comfort him or a solution or offer him, she thought, perhaps, she could still help to put his mind at ease.

It seemed to work. There, enveloped in the sweet springtime air, she could almost feel the tension and worry evaporate from his body. She kissed him again and again, and he kissed her back in a way that made her feel that she, her touch, her energy, could revive him.

Maybe that was why, in the grand scheme of fate and meant-to-be, she was with him. She'd always believed that things happened for a reason. Life was full of instances and moments and random happenstances, but nothing was a coincidence. Michael Sinclair could see and communicate with the dead because he was supposed to. It was something he was meant to do. Maybe she was there with him, not just because she loved him, but because he needed her. Maybe she was supposed to be with him for the moments like these. He was meant to help the lost spirits of the dead. Maybe she was meant to be there to help him.

The ghosts put a strain on him. They always had. From the energy he'd spent trying to avoid them all those years to the times that left him lost and confused, it wasn't an easy life, and she was certain, beyond the shadow of a doubt, that it had influenced his character and made him the person that he was. And she loved that person. She loved him with all her heart. And yet, she still ached for him because she knew his life would never be simple.

On the one hand, he knew truths that others could barely dare to fathom. On the other hand, such knowledge and experience came with a price. Exactly what that price was, Kate still wasn't completely sure.

The one thing she did know was that she wasn't going to let Michael go it alone.

Gently, she pulled her lips away from his and whispered, "Do you want to stay with me tonight?"

He simply nodded.

Chapter 12

Before, Michael had never felt comfortable enough in a relationship to consider spending a night with a girl, but that had changed with Kate. He'd initially thought it was because of how long they'd known each other and everything that they'd been through. It wasn't until recently that he realized his feelings had nothing to do with the amount of time they'd spent together. It was her. She felt like home. She always had.

Luke, thankfully, had understood that Michael and Kate needed to spend a bit of time alone together. In fact, he'd seemed almost relieved when Michael came to retrieve his bags from their condo.

"I've got some serious research to do tonight, anyway," Luke had said. "I want to know everything about this place, the people running it, and the ghosts that might be haunting it. Starting with Claire Tellers." Michael had told him and Kate briefly about the girl's attack on Chance McDermott. "I also want to monitor all the social media outlets."

"What for?" Michael asked.

"Because of that pitiful scene that Chance McDumbass had the gall to stir up earlier," Luke grumbled. "Calling you out for something he knows you didn't do? Just to get a rise out of people. Or maybe it was to cast himself as some sort of victim, try to make people feel sorry for him. Who knows? The guy is evil."

"So you've said," Michael remarked.

"I'm just looking out for you, Mikey. You're still so young and innocent in the ways of the cold, cruel world."

"Twenty-four hours ago I was old and decrepit."

"Yeah, well, a lot can happen in twenty-four hours," Luke reminded him.

Michael didn't like the dark, prophetic tone in his friend's voice, but he tried to put it out of his mind as he returned to Kate. She had already showered and changed into pajama pants and a sweatshirt by the time he arrived. Her hair was tied up in a knot on top of her head and her face bore no makeup.

"Sorry," she apologized from her spot on the bed. "I had to get comfy."

"Don't apologize. You look beautiful." And she did. Others might disagree, but to Michael, although she was always gorgeous, she looked best when she wasn't dressed to impress. He loved her cozy, natural look. Best of all, it let him know that she felt comfortable enough around him to let her guard down and be herself in any form.

She rolled her eyes, but smiled nevertheless.

"Did Brink come back with you?" she asked.

"Um, no. I'm not sure where he's run off to." Typical.

"So we're all alone..." she trailed off, gazing up at him from the bed.

She didn't have to beckon him. In a heartbeat, Michael had crossed the room and taken her up in his arms. For a few fleeting moments, he simply savored everything about her: the warmth of her body pressed against his, the smell of vanilla in her hair, the tracing of her lips on his neck. And suddenly, it was like nothing bad had ever happened to him at all. All that existed to him in those precious moments was Kate.

"I love you," he whispered.

"I love you, too," she replied, pulling away ever so slightly to look him in the eye. "Are you feeling better?"

"Yes," he answered honestly.

"Good." She kissed him softly. "Is it okay if I ask what really happened earlier?"

"What do you mean?" he asked.

"With McDermott. I know you didn't do anything to him. You couldn't have," she said. "Was it a ghost?"

"Yeah, the acrobat girl again. Claire." Michael had to admit, it wasn't exactly what he wanted to be talking about. But if Kate had questions, he wasn't going to let them go unanswered. He owed her that, especially after the day they'd just endured.

"What is going on with her? Has she spoken to you? Tried to contact you at all?"

"No. Every time I see her, she just looks at me. She was the one who attacked McDermott."

"Attacked? You mean, kind of like how Trevor was draining Gavin's energy last year?" Kate asked.

"No, this is different. Yeah, Trevor did feed off of Gavin's energy enough to make him ill, but this was aggressive, intentional. I think she *wanted* to hurt him," Michael explained with a shiver.

"Why? I mean, I totally understand why someone would want to smack some decency into him, but what do you think her motivation was? Do you think she was defending you?"

"I don't know. Maybe she'd had a previous encounter with him and knew how much of a jerk he could be." He sighed. "Whatever the reason, I just hope the worst is behind us."

"I do too," Kate said, sinking back down onto the bed. Then, she tucked a few stray strands of hair behind her ear and glanced down at the floor.

"What is it?" Michael asked her.

"You don't think..." She took a deep breath, but she still couldn't meet his eye. "You don't think that Rasia was right, do you?"

"About what?"

"About everything. Think about it. Luke will encounter his worst fear? What could be worse than Chance McDermott? And then you almost getting run over by that cart? What if something bad is going to happen to you?" She almost sounded like she was about to start crying.

Michael took a seat next to her on the bed and took her hand. Finally, she turned tearful eyes back to him.

"What about you?" he asked her. "Was Rasia right about you? And Trevor?"

"I don't think so," she replied. "I don't know. It could be that she put the idea in my head. Sort of a self-fulfilling prophecy. But I have no doubt in my mind that I want to be with you. You're who I'm supposed to be with, Michael. I know it."

That was enough for him. Without another word, Michael cradled her face in his hands, leaned in, and kissed her. She returned his kiss wholeheartedly, and as Michael pulled her closer, he could feel the tension and nervous energy evaporating from her body.

He had no idea what the future might have in store for them, but there, in her embrace, he felt confident that no matter what happened, they'd make it through.

~*~

Hours later, Michael woke with a start.

At first, he thought it may have been the tree branches scraping against the window, but the night was calm and very, very still. And it was silent. Too silent. Michael knew what that meant.

It wasn't Brink. He was sure of that. Michael didn't recognize the energy.

It must have been that girl. Or maybe the little boy from the night before. Either way, Michael knew he and Kate were no longer alone. Thankfully, Kate hadn't stirred. She still slept peacefully in his arms.

But whatever or whomever was inside the building was gaining energy and on the move. Michael couldn't be sure how he knew, but he sensed more so than heard the presence making its way through the condo. Within moments, a shadowed figure appeared at the edge of the bedroom, peering around a corner toward the bed.

Instinctively, Michael shut his eyes, but he could still feel the spirit watching him. How had it found him there? Had it been following him the entire time? Or could it be just another wandering spirit, just passing through? He hoped it was the latter, but somehow, he doubted it. Regardless, the longer the person stood there, the more uncomfortable and tense Michael began to feel, and it became harder and harder to lie still and act like he was asleep.

With his eyes closed, every one of Michael's other senses was on high alert. When the ghost finally gave up on waiting and began to move into the room itself, Michael heard it. It wasn't footsteps. Instead, it was a soft whisper of a light breeze or a distant voice. The entity moved slowly around the foot of the bed to the side where Michael pretended to sleep. Even with his back turned, Michael could feel the ghost standing over him. His heart pounded with a strange sense of dread and anticipation. He knew the ghost wasn't there to hurt him, but its presence there was still unnerving.

It was only then that Kate seemed to sense it as well. She shifted in Michael's arms and buried her face in his neck.

"Michael?" she whispered.

"I'm here." He tried to keep his voice as low as possible.

"'S'there someone else here too?"

Michael bit his tongue. He didn't want to lie to her, but he didn't want her to be frightened, either.

"No, there's no one," he murmured. "Go back to sleep."

"M'kay. Love you."

"I love you, too."

He knew the ghost had heard every word. He also knew it was for that very reason that it probably wouldn't be departing any time soon. It would stand there as long as it needed to.

It was going to be a very long night.

~*~

Kate woke the next morning feeling tired and out of sorts. It wasn't that she hadn't slept. She had. She always slept better when Michael was around. His presence soothed her. But her dream had been so stressful and had seemed so real that she barely felt that she'd gotten any real rest at all.

93

The dream, or nightmare as it had been, had involved a banquet in a grand ballroom. It was exactly like a fairy tale. The room was tall, at least three or four stories, and the windows were so large and clear that she could see straight out into the bright starry sky. Her sparkling diamond and sapphire gown seemed to mimic those stars as she wandered through the crowds of people, searching for her love.

Finally, she found herself at the center of the ballroom, glancing around at the intricate interior artwork and fabulous velvet curtains when he finally approached her.

He was tall, dark, and dashing in his suit. His eyes were beautiful and bright, his smile stunning, and yet his hair was still adorably messy as he reached out his hand for a dance. She took it and he immediately swept her in his arms and began twirling her around the dance floor.

Suddenly, they were the only two in the entire room. That was just fine by Kate. She moved closer to him and wrapped her arms around his neck. He kissed her neck, then her cheek. But right as he went to kiss her lips, the room went dark, and a thunderous pounding sounded from the door at the top of the stairs.

Startled, terrified, Kate turned away from him to look to the door, searching for the source of the noise, but there was none that she could see. She felt it though. Something was there, just out of sight, and just out of reach, and it knew they were there.

"What is that?" she asked. "Do you hear that?"

She turned to look back at him, but he was no longer the man she loved. His handsome features had become sickeningly sunken and pale, his hands cold and crooked, his eyes blank and unseeing and totally...

Dead.

She'd gasped and woken up, her heart racing. The room was still dark, barely morning. Frantically, she glanced down at Michael who slept soundly beside her, warm, healthy, and very much alive.

Kate heaved a silent sigh of relief, leaned down, and kissed him lightly on his forehead. He didn't stir. She wondered if he'd had a restless night as well. Lying back down, she snuggled up next to him and listened to the reassuring sounds of his heart beating and his deep, even breathing as she slowly convinced herself to relax again. She even managed to fall back asleep for a few hours, but she kept seeing him over and over as a dead man, a cadaver, a living corpse.

No. No, not a corpse.

A ghost.

Chapter 13

Morning came too soon for Michael. If it hadn't been for the smell of freshly-brewed coffee and the promise of a hot, relaxing shower, he would have opted to stay in bed all day. Still, a part of him dreaded opening his eyes. What if the ghost from the night before was still in the room? What if today turned out to be just as dreadful and draining as the day before? What if Chance McDermott and Rasia were waiting to ambush him with prophecies and mind games and insults that he once thought he'd only hear in a seventh grade locker room? What if, what if, what if?

A swift breeze past the bed, however, reminded him that he wasn't alone. He still had Kate. And no matter what, she somehow made everything worth it.

Slowly, he opened his eyes to a wave of blond hair and bright blue eyes staring down at him.

Wait. Blue?

"Rise and shine!" Brink greeted him loudly.

"Ugh," Michael moaned and buried his face back into his pillow. "I thought you were Kate."

"Thought who was me?" Kate called from the kitchen.

"Brink," he replied, his voice muffled by the pillow.

"Aw. Hi, Brink. I missed you yesterday!" she greeted him.

"Tell her I missed her, too," Brink said.

"No."

"Why not?"

"Tired."

"Well, that's what happens when you let girls 'lead you into temptation,'" Brink snickered, echoing Mrs. Grout's words from a few nights earlier.

"Bite me."

"*What* are you boys talking about over there?" Kate asked.

"Nothing," Michael assured her, summoning up every ounce of will power he possessed to drag himself out of bed. Then, glancing at Brink, he asked, "Were you here last night?"

"Nope. I went back to the other condo because I thought *someone* was supposed to be sleeping there."

"So what, did you pal around with Luke all night?"

"Nah, he never even noticed I was there. But he was up pretty late. Which is what I came to talk to you about."

Before Michael could ask what he meant by that, however, someone pounded loudly on the front door.

"Mikey? Kate? Open up, it's me!"

"Oh, speak of the devil," Brink commented as Kate went to answer the door.

Luke stood there, looking disgruntled and out of sorts, but nevertheless, wide awake. Michael realized then that he was the only person in the room still dressed in his nightclothes. And his nightclothes were boxers and a white undershirt. Not that any of his friends cared all that much. Still. It was a bit awkward.

"Have either of you been online this morning?" Luke asked, barging into the condo without so much as a 'Good morning.'

"No," Kate replied.

"Why would we? We're on vacation," Michael reminded him.

"Oh, that's right. You're allergic to social media," Luke commented. "Well, as someone who makes their living existing in the public eye, part of my job is keeping up with everything that is

97

going on in the world, particularly that which pertains to me, my career, my team, and in this case, my friends."

"I thought he made his living chasing ghosts," Brink quipped.

"I think he's making a point," Michael muttered under his breath.

"Okay, so what's going on?" Kate asked.

"Chance McDermott! That's what's going on!" Luke exclaimed.

Oh, great. Michael hadn't been awake for five minutes and he was already sick of Chance McDermott.

"Elaborate, please," he requested, rubbing his eye with the heel of his hand.

"I had a bad feeling after that ridiculous scene he made last night, so I've been keeping an eye on him and his various social media accounts, Facebook, Twitter, what have you. Sure enough, he posted this a few hours after midnight." Luke cleared his throat and began to read, "*Finally recovered after vicious psychic encounter with American Medium, Michael Sinclair. Don't let the boy-next-door facade fool you. He is more powerful and dangerous than he seems.*"

"What?" Kate demanded, sounding angrier than Michael had ever heard her sound before. It was a little scary.

"It gets worse," Luke warned them. "Mikey's name started trending on Twitter around three AM."

"Are you *kidding* me?" Kate asked, whipping out her phone.

"What does 'trending' mean?" Michael asked.

"It means a lot of people were talking about you last night," Luke translated.

"Why?"

"Because, Mikey, thanks to Chance McDermott, the entire nation thinks you're a *very disturbed individual*." Luke didn't even try to hide his exasperation. "God, today is going to be a nightmare. I only hope it's not a slow news day, because if it is, you're going to be dodging the press all day."

"Unless..." Kate spoke up, but then she reconsidered.

"Unless what?" Luke asked.

"You don't think this was the plan all along, do you? Get Chance McDermott to stir up some trouble? Get Michael in the headlines and generate a little publicity for Van Dalen and the circus?"

"Oh my *God*, why didn't I think of that? Of course! It's so obvious," Luke exclaimed. "*That's* why Van Dalen didn't ask the *Cemetery Tours* crew to be a part of the opening weekend. He knew we were friends so he must have figured I'd never go behind your back or betray you for some stupid publicity stunt. Man, everything makes sense now!"

"Who's Chance McDermott?" Brink asked.

"You don't want to know," Michael told him.

"Is that Brink? Did you tell him to stay away from strange men with cameras?" Luke asked.

"No, but that's probably good advice for everyone," Michael remarked with a huge yawn.

"Good to see you haven't lost your sense of humor, Mikey," Luke said. "Now, here's what I think we should do. We go about our day as if we are totally and completely unaware of anything that is happening in the world. Don't talk to anyone. Don't talk to patrons, don't talk to Van Dalen, and especially don't talk to reporters."

"Wait, we're going back out there?" Michael asked.

"Of course. What did you think we were going to do?"

"I was hoping for something along the lines of stay in bed all day and marathon *Firefly* on Netflix."

"And how do you expect to get Netflix here, Mikey? Huh?"

"Kate has a Kindle Fire."

"Yeah, but I forgot the charger," Kate told him. "Besides, *Firefly* is kind of boring."

Brink gasped, "Blasphemy!" while Luke took a step back, clutching a hand over his heart.

"How are we friends?" he asked, sounding utterly appalled. Then, he turned to Michael. "How are you dating her?" And then, back to Kate again, "This one cuts me deep, Avery. I thought you were one of the good ones."

"Oh, for Heaven's sake," she laughed. "Look, I tried watching a few episodes. I just couldn't get into it."

"But it's such a great show."

"If it's such a great show, then why was it canceled?" Kate asked.

"Because the universe is cruel and life's not fair," Luke argued.

"I'd drink to that," Michael piped up. Finally, something he and Luke could agree on.

"We're getting off track here. Why do you think we need to spend another day out there? Especially if you believe that this is all intentional?" Kate asked Luke.

"He wants to spy on McDermott," Michael answered before Luke could think up another plausible argument. Not that there really was one. Wanting to keep an eye on his arch-nemesis wasn't even really that good a reason to risk public speculation, ridicule, and quite possibly, panic.

No, it would definitely be best if he didn't show his face that day.

"Don't think of it as spying," Luke said. "Think of it as protecting the good people of Oklahoma from his dastardly tendencies. You wouldn't this to happen to someone else because of him, would you?"

"Honestly, I really don't care," Michael said.

"Well, I do! There are enough problems in this world without the likes of Chance McDermott and his fellow miscreants."

"Luke, no offense, but you're beginning to sound like a one-hit wonder," Michael told him. "We get it. You don't like the guy. I don't either. He's a jerk. And because he's a jerk, I really don't feel like running into him." Or Rasia. Or Alfred. Or Claire. Or anyone who might have a Twitter account.

"And I know you probably don't even want me bringing her up, but I'm still concerned about what Rasia predicted," Kate frowned. "What if she - "

"Kate, I'm going to stop you right there," Luke interrupted. "I think Rasia was right, also. I think Mikey is in danger. But I think it's more of a social danger. You know, like his reputation being at stake and whatnot. You get what I'm saying?"

"Sort of. But what about what happened yesterday with the cart?"

"That was just a freak accident. Could have happened to anyone," Luke answered.

"But it didn't happen to anyone. It happened to Michael," Kate reminded him. As she argued, Michael began to see a bit of the overprotective Kate he'd met when she and Gavin first moved in next door to him. The one who cared deeply and showed fierce concern for everyone that she loved. That was the Kate you didn't want to antagonize, because she was smart and she was snappy.

"There's a lot of stuff that you haven't told me yet, isn't there?" Brink asked Michael.

Luke, meanwhile, asked, "So you think we should hide out here all day like hermits? Even after that happy-go-lucky, smiley sunshine routine you tried to pull yesterday?"

"Okay, well, that was before my boyfriend almost got flattened by a runaway popcorn cart," Kate replied. "I'm not risking his life, especially for Chance McDermott."

"Fine. Mikey can stay here. You go with me."

"How is that a good idea?" Michael asked.

"It's not. It's a terrible idea!" Brink interjected.

"Don't worry, I'm not gonna try to steal your girl," Luke assured Michael. "But she and I can at least do a bit of scouting, see if it's safe for you to come out of your hidey-hole."

"Will they even let us in without Michael?" Kate asked.

"Sure they will. I'm Luke Rainer."

Kate glanced back at Michael. He could tell by the look on her face that she was just as apprehensive about Luke's plan as he

101

was. But he had a feeling she would go along with it. She was a fixer, after all. He just wished she didn't have to be, especially for him. Even the idea of sitting alone in the condo all day while they went out and tried to figure out what was going on made him feel like such a coward.

"Maybe I should go with you," he said.

"Mikey, no. Stay here. Get some rest. No offense, but you look like you could use it," Luke told him.

"Does he *want* to be alone with her?" Brink asked, eyeing Luke with newfound suspicion. Michael didn't think he did. At least, not in the way Brink was insinuating. Still. It was kind of an odd suggestion on Luke's part.

"Kate? What do you think?" Michael asked.

She chewed on her lower lip for a moment before meeting his gaze. "I would feel better if you stayed here," she answered, sounding almost apologetic. "After what happened yesterday... I just don't think we should take any chances."

"But what about you?" Michael asked.

"I'm not the one whose life might be in danger," she reminded him.

"She's also not the one Twitter is obsessing over," Luke added. "Trust me, Mikey. I'll take good care of her."

Michael wanted to inform Luke that Kate didn't need anyone to take care of her, that she could take care of herself better than most people he knew. But he didn't want to make the situation any more awkward or uncomfortable.

"Okay," Michael finally rose up off the bed and pulled Kate into an embrace. "I love you."

"I love you, too." Then, she kissed him softly on the mouth. "We won't be gone long. I promise."

Chapter 14

Okay, so maybe it was a little crazy, making Mikey stay locked up in Kate's condo all morning while they scoured the circus for any signs of foul play. Still, ever since three AM when the incident went viral on social media, Luke had known that something wasn't right. Hell, he'd known that since the moment Chance McDermott reared his ugly face almost twenty-four hours earlier.

"So, what exactly are we hoping to accomplish?" Kate asked as they walked the semi-familiar grounds of Cirque Somniatis. Luke recognized a few of the performers and merchants, but none of them seemed as though they were harboring a dark and scandalous secret.

They would just have to dig a little deeper.

"We are going to find proof that Mikey is being exploited by McDermott or Van Dalen or both and we are going to expose them for the frauds that they are."

"And how do we do that?"

"Kate, I've gotta be honest with you. I am making this up as I go along," Luke told her, glancing around for any signs of Van Dalen or the Grave Crusaders. "But you know, that is basically how I've lived my entire life. I wing it."

"You don't make plans? You just... go with it?" she asked.

"Pretty much."

"Huh." Kate considered that.

"You've never just gone with it?" Luke asked.

"No, I guess I have. But you know, I'm a girl. I like schedules. I'm also a bit of a control-freak. I try to deny it, but I know I am."

"So, falling in love with a guy who can see ghosts...?"

"Definitely not part of my original plan," Kate laughed. "But I'm glad it happened."

"Really?" Luke asked.

"Really," Kate replied. "Even with all the craziness that seems to follow him around. Even though it's meant stepping into the unknown, which is just about the scariest thing in the world to me. I'd rather be with him and endure all that than not be with him. You know?"

"Yeah," Luke answered, although he really didn't. Part of him wished he did. He had no idea what it was like, the idea of being better off with someone than without them. He'd been exceptionally better off without all of his past relationships, and they were most certainly better off without him. Dating was just too messy, too complicated, especially in his line of work. "You're lucky that you found each other."

"Yeah, we really are," Kate smiled.

"Do you think you'll get married?" He wasn't even sure why he asked the question. After all, he was fairly certain he'd never get married.

"We haven't talked about it, really. But I've always kind of believed that when you're with the right person, you'll know it. And I'm not sure if I felt that way with Trevor or not. I like to think I did, otherwise I wouldn't have agreed to marry him. But... I definitely feel it with Michael."

"You make it sound so simple," Luke told her.

"In a way, I guess it kind of is. But at the same time, no relationship is ever easy. I still have insecurities. I still get paranoid if he takes too long to return a text message or if I think he's irritated or upset. We're kind of an unconventional couple, but in a lot of ways, we're exactly the same as everyone else."

104

"And what way is that?"

"Still trying to figure out how life really works."

"I'm not sure we're meant to figure that one out," Luke grinned. The smile swiftly faded from his face, however, as he caught sight of McDermott's blue-haired flunky standing a few meters in front of them, snapping photos with his smart phone. "Hey!" Luke called out.

But as soon as the thug realized he'd been spotted, he took off sprinting into the crowd behind him. Luke didn't think twice. He bolted after him, dodging past patrons, balloons, and giant stuffed animals along the way.

"Luke!" he heard Kate's voice call his name, but he didn't respond. He was going to catch that crusading crony even if it sent *him* to an early grave.

It didn't take Luke very long to catch up to McDermott's lackey. Luke was faster and in much better shape than the stocky cameraman. Still, he wasn't going down without a fight.

"Hey, come'ere!" Luke growled, tugging on the guy's black and gray camouflage-pattered T-shirt. The lackey tried to fight him off, but Luke was too strong. Meanwhile, another crowd of concerned (or nosy) spectators began to gather as Luke wrestled the blue-haired flunky to the ground.

"Luke, stop it!" Kate cried, having finally caught up to them.

"Just what do you think you're doing, spying on us, huh?" Luke demanded.

"What have you got to hide, Rainer?" the cameraman shot back.

"*What* is going on here?" The crowd parted to reveal a young man, dressed in burgundy, whose brown eyes stared incredulously at the scene before him. It took Luke a moment to realize that the kid, who couldn't have been older than twenty-five or twenty-six, was in fact the one and only Alfred Van Dalen. "Luke Rainer? Dashiell Shepherd? Exactly what is the meaning of this?"

The two older men were on their feet in an instant. For a guy so young, Van Dalen certainly had the whole Disappointed-Authority-Figure tone working for him.

"I don't know!" the cameraman, whose name was apparently *Dashiell*, began. "I was minding my own business - "

"Oh, that is crap!" Luke interrupted.

" - when all of a sudden, Rainer here totally freaks out and starts chasing me!"

"You were snapping pictures of Kate and me on your phone. Don't even *try* to pretend that you're the innocent party here."

"Why would I do that?"

"Yeah, why would he do that?" Chance McDermott asked, appearing out of thin air. Some stupid bystander must have uttered his name three times, just like Beelzebub. "Unless, of course, you're hiding something. Are you hiding something, Luke?"

"I could ask you the same thing, McDermott."

"This again? You trying to throw these childish accusations back in my face? You've got to give it a break, Luke. After all, it was your friend who attacked me last night. And now you're the one strolling around, getting cozy with that same friend's girlfriend. Yet somehow, you're pointing fingers at me?"

"First of all, Michael didn't *attack* you," Kate spat. "That was a spirit. The girl you've supposedly been communicating with."

"Oh really?" McDermott crossed his arms and stared her down with an egotistical, condescending smirk. "If your darling Michael Sinclair is innocent, why isn't he here with you?"

"He didn't want - " She paused mid-sentence and cleared her throat. "He wasn't feeling well. He didn't want to take any chances."

"But he knows the two of you are out here? Together?"

"Of course," Kate snapped.

"Okay," Chance remarked lightly, holding his hands up in mock surrender. Luke felt his blood boil.

106

"Secondly, why would you go out of your way to stir up trouble for him? You don't even know him," Kate continued.

"I know he's a friend of Luke's. And any friend of Luke's is *not* a friend of mine."

"You wanted him on your show just yesterday," she reminded him.

"Yeah. And then he attacked me so I changed my mind. I don't want your weirdo of a boyfriend anywhere near me *or* my crew. In fact, that pretty much goes for you, too. Luke can stick around though. I might be able to show him a thing or two about real ghost hunting."

"If you were any sort of a *real* ghost-hunter, you'd know what a psychic attack feels like," Luke snarled.

"That's enough!" Van Dalen interrupted. He'd been so silent that Luke had almost forgotten he was standing there. "Now I am going to try to phrase this as courteously as I can. You, Chance, and Michael Sinclair and his friends, are all here on my invitation. You are my guests. But if this disruptive behavior continues, I will ask you all to leave. And I will no longer permit you to use the footage you filmed here in your television program. Is that understood?"

"Yes."

"Yes, Sir." Luke and McDermott replied as one.

"Excellent," Van Dalen smiled. "See to it that Michael receives the message as well."

And with that, Van Dalen turned on his heel and vanished into the crowd.

~*~

Michael tried to get some rest while Kate and Luke were out, but it was difficult. It should be him out there, not them. If not for him, none of them would even be there. He wasn't about to let Kate know, but this whole experience had pretty much ruined him from ever taking a vacation again.

Once he realized he wasn't actually going to get to relax, he stood up and began pacing around the condo. He glanced out the window. He wandered into the kitchen. He even stepped into the bathroom to see if his hair looked any less horrible than it had the day before.

It didn't.

When he emerged from the bathroom, he was startled to discover he was no longer alone. The beautiful young acrobat girl stood in the bedroom directly across from the door where Michael stood.

He must have looked as shaken as he felt because she held her hands up and exclaimed, "I'm sorry! I didn't mean to frighten you. Please don't be afraid." She took a few cautious steps toward him.

"I'm not. I - I mean, it's okay. I mean... Hi. I'm Michael."

"Oh, I know that. She told me about you."

"She?" Michael asked, although he had a feeling he already knew.

"Rasia. The seer."

"Of course," he muttered. "And um... what did she tell you?"

The girl took another step forward. She was smiling at him in such a way that Michael took an automatic step back. It wasn't that he felt threatened, or that she was even remotely frightening. Quite the opposite, in fact. She was even more beautiful up close. No, he stepped away from her because she was looking at him like he was her last hope, her one true salvation. And that terrified him.

"She saw you and your future," the girl smiled. "She said that you came here for me, that our paths were meant to cross."

That was odd, especially considering the ominous prediction she'd made concerning his well-being.

"Why does she think that is?" Michael asked.

"She didn't say."

"And um... I hope you don't think I'm rude, but do you mind if I ask you your name?"

"You know my name. Rasia told you. It's Claire," she replied. "Claire Tellers."

"Right. I was just double-checking. You know. You can never be too careful when it comes to names and awkward situations."

Claire giggled. "You're funny."

"Oh. Thanks." Michael cleared his throat. "Anyway, Claire. Um... I know you've probably talked this over with Rasia a bit, but I was wondering, why are you here? What... What can I help you with?"

"Help me?" Claire asked, tilting her head slightly.

"Yeah, like... What is your unfinished business?" If that wasn't a cliché to top all ghost clichés....

"Oh. Well, I don't know. After I died, it was like waking up into a dream. Nothing seemed real. I couldn't remember what had happened or how I'd gotten to where I was. Time had simply stopped. When I finally realized what I had become, I was devastated. But it's been so many years... I can't even tell you how many. Once Rasia came to me, however, she explained that I was still here because my journey wasn't over yet. She assured me there's a greater purpose and that one day, I would understand the meaning of it all.

"And what do you think that is?" Michael asked.

Claire gazed up at him with wide gray eyes.

"I was hoping you could tell me."

"Oh... Wow, um..." That was a big question, one that deserved an even bigger answer, and Michael wasn't altogether certain that he was qualified to provide one. "Claire, what you're asking... Life and death, they aren't that simple. And meaning and purpose, I mean, those are different matters entirely. Now, do I believe that everything happens for a reason? Yeah, I'd like to think I do. But I can't even pretend to understand most of it or know what any of those reasons are."

"But you do believe there is something left for me?" the lovely ghost asked, hopefully.

"Well, yeah. I think there's something left for everyone."

"What is it?" she asked.

"That, I can't tell you. It's just something you'll have to figure out."

Claire smiled sheepishly down at her bare feet before glancing up at him through her tumbling brown hair.

"Then perhaps you and I can figure it out together."

If she sensed his discomfort, she didn't acknowledge it. Instead, she bade him a wistful goodnight and vanished, leaving the room as calm and quiet as any empty space.

Chapter 15

"I think we should head back," Kate said once the chaos surrounding the scuffle had finally died down.

"You feeling okay?" Luke asked.

"Yeah, I'm feeling fine. I just don't think we should be out here without Michael."

"Are you worried about what people are going to think?"

"What are you talking about?" Kate asked. Then she remembered why the fight between Luke and Dashiell had broken out in the first place. The Grave Crusader had been recording them. "No, I don't care about that. Are *you* worried about that?"

"I'm not particularly *thrilled* about it..." Luke muttered under his breath. "I can see the headlines now: *Scumbag Luke Rainer Makes Off With Best Friend's Girl.*"

"Stuff like that gets written all the time. It's rarely ever true."

"Yeah, but people like to believe it anyway."

"Luke, if it makes you feel better, I will issue a statement to People Magazine telling them about what a great guy you are and that you'd never snake away a friend's girlfriend. But for now, I just really think we need to get back and make sure he's okay."

"You know he's fine. Brink is there with him, right?"

"Okay, then. We need to get back and let him know that we're okay."

"Why can't we just text him?"

"Luke!" Kate snapped. "I'm sorry, I'm sorry, but you are really stressing me out. If you don't want to go back, fine. Stay out here. Pick more fights. See if I care. But I'm going to..."

But the words died on her lips when the wail of a distant siren struck her ear. She told herself that there was nothing to be concerned about. They were just on the outskirts of town. It wasn't unnatural to hear sirens. They may have even been close to a medical center.

Then why do they sound like they're getting closer?

She didn't have to wonder long as she watched Luke's face fall.

"Holy..." he trailed off, his eyes wide and fixed on something behind her.

Kate whirled around to see a dark, thick, billowing cloud of smoke rising up just beyond the perimeter of the fairgrounds. As she gasped, a few of the circus-goers surrounding her began to scream while several stopped to take pictures with their smart phones.

"Call 911!" a woman cried out.

"They're already here!" a man responded.

"Is that a fire?" a little boy, no older than four or five, asked.

"Cool!" another boy exclaimed.

"No, no, no..." Kate could barely breathe as she took off sprinting toward the condos and to the massive cloud of smoke that seemed to engulf them.

As she raced through the crowds, she could feel tears streaming out of the corners of her eyes. This couldn't be happening. This was supposed to be such a wonderful weekend. It wasn't supposed to be all this fighting and hatred and fire and brimstone. They should have stayed home. If they had just stayed home, then everything would be alright. She and Michael might have taken a springtime hike through the nature preserve or stayed in for a movie night. They might be ordering a pizza while he tried to persuade her to give *Firefly* one more shot.

Please, oh please God, let him be alright, she prayed harder than she'd ever prayed in her life. *I'm sorry. I'm sorry for every bad thing I've ever thought or ever done. Please just let Michael be okay. I promise... I'll watch every single episode of* Firefly *AND* Babylon 5 *straight through without complaint. Just let him be okay.*

By the time she made it back to the complex, she was completely winded. Her legs ached and several loose strands of hair stuck to the sides of her flushed, sweaty face. Blinded by tears, it took her a moment to realize that the condo where she had been staying, where she and Luke had left Michael, was still standing, untouched by any flame. The condo that had been set ablaze sat all the way at the other end of the street.

Already, a crew of firefighters were in motion to extinguish the roaring fire that threatened to spread to other condos.

It's not him. Thank you. Thank you, God. She heaved a heavy sigh of relief as she bolted into her condo to find Michael.

He wasn't there. The condo was completely empty.

Kate felt her blood run cold.

It's alright. Don't panic, she told herself. *He's probably outside. He must have heard the sirens and went out to see what was going on. He's okay. He's got to be okay.*

She ran back outside just in time to see a breathless Luke jogging up the street.

"Did you find him?" he panted.

"No," she replied. "He's not in there."

"Where else would he... Oh shit," Luke muttered. "That's our condo."

"What?"

"Our condo! The one where Mikey and I were staying. That's that one!" he pointed to the diminishing flames.

"No... Are you sure?"

"Positive!" Luke called back to her.

"But you think Michael's alright, don't you? I mean, he wouldn't have any reason to go back there, would he?" Luke didn't answer. Kate pressed on. "Luke? He wouldn't go back there, would he?"

"Not unless he left some of his stuff there by mistake last night."

"Oh my God..." Kate felt sick to her stomach.

"Hey, listen to me," Luke commanded, steadying her with his strong grip on her shoulders. "I'm sure he's fine. Everything is going to be fine. Let's just get down there and see what we can find out, okay?"

"Yeah. Yeah, okay," Kate replied, hoping she didn't sound as woozy as she felt.

Terrified, she followed Luke down the street as he approached the firetruck and the smoldering remains of the condo. Most of the flames were gone, but the firefighters weren't taking any chances. A mad rush of water still arched through the air and pounded down onto the charred walls and foundation of the building.

"Excuse me," Luke called to the firefighters.

"Sir, you're going to need to step back!" one of the firefighters shouted back to him.

"This is my condo! This is where I'm staying!"

The fireman who had responded turned and muttered something to one of his partners, who began to approach them. Kate felt herself beginning to panic again. What if he told them that they'd found a body inside the condo? What if he said that the fire was set intentionally?

Before she could ponder further, the fireman asked, "This is your place?"

"I'm renting it for the weekend," Luke explained. "Can you tell me what happened here?"

"More than likely, it was just a freak accident. Maybe someone tossed a cigarette a little too close. There may have been some faulty wiring. It's hard to say," the fireman replied.

"But you don't think this was arson?" Kate asked before she could help herself.

"Given the state of the building, it's hard to say, but as of right now, we have no reason to suspect that."

By that point, news helicopters were flying overhead and prudish old Mrs. Grout was pattering over to inspect the damage. Meanwhile, Kate was feeling dizzier by the second. She still didn't know. She still didn't know if Michael was okay. Where he was. Why he wasn't there.

And then, as though he'd been summoned by her thoughts, he appeared, sprinting down the street as fast as he could.

"Michael!" Kate shrieked and practically flew to him.

"Kate! Oh, thank God," he sounded as breathless as she felt as she threw her arms around him and buried her face in his neck.

"I didn't know what had happened to you. I was so worried..." she sobbed.

"It's okay. It's okay. I'm here," he whispered, running a comforting hand through her hair.

"I was so scared," she whimpered. "I thought..."

"I know. I'm sorry."

"Mikey!" Luke called as he ran over to them. "Just about gave us a heart attack there, pal. Where were you?"

Michael's reply came as a surprise.

"I was out looking for Rasia."

"Rasia?" Kate asked, wiping her tear-stained face with the back of her hand. "Why on Earth were you looking for her?"

"Claire. I'll explain it to you later. What happened here?" he asked, indicating the fire.

"We don't know," Luke told him. "The guy said it looks to be some sort of freak accident. Probably a messed up wire or something. But now that I know you're safe and sound, I won't feel like a total tool lamenting all the equipment that I had stashed away in there."

"Do you think any of it survived?" Kate asked.

"Probably not," Luke muttered. "I think I've got insurance on some of it, but the rest..."

115

"Maybe your producers or the Discovery Channel will replace it for you," Kate said.

"Nope. This was all my personal equipment. Nothing that I used for the show," Luke replied, shoving his hands into his pockets. "Oh well. The good news is Mikey is here and no one got hurt. Although..."

"Although what?" Kate asked.

"If it's not too much trouble, we're going to have to make a trip into town. All of my extra clothes just went up in smoke."

~*~

Michael had known that running off without telling Kate or Luke where he was going had been a dumb idea, but he couldn't stay there in the condo, not after the encounter with Claire. He wanted to know exactly what Rasia had said to her that had given her the impression that he could be the one to save her or alter her destiny or whatever it was she wanted from him. He wasn't even certain that Claire understood what Rasia had conveyed to her.

But as soon as he saw the billowing black smoke rising up from the street, all thoughts of confronting Rasia had been abandoned. The pressing issue now, he realized, was getting out of Hugo, Oklahoma in one piece.

Kate seemed to be on the same page.

"Luke, I know you need to replace what you lost, but maybe we need to reevaluate exactly what we're doing here," she said, pouring herself a drink of water inside the kitchen of their condo.

"What do you mean?" Luke asked.

"I mean, maybe we should just take this as an opportunity to quit while we're ahead. Maybe we should just go home."

"I think that is a good idea," Michael agreed. In fact, anyone else on the planet would probably agree that after the place you're staying burns down, it's time to cut your losses and leave. "We only have one more night here anyway."

"Exactly. We only have one more night. That's why we have to stay!" Luke insisted as his cell phone began to chime in his pocket. He ignored it.

"Luke, do you really think it was a coincidence that the one building to burn to the ground was the one assigned to you and Michael?"

"I get what you're thinking Kate, but need I remind you that Mikey moved out last night? If the great Powers That Be really had it out for Mikey, then your condo would have been the one to catch fire, not mine."

"Regardless, I think we've been tempting fate long enough," Kate pressed on.

"Kate, if this was a random instance of faulty wiring or a discarded cigarette butt, I'd agree with you. But like you said, what are the odds that it was our building to burn down? *What are the odds*?"

"What are you saying, Luke?"

"I think someone burned that condo down on purpose, either to scare us or to drive us away."

"That's crazy. Who would do that?"

"Who do you think?" Luke asked, his phone chiming even more incessantly. Finally, Luke pulled it out to silence it. In doing so, he caught a glimpse at the screen. "Well, that didn't take long."

"What didn't?" Michael wondered.

"*Looks to me like Luke Rainer is getting a little too close to Michael Sinclair's girlfriend,*" Luke read. Then, he showed them the image on the screen: a snapshot of Luke and Kate walking through the circus grounds earlier that day. "I'm going to kill that guy!"

"Did Chance tweet that?" Kate asked.

"No, Dashiell. Guess McDermott is too cowardly to do his own dirty work," Luke spat. "Thankfully, he's still pretty much a nobody. No one seems to be paying him much attention."

"So let me get this straight. Chance McDermott is so evil that he burned our condo down... And had his henchmen start a stupid internet rumor," Michael commented. Somehow, it didn't quite add up.

"What's with the tone, Mikey?" Luke asked.

"I'm just saying, I can see a person being responsible for one or the other, but not both." And a spineless weasel like Chance McDermott was definitely going to go for the safe approach. In other words, spreading lies around online fit right into his mode of operation. Burning down condominiums? Not so much.

"So now you think the fire was an accident," Luke translated.

"I think that this weekend has been a lot more trouble that it's worth," Michael admitted.

"Okay, yeah, I get that. This weekend has sucked. But you still want to talk to Rasia, right? About Claire?"

"Well, I did, but to be honest, I'd rather go home."

"That's too bad. Forget about going home. You want to talk to Rasia. I need to confront McDermott about this. What I'm suggesting is - "

"You can't," Kate spoke up.

"I'm sorry, what?"

"Van Dalen said that if you and McDermott get into any more fights, he'll throw you both out, remember?" Kate said.

For a brief moment, Luke looked discouraged. Then his face lit up just like the Grinch's when he decided to steal Christmas from the unsuspecting Whos.

"Oh, well now I *have* to talk to him."

Chapter 16

It was a new low. Luke fully acknowledged that. But sometimes a guy had to play dirty, especially when his opponent was a rotten, cheating scumbag who might also have a flair for setting buildings on fire.

Granted, he wasn't *entirely* positive that it had been McDermott to start the fire. It was possible that it had been Dashiell or the other crony, whose name escaped him. Maybe they were trying to impress their boss by stirring up trouble for Luke.

Or it could have been Rasia. He hated to admit it, but Luke hadn't quite ruled her out as a potential suspect. Maybe she'd put Claire or one of the other spirits supposedly crawling around the circus up to it in some twisted attempt to make her prophecy come true. Then again, it wasn't as though her prediction had been made publicly, or that she had anything to prove to anyone.

That only left Van Dalen. It was possible this was another attempt to stir up some publicity. Luke had caught a glimpse of him speaking with reporters before they headed back out to the fair grounds in search of Rasia. Even if she wasn't responsible for the fire, she was still sending spirits after Mikey; spirits who, from what it sounded like, had been out of touch with nice, normal, rational human beings for a little too long.

The bottom line was that Rasia had a motive. Everyone had a motive. Some wouldn't admit it, but most people very rarely acted out of pure selflessness. Rasia may have truly wanted to help people, the living and the dead alike, but she'd also made a fortune in doing so. Alfred Van Dalen had graciously invited them to the opening of his circus, but that certainly hadn't been a selfless gesture. As for McDermott and his ilk, they didn't even try to pass off anything they did as selfless. They were unabashedly selfish and self-motivated one hundred percent of the time.

That was why Luke had to confront them at least once more. As Kate had so graciously reminded him, Van Dalen had threatened to kick both of them out if they stirred up any more trouble. Well, he hoped that wasn't an empty threat, because trouble was brewing. Big trouble. It didn't matter if he got kicked out because his friends wanted to leave anyway. That wasn't the goal. The goal was to get McDermott kicked out. Not only that, but to expose him for the creep and possible felon that he really was. If that happened, not only would they not be able to finish filming their stupid two-hour-long season finale, they might even get pulled from the air altogether.

It was devious and deplorable, but desperate times called for desperate measures.

Meanwhile, his phone was still blowing up with Twitter notifications, not only concerning his "romantic afternoon" with Kate, but now rumors were circulating that they'd both died in the fire while consummating their newfound secret passion. Michael was the lone survivor and despite the devastating betrayal and his ability to see ghosts, was heartbroken over the loss of the two people closest to him.

Luke figured that neither Kate nor Mikey really needed to know any of that. He would deal with it later. He'd already sent out a Tweet denying all the rumors, but somehow, they still persisted.

Oh well.

After a quick trip into town to replace Luke's personal belongings, they returned back to Kate's condo (now *their* condo) to find none other than Alfred Van Dalen waiting for them.

"And here I thought this opening weekend would be relatively uneventful," he broke the ice with a quick grin. "I hope you're all alright."

"Oh yeah, we're fine," Luke answered. "Can't say the same for all my stuff..."

"Yes, and I hope you know that we are fully prepared to reimburse you for anything you lost," Van Dalen assured him.

"Wow, thank you. That's very considerate of you. But it's not necessary. Really," Luke replied.

"Nevertheless, I do want to apologize for this mishap. I feel just horrible and I hope you'll stay."

"Of course we will. We're not going anywhere. Right, guys?" Luke asked Kate and Mikey.

He could tell that Mikey was fighting a very strong impulse to chew him out, but Kate, bless her heart, smiled her sweet smile and replied, "Of course, we're delighted to stay."

"That's wonderful. Because you won't want to miss the closing performance tomorrow night under the Big Top. It's going to be spectacular. But you know, I've really got to be going now. The contortionists' act is about to begin. Stop by if you find yourselves around Tent B. And if you've got a strong constitution."

Then, with a tip of his top hat, Alfred Van Dalen strolled down the sidewalk and back toward his circus.

"I'm not the only one, right?" Luke wondered.

"The only one what?" Kate asked.

"The only one who is *seriously freaked out by that guy*!" Luke hissed.

"Wait a minute," Mikey eyed him. "If he freaks you out so much then *why did you tell him we were going to stay*?"

"Because, not unlike your spirited spirit friends, we too have unfinished business here," Luke reminded them.

Mikey stared at him. "You have so many problems."

"Perhaps I do, Mikey. But I'm right about this."

"Right about what?"

"I don't know yet. That's why we need to interrogate our other suspects. Starting with the superstitious psychic herself, Rasia Leyland."

~*~

Although he didn't come out and admit to Luke, and especially to Kate, Michael had actually been hoping to talk to Rasia alone. It wasn't that he had anything to hide from his friends, but his encounter with Claire had left him a little confused and uncertain. He didn't want to say it out loud, but the way Claire had been looking at him... It reminded him an awful lot of how Kate looked at him.

That wasn't a good thing. And it wasn't something that Michael really knew how to deal with. As far as the afterlife was concerned, he'd been fairly certain he'd seen it all: children seeking parents, murder victims seeking justice, guilty consciences seeking absolution. But he'd never expected a ghost to fall in love with him.

That wasn't the part he was afraid to say out loud, though. He'd been captivated by Claire Tellers when she danced through the air the night before. She was beautiful and breathtaking and he'd barely been able to tear his eyes away from her. Michael wasn't in love with her, but he had been enchanted by her. And that was something he never, ever wanted to confess. Not only because of Kate. He didn't want it somehow getting back to Claire.

They found Rasia speaking with a pair of young women, both of whom stared at her in awe and gratitude. But it was the fourth, smaller figure that caught Michael's attention. The ghost of the young boy was back, staring up at Rasia with wide, curious eyes. As soon as he noticed Michael staring, however, he gasped and ran away.

Odd.

"Don't worry, my dears. Your grandmother is with you every day and she is very, very proud of both of you," Rasia told the girls. Then, she glanced over at Michael, Kate, and Luke. "There you are. I've been expecting the three of you." She bade the two girls farewell before walking over to meet them, her long skirt sweeping and swaying behind her. "I see you're still here, Michael Sinclair."

"Sort of against my will. But yeah," Michael responded before he realized how rude that sounded.

"You're either a very brave soul or a very reckless one," Rasia remarked, raising a thin, penciled-in eyebrow.

"Well, it's definitely not the first," Michael tried to joke, but it came out as more of a grimace.

What is wrong with me? Why am I so nervous?

Kate must have sensed his jitters, because she asked, "Rasia, we were wondering if you might tell us a little more about the ghosts here. You mentioned a girl named Claire?"

"Yes. Such a dear girl. Lovely. Such a tragedy what happened to her."

"And what was it that happened to her exactly?" Kate asked.

"Why it was right here on these very grounds. Back in the early fifties. Claire was a dancer and trapeze artist, one of their youngest. And most beautiful."

Michael shifted uncomfortably and hoped that nobody noticed.

Rasia continued, "It was one of her very first performances with that particular circus. Claire leapt off the platform, but her fingers slipped as she tried to grasp the trapeze. She plummeted to the ground, breaking her neck in the fall. She died instantly."

"Oh my God," Kate whispered, clasping a hand over her mouth.

"That's terrible," Luke said.

Michael didn't speak. He couldn't. Rasia's vivid description of Claire's death echoed in his ears, and in his mind, he could see Claire, dressed in white, her eyes wide and alert with passion. He saw her take that final leap, and the look on her face as she realized she wouldn't survive the fall. He saw the darkness of the empty air below rise up before the cold, hard ground claimed her lifeless body.

"Yes, the poor thing has been through quite an ordeal. That's why I've been trying so hard to help her, but I'm afraid that I won't be the one to do so," Rasia said, turning her gaze toward Michael.

"Me?" he asked. "Why do you think it will be me?"

"I don't think, dear boy. I know these things. You are the one who is destined to be her guide to the other realm. You are her hope."

"Wow. No pressure, Mikey," Luke remarked. Michael wanted to smack him.

"What *exactly* did you tell her about me, Rasia?" He'd just about had it with all her vague, mystic non-answers. They were so incredibly unhelpful that Michael wasn't even sure why she bothered in the first place. What he needed was for her to give it to him straight. No fancy words. No prophecies or metaphors or ghostly knock-knock jokes. Just straight answers.

But apparently, that was too much to ask from Rasia.

"I told her that you'd both been called here for a reason. The winds of fate do not blow haphazardly, Michael. Every path in life is laid out perfectly to direct you toward your destiny. You may take many roads, but they will all lead you to where you are supposed to be."

"And I'm supposed to be here? Even though I'm in grave danger here?"

"My dear, I am a messenger. Not an interpreter. When I receive a message from the other realm, I convey that message. Rarely am I told what it means. That's up to you to discover."

"So, as far as how to deal with Claire, you've got nothing," Michael translated. He was beginning to think that this entire conversation had been a colossal waste of time. Instead of even the smallest inkling of how he was supposed to handle Claire, he just had an incredibly bothersome headache.

"Did she appear to you?" Rasia asked.

"Yeah, she did. And she seemed pretty convinced that I'm going to somehow change her life. Or death, as it were."

"Then perhaps you should listen to what she has to say," Rasia advised.

"And what if I don't?" Michael demanded. He was beginning to feel like Rasia was playing games with him, and it was kind of starting to tick him off. She was supposed to be just like him. Sort of, anyway. She'd been dealing with the mysteries of the afterlife as long as he had. Longer, considering her age. She should understand how confusing and frustrating it could be, and how clueless and helpless it could make a person feel.

"What do you mean, Michael?" she asked.

"What if I do what you said originally? What if I just packed up, left, and never looked back?"

"I'm not sure you can anymore," Rasia responded. "I'm afraid that something might be holding you here. I can't see for certain, but there are forces here demanding that you stay. Whether they are dark or light, I cannot say."

"Chance McDermott," Luke muttered under his breath.

"Do you think Michael is still in danger?" Kate asked. "I mean, if he stays, will he be alright?"

"I hope so, my dear," Rasia answered her. "I truly hope so."

Chapter 17

The rest of the day passed, surprisingly, without a hitch. Michael wasn't sure what that was supposed to mean. It seemed a bit too good to be true, especially after the disastrous morning they'd all endured.

Of course, once they returned to the condo, Michael remembered that now, instead of just him and Kate, it would be him and Kate and Luke, all crammed cozily together in a bedroom barely big enough for two. And that was without the additional ghosts.

Brink was waiting for them when they arrived.

"Where have you been all day?" Michael asked him as Kate excused herself for a shower and Luke stepped outside to make a few phone calls.

"Just wandering. There's so much to see here. Although, you know, earlier in the day, I could have sworn I spotted smoke not too far from here."

"That's because one of the condos down the street burned down."

"Oh, really?"

"Yeah." Briefly, Michael told him not only about the fire, but the events leading up to it, as well as their interaction with Rasia.

"Damn, bro. That's rough," Brink told him. "I wish I'd been around. I might have seen who started it."

"The firefighters seem to think it was just a freak accident."

"Yeah, but freak accidents don't just happen. Not to you, anyway," Brink reminded him. "With you, it's always going to be something weird." Michael wanted to argue, but unfortunately, he knew his friend was right. "If you ask me, I think you should be a little more wary of that girl you mentioned. Claire?"

"What about her?" Michael asked.

"Dude, the way you described her, it makes her sound like some sort of nut job. Are you sure that you can trust this girl?"

"No more or less sure than anyone else I might meet. Why?"

"I don't know," Brink replied, uncharacteristically somber. "It just sounds to me like she might be a little out of touch with reality. And by 'a little,' I mean 'stark raving crazy.'"

"Okay, so what's your point?"

"My point is what if she's the danger that Rasia has been warning you about? You already know she's been stalking you. What if she's also trying to hurt you? Or the people you love?"

"Why would she do that?"

"Maybe to get you all to herself. If you're right and she's got a weird, inter-mortality thing for you, who knows? Stranger things have happened."

Michael stared at the eighteen-year-old ghost standing before him. He might have a sort of plausible theory, but it was just as likely that the fire had been a consequence of bad luck.

"Brink, where do you come up with this stuff?"

"I watch a lot of TV and I analyze the hell out of things. It sounds stupid, but trust me, I've got a lot of time to sit around and think about stuff."

"Fair enough," Michael replied as Kate emerged from the bathroom dressed in sweat pants and an oversized T-shirt. Her hair was tied up in a knot on top of her head.

"What's fair enough?" she asked, giving him a swift kiss. Brink pretended to gag.

"Brink having a lot of time to sit around and think."

"Oh yeah? What have you been thinking about, Brink?"

Even though he knew she couldn't hear him, Michael knew that Brink appreciated it when Kate spoke to him as though she could.

"Tell her something that makes me sound really smart," Brink said.

"Something about who's going to get the final rose on *The Bachelor*. I didn't ask," Michael answered.

"Thanks, man," Brink muttered.

"Ooh. I think it will be Christina. But Lindsay is a close second," Kate grinned.

"Oh my God, please tell her I don't care!" Brink demanded.

"He says he agrees with you."

"Dude!"

Michael couldn't help it. He snickered.

"What's so funny?" Kate asked, wrapping her arms around his waist.

"I don't know, exactly," Michael told her.

"Well whatever it is, I'm happy to see you smile." She sighed and rested her head against his chest. "It's been a trip, hasn't it?"

"It really has. I'll be happy when we're home." He kissed the top of her head, her hair still cold and wet from her shower. Then he mumbled, "I wish Luke wasn't staying here tonight."

Kate just laughed.

"I wish Brink wasn't staying here tonight either," Brink remarked from the sidelines. "Would either of you like to turn on the TV so I don't have to listen to your mushy gushiness?"

Michael fought the urge to roll his eyes. Being haunted was kind of like having a puppy. You had to walk it, play with it, and leave the TV on so it wouldn't get lonely. The only difference was that everyone wanted a puppy. Michael didn't know anyone, except maybe Luke, who wanted a pet ghost.

But Michael obliged, turning the television on to a local news station. He wasn't surprised to see aerial footage of the condo fire being played back to him from the screen.

" - the Cirque Somniatis, which is celebrating its grand opening this weekend. Circus-goers have traveled from different cities across Oklahoma and even neighboring states for this event.

"Local authorities have confirmed that there were no injuries in the fire and that it has been ruled an accident.

"We spoke with Alfred Van Dalen, the founder and owner of Cirque Somniatis - "

"Hey, hey turn that down!" Luke ordered, reappearing in the entry hall. "I've got a new lead."

"A lead on what?" Kate asked.

"I have it on good authority that Chance McDermott and his corrupt crew are filming tonight at Showmen's Rest."

"What's Showmen's Rest?" Michael asked.

"It's the section of Mount Olivet Cemetery reserved for circus burials. It's supposed to really be something to see, with a whole lot of circus-themed gravestones and such. I think we need to go check it out."

"What, now?" Michael said.

"Yes, now."

"But it's so late."

"Your point?"

"My point is we've had a really long day and I'm exhausted."

"*And* I already showered," Kate piped up.

"Okay, that's fine. You senior citizens clearly need your beauty rest. You two just stay here with your cozy jammies and settle down in your nice warm bed, maybe watch some *Dateline*. I'm going to go catch a psychopathic paranormal pretender before he burns down another condo," Luke announced before he turned and walked right back out the door, slamming it shut behind him.

"He just called us old," Kate said.

"Don't let it get to you. He's been calling me old all weekend," Michael told her.

129

"We're *not* old," Kate insisted.

"I know that. But not wanting to go crash the *Grave Crusaders'* season finale in a spooky circus graveyard in the middle of the night does not make us old. It makes us rational. Besides, he has absolutely no guarantee that they're even out there. He probably just wants an excuse to go run around a creepy old cemetery because he's Luke Rainer and that's what he does!"

"I don't know, Michael. Maybe we should go after him..."

"Kate, no. I love you. But don't let him get inside your head like that. This is what he wants. He wants us to go after him."

"But what if he's walking into something dangerous?"

"Well, it wouldn't be the first time. We're talking about a guy who once hired a witch to open up a secret portal to hell," Michael argued. Not that he really believed in witches. But then, there were people out there who didn't believe in ghosts either.

"That's true. But at the very least, we'd better go and make sure he doesn't end up in jail," Kate said.

Brink, who'd been listening in the whole time, looked over at Michael.

"You know you're not going to win this one."

Michael sighed.

"I'll lock up the condo."

A few minutes later, they walked out the front door into the cool, springtime night, only to find Luke waiting for them by his car. He had his smart phone out and was scrolling through Twitter. He glanced up when he heard them approaching.

"Finally. I was beginning to think y'all were actually going to make me do this all by myself."

"Oh, come on, Luke. It's like you don't know us at all," Michael remarked.

"I'm detecting sarcasm, though I'm willing to overlook it."

The drive to Mount Olivet Cemetery was a short one, barely five minutes. When they arrived, Michael was surprised by how peaceful he felt. It was actually a really beautiful night.

The air was cool and fresh and smelled of the surrounding trees and the sky was so clear he was certain he could see every star.

The cemetery itself was as still and quiet as most Michael had visited throughout the years. Although the ghosts themselves did not walk among the headstones, it felt to Michael as if the ground knew and remembered all those buried beneath it. It was a strange sensation, being so close to so many who had died. And yet, they weren't really there.

Luke had been right, though. Showmen's Rest was truly something to behold. Throughout the entire yard, statues and carvings of elephants, clowns, and tight-rope walkers danced on the gray and white surfaces of tombstones and grave-markers. For the first time, Michael got the feeling that the men and women who'd been buried there were probably really happy with their final resting place. It was a touching tribute, one that honored their passion in life and that had been constructed out of love and respect.

"I never expected to say this about a graveyard, but this is cool," Kate whispered.

"Told you," Luke smirked.

Michael meanwhile, meandered around, observing the individual grave markers. He wasn't sure if he was looking for hers, or if something drew him to it, but he soon found himself standing over the grave of Claire Annette Tellers. The headstone was tall, at least four feet, and beautifully engraved with an image of a graceful trapeze artist diving through the air.

And then, just like that, she was there, smiling at him over her tombstone.

"You found me."

"Oh. Um... Yeah, I did," Michael replied, unnerved by her sudden appearance. He hadn't given much thought to Brink's earlier reservations about her, but now, staring into her wide gray eyes, he began to feel a little apprehensive. How had she known he was going to be there? Had she followed him? How long had she been around?

131

Still smiling, she took a step forward, through her own headstone, and gazed up at Michael.

"I've missed you."

"Really? I mean... We don't know each other very well."

"We will," she assured him.

"Look, Claire, this really isn't a good time..."

But she acted like she didn't hear him. In fact, she ignored him completely as she glanced over his shoulder toward Kate and Luke.

"Who are they?" she asked him. "I see you with them a lot."

"They're two of my best friends," Michael answered. "Luke is a paranormal investigator. And Kate..." he trailed off. If this girl was as unstable and volatile as Brink suspected, he wasn't sure how much he should tell her about Kate. Granted, she'd seen them sharing a bed the night before. But there was something about Claire that wasn't quite *there*. She was dreamy, aloof, and she never seemed fully aware of her surroundings. So instead of confessing his romance with Kate, he simply told Claire, "She's a really good friend."

"Did you tell them about me?"

"Uhh... A little," he answered. Then he heard Luke call his name. He and Kate were beginning to move away from him. They must have spotted Chance and his crew. "Listen Claire, I'm sorry, but I really need to be going. Maybe you should go talk to Rasia again."

"She doesn't look at me the way you do. Besides, I want to come with you."

"No! I mean... I just... I'm really busy right now."

"Well, why does that mean I can't come too?" she pressed on.

Michael chose his next words carefully. "Claire... I don't know how to help you."

"Maybe I don't want your help. Maybe I just want you."

Flattering though her sentiment was, Michael felt the icy grip of panic inside his chest. How do you let a ghost down gently?

"That's really nice of you. But I can't give you what you want. I'm sorry," he told her, trying to ignore the pain etched across her pretty face. "I need to go."

And with that, he left her standing alone, heartbroken and confused, in the long, dark shadow of her tombstone.

Chapter 18

The night was quiet. So quiet that Kate suspected if she were to listen closely, she'd hear the soft shuffle of ghostly feet through the grass and fallen leaves. She wanted to ask Michael if there were any spirits around, but he seemed distracted, lost in thought. He'd barely said a word since they arrived, and she was beginning to worry about him. She kept telling herself that he'd had a long day and a stressful night and that he was just exhausted, but she couldn't shake the feeling that something was seriously wrong.

Meanwhile, Chance McDermott and his crew hadn't figured out that they weren't alone yet. Or if they had, they weren't letting on that they knew.

Kate could barely see them through the pitch darkness of the cemetery, but as they drew closer, she began to hear tidbits of McDermott's dialogue.

"Since the 1930s, this small town, known as Circus City, USA, has served as the winter home for traveling circus folk and their caravans. And here at Showmen's Rest is where the dedicated and talented performers take their final bow. For years, this - Did you hear that?"

"Oh please, he didn't hear anything," Luke hissed. "Mikey, are there any ghosts out here at all?"

"I uh... I can't really tell."

"It could have been us," Kate whispered.

"Why are they even filming out here anyway?" Luke muttered.

"Because it's a fascinating place filled with fascinating stories," McDermott answered, striding over to them. "Fancy seeing you out here, Luke. And Kate." But he stopped walking and glared when he spotted Michael. "Sinclair. You know, I'd feel a lot more comfortable if you'd stay away from me."

Michael didn't respond.

"I think the feeling is mutual," Kate informed McDermott.

"Hey, I've done nothing to him," Chance defended himself.

"Oh yeah? Are you sure about that, Chance?" Luke asked. "You haven't been trash-talking him online? Spying? Spreading rumors? Are you sure you don't have access to matches and a bit of lighter fluid?"

"Wait a minute, *that's* why you're out here? You think *I* started that fire?"

"Well, if the arsonist's boot fits..."

"Damn, Rainer. You know, I always had you pegged for a dumb pretty boy, but I never figured you were actually *that* stupid."

"What the hell does that mean?" Luke demanded.

"It means you saw us on the opposite end of circus mere moments before that fire started. The only reason you're standing here accusing me of something we both know is impossible is because it fits perfectly into your scheme of painting me as the villain."

Kate didn't want to say it out loud, but he sort of had a point. Granted, Chance McDermott had more than earned his rotten, villainous reputation. But Luke did seem pretty eager to place the blame on Chance even when, as Chance pointed out, his findings were illogical.

"So you're denying it," Luke said.

"Of course I'm denying it. I may be petty, but I'm no criminal."

"You'll just lie and cheat and do whatever it takes to make it."

"Yes," Chance answered shamelessly. "I don't know a soul in the business who wouldn't."

"*I* wouldn't."

"Oh, please." Chance rolled his eyes. "The entire paranormal community knows how you operate, Luke. How you've been begging and manipulating Michael for years to become a part of your team. How you cozied up to the girl he liked to get what you wanted out of him. And how this person whom you claim to be your best friend doesn't even watch your show. What are we to make of that?"

"That's not true!" Kate exclaimed. Even in the darkness, she could see that Luke was seething. She wouldn't have been surprised to see steam rising up out of his ears.

"Which part, Sweetie?" Chance asked. "The part where you dumped him for the weird, skinny guy who lives next door? No offense, Sinclair, but you know there's got to be something wrong with Rainer when a babe like her dumps him for a guy like you."

"Why do you do this?" Kate asked. "Do you just like to get a rise out of people? Is that it? Do you get some sort of kick out of being a jerk?"

"Now that you mention it, it is enjoyable to watch brainless oafs like Rainer squirm. But you know, I don't see myself as being a jerk. I'm just calling it like I see it. And the way I see it, Luke Rainer is a washed up, over-exposed, self-important has-been." McDermott crossed his arms and smirked down at her. "Now you? I'd say you're just about as insecure as they come."

"Excuse me?"

"You're too uptight. Very defensive. I'd say you're not sure about anything. Not Luke Rainer, his credibility. And certainly not your relationship with Sinclair over there."

"How can you *say* that? You don't even know me!" Kate hissed.

"Like I said, you're defensive. If you had any confidence in your friends or relationships, you wouldn't be so uppity. But don't feel bad. I don't think your boyfriend is one hundred percent sure about you either."

Even though Kate knew he was just trying to get into her head, that she had absolutely no reason to give him or anything he said the time of day, that last comment made her blood freeze in her veins.

"What the hell does that mean?" Michael demanded.

"What? You think that just because Claire doesn't have a heartbeat, she can't make a man fall in love with her?"

"Claire?" Kate asked. "What does she have to do with anything?"

"Unless Dashiell and Robert are mistaken, your darling Michael was enjoying a secret rendezvous with her just a few minutes ago. Isn't that right, Michael?"

"What? No! How did you know about that?!" Michael stammered.

"It's true?" Kate asked, all the while willing her heart not to shatter into a million pieces. It wasn't true. It couldn't be. Michael loved her. She loved him. They were meant for each other.

"No! Kate, of course it's not true. I mean, yeah, she was here. But she just appeared. I think she's been following me."

"And why wouldn't she follow you after the way you've been looking at her?" Chance asked. "She's pretty, isn't she? I know. I came across a few pictures of her while I was researching this place. She's gorgeous. I might go so far as to say *enchanting*. You can't really blame him for being smitten. He's only human after all..."

No. No, this wasn't happening. Kate knew him. They'd been through too much together.

Stop letting him get to you. This is what he wants.

But the fact of the matter was, Kate was only human too. And the mere thought of the guy she loved looking at another girl, even one that posed no actual threat, hurt more than she

137

could adequately express. It wasn't even a sense of betrayal or jealousy. It simply broke her heart.

"Kate, don't listen to him," Michael insisted.

"Is she pretty?" Kate didn't know why she was asking, but something inside needed to know.

"No! I mean... Well... Yeah. I mean, she's okay. But she's *not* you. There is nothing like that at all. Come on you... You can't be taking him seriously! Please, Kate," Michael begged. "Please. I love you. Only you. Claire... She's nothing to me. Agh!" Suddenly, Michael cried out and grasped his head. "What are you - Agh!" Kate watched in horror as Michael sank to his knees, his face twisted into a pained grimace.

"No!" she gasped and dropped down next to him.

"What the hell is wrong with you people?" Chance demanded.

"I think this is what happened to you last night," Luke shot back.

Michael, meanwhile, was gasping, pleading, with the girl that only he could see. "Stop... Stop... I'm sorry. I shouldn't have... No! Please, don't..."

Kate wanted to protect him. She tried. She wrapped her body around his in an attempt to stop the attack, but she knew it wouldn't help. More often than not, the ghosts they met were good, genuine, harmless souls. But when they got angry or scared or hurt, then there was nothing any living being could do to stop them. Trevor had proved that. Sterling had proved that. Now it was Claire's turn.

Finally, Michael relaxed in her arms. He was breathing heavily and his skin felt cold and clammy.

"Kate..." he whispered.

"I'm here," she promised him. "Are you okay?"

"No... Claire..." he tried to talk, but before he could get another word out, his body heaved and he threw up onto the ground in front of him. Kate flinched, but she stayed beside him, rubbing his back as he gagged again.

"We need to get you home," Luke announced, kneeling down to help Michael to his feet. "I'm sorry. I shouldn't have dragged you guys into this."

"Damn right," Chance smirked. "Now do you believe that I had nothing to do with your rotten luck?"

"No, I don't," Luke snapped back. "You may not have started the fire, but you are deliberately trying to stir up trouble for me and my friends. And I'm not gonna put up with it!"

"Ooh, what are you gonna do? Sic your pathetic posse on me?" Chance laughed. "For the record, Luke, you've brought all of this upon yourself. If you were maybe a little nicer, a little more considerate of people's feelings, then maybe none of this would be happening. Karma is a bitch, my friend. Those receipts tend to pile up."

"What is he talking about?" Kate asked Luke.

"Nonsense, as usual," Luke spat. "Come on. Let's get Mikey back to the condo."

And without another word, Luke and Kate, each supporting Michael on one shoulder, turned and began to make their way back through the graveyard.

"Oh, and by the way," Chance called after them. "Aside from the part where you accuse me of being a serial arsonist, that whole scene is going to make for some great ratings. Thanks, Luke."

"Bite me," Luke grumbled.

~*~

None of them talked at all during the short drive back to the condo. Michael was grateful for the silence. It made it easier for him to concentrate on not being sick again. He was lying down in the backseat of Luke's car, still shivering from the dreadful attack.

There was an old saying he knew about hell and fury and a woman's scorn. Well, whoever came up with it was dead on. No pun intended.

He knew Kate was still worried about him. She kept glancing back every few seconds to make sure he was okay. He just hoped that she wasn't still thinking about what McDermott had said. Michael didn't understand. He'd met plenty of jerks in his time, but none that went out of their way to stir up trouble the way Chance McDermott did.

The real question that Michael wanted to ask was *why*?

Perhaps there was no *why*. It was possible that Chance McDermott was just a bully. But after what he had said to Luke about karma and being more considerate, Michael was beginning to wonder exactly what Luke hadn't told them about his relationship with McDermott and his Grave Diggers or whatever they were called.

When they finally made it back to the condo, Kate instructed Michael to lie down in bed while she made him a tall glass of water. Luke, meanwhile, excused himself to take a shower.

"You should try to sleep," Kate said to Michael when she returned with his water. She sat down on the edge of the bed and brushed a few locks of dark hair away from his forehead.

"I know," Michael replied. The problem was, even though he was totally drained, he couldn't relax. His mind was racing a mile a minute and he was still feeling a little queasy.

Kate glanced off toward the tiny hall that led to the bathroom. Michael wondered if she was thinking about Claire. Thankfully, Michael hadn't seen hide nor hair of her since she disappeared after the attack. He knew she'd be back though. She'd promised she would be.

What did that mean? Michael wasn't sure he wanted to know. He'd only caught a glimpse of her face as she rendered him utterly defenseless with a white, blinding, crippling headache. All the light and beauty and innocence that he had seen in her had vanished, and contempt, bitterness, and unadulterated fury had moved in to take their places.

"What did she say to you?" Kate asked, her voice snapping him out of his stupor.

"What?" Michael asked. He wasn't sure he understood the question.

"When Claire was attacking you, it sounded like you were pleading with her. What did she say?"

"I didn't catch all of it. She was screaming so loud that it was kind of difficult to understand her. All I caught at the very end was, 'You'll be sorry... You'll be sorry.' And then..."

"Then what?"

"Then she promised she'd be back. And she vanished."

"So she was threatening you?" Kate asked. Michael nodded. "Maybe we do need to get out of here. As soon as possible."

"We can't," Michael muttered.

"Why not?"

"Because no matter what we do or where we go... I'm afraid that Claire will follow us. And I'm not leading her back to where I live. To where we live."

"But she's not here now, is she?" Kate asked.

"No, but she's close." Michael wasn't sure how he knew it. He just did. She'd used up almost all of her energy in the attack, but she wouldn't let him get far. Michael leaned back against the pillows and with a deep breath said, "We have to talk to Rasia again."

"Do you really think she'll know what to do?" Kate asked. "Last time we went to her with questions, she answered in riddles. I don't know what her game is, but honestly, I don't feel like playing."

"But she's the only other person who's had any sort of communication with Claire."

"What about Van Dalen? I mean, he did invite you all out here for a reason," Kate reminded him. "Maybe he and Claire are closer than you think."

"Maybe," Michael echoed.

It was possible. Anything was possible. Especially in this haunted world, full of lies and tricks and secret ambitions. Why couldn't everything just be simple and straightforward? Why had this weekend turned into such a mess? The fire, Claire, Chance McDermott, Rasia and her prophecies, Van Dalen and his mysterious invitation, not to mention Luke and whatever he'd done to make McDermott believe he deserved retribution. It was all so overwhelming.

But dwelling on any of it further tonight wouldn't do him any good. It would only keep him awake, when what he truly needed was to rest. His head still swimming with faces and ghosts and words and accusations, he closed his eyes and drifted off into an uneasy sleep.

Chapter 19

When Luke emerged from the shower, Kate was still awake, absently scrolling through her Kindle, but Mikey was out. After what he'd been through, he definitely needed it.

"Hey," Luke whispered.

"Hey," Kate murmured back without glancing up.

"Whatcha doing?"

"Trying not to think," she replied.

"About what?" Luke asked. Finally, Kate looked up at him. "I know, that kind of makes it harder to not think about whatever it is you're trying not to think about."

"Just a little," Kate remarked with a wry grin. "Michael doesn't think that we can leave until he talks to Rasia again. About Claire."

"Because of what happened tonight?"

"Yeah," Kate sighed and averted her gaze.

Luke must have known, or at least had idea of what she was thinking, because he knelt down next to the bed and looked her in the eye.

"Hey. You know McDermott was just trying to mess with you tonight, right?"

"Yeah, I know." And rationally, she did know. She knew that there was nothing Claire, or anyone, could do to make Michael love her any less. But that didn't make her raw, emotional side feel any better. If anything, it made her feel worse.

"Mikey loves you more than anything."

"I know," Kate repeated. "I guess it's only fair though, right? First Rasia accusing me of still being in love with a ghost. Now McDermott suggesting that Michael's having an affair with one."

"Unfortunately, when you date a guy like Mikey, ghosts are always going to be there. Ghosts are always going to be there anyway, but with him, you're a lot more aware of it."

"Are they always going to be interfering in our relationship too?"

"Sometimes," Luke answered. "You know, I once dated a girl when we were first starting out. I brought her over to my apartment one night. I set the mood. Candles, wine, slow jazz. Very romantic. Anyway, we're on the couch, and right as I lean in to kiss her, she jumps up, screaming her head off, and swearing that something grabbed her shoulder. I should preface this by saying my hands were nowhere near her shoulders."

"Charming," Kate quipped.

"Hey. Don't make this dirty," Luke scolded.

"I'm sorry. Please continue."

"Anyway, she's crying and screaming and I'm trying to calm her down. Then she tells me that she's felt uncomfortable there all night, like something was watching her, or like we weren't alone. Now who does that sound like?" he asked, grinning at Kate.

"She's a sensitive?"

"Even more sensitive than you. Now, I had told her what I did, but she'd just brushed it off, like she thought it was a cool hobby or something. But once I got her into my apartment... She was done. She became a believer that night. She also became my ex-girlfriend."

"Aw. I'm sorry."

"Not your fault. And no big loss. If a woman can't handle what I do for a living, she's not the right woman for me. The point is though, when you're involved with the paranormal, don't be surprised when the paranormal becomes involved with you."

144

"Super," Kate muttered. Weren't relationships complicated enough *without* the addition of ghosts and spooks and things that went bump in the night?

"You're not having second thoughts, are you?" Luke asked her.

"No! No, of course not. It's just... I always figured there'd be at least a few other girls vying for Michael's attention. Especially since he's America's Medium now, or whatever. I just never thought that I'd be competing with a ghost. Or rather, I never thought that we'd be haunted because of it."

"First of all, there is no competition. Mikey loves you. Secondly, I know that this situation isn't exactly... ideal... But we will get through it. You'll see."

But even as he spoke the words, Kate felt a childlike fear of uncertainty and monsters and everything in between take hold of her. She curled her legs up to her chest and wrapped herself into a ball, resting her chin on her knees.

"What if she tries to hurt him again?" she asked, her voice small and pitiful.

"Then we'll figure out a way to protect him."

Kate simply nodded in response. Luke sounded confident, but Kate had a feeling they both knew that was easier said than done. They hadn't been able to do anything for him tonight except hold him when it was over. What if the next time was worse? She didn't even want to think about it.

"So what did McDermott mean?" she asked him, changing the subject. "You know, when he said all that stuff about karma and being considerate?"

"I've got to be honest with you, Kate. I have no idea," Luke answered, running a hand through his short hair. "I've been wracking my brain all night trying to remember if I said something or if I've done something. But I'd never even met the guy until a few days ago! I'd heard of him, sure. Didn't care for him, or what I knew about him. But I never went out of my way to make his life miserable. Unlike him."

"I guess Rasia's predictions all came true then," Kate stated. "You met your worst fear. I'm hung up on a ghost, though not the one that we initially assumed. And that same ghost is putting Michael's life in danger."

"Do you really think he's in danger?" Luke asked.

"Do you really think he isn't?"

"I don't know. I'll admit, there's been a lot of weird stuff this weekend."

"Enough to wish we'd just stayed home," Kate murmured.

"Yeah, but you know, even when stuff like this does happen, you can't be afraid of experiencing new things, or of getting out and seeing new places. You can't spend your entire life hiding away because you're afraid that something might go wrong. Mikey would be the first one to tell you that. He's shut the world out his entire life. Until he met you, that is." Luke winked. Kate couldn't help it. She smiled. "I guess what I'm saying is don't let this one experience deter you from future adventures. I know you. You're not a sit-at-home-and-knit kind of girl. You need excitement. If I said I was going to do something crazy, like spend a night in Dracula's castle in Transylvania - which I fully intend to do one day - you'd be the first one asking if you could come along too. And you know you and Mikey would both be invited, right?"

"Thanks, Luke," Kate smiled.

"Any time, Beautiful. Now I don't know about you, but I'm wiped. I think it's time for bed."

"Do you want to sleep up here? I can take a spot on the floor," Kate offered.

"What kind of gentleman would I be if I allowed a lady to sleep on the floor while I took the bed?" Luke asked, sounding horrified. "Besides, I can guarantee you Mikey would rather wake up next to you than me."

Kate laughed. "Fair enough." Then, she handed him a pillow and the throw blanket at the foot of the bed. "Goodnight, Luke."

"Goodnight, Kate. Sleep tight."

The circus haunted Michael's dreams that night.

It all began back under the Big Top. He was sitting in the audience, but somehow, he knew he was the only living soul in the crowd. The people around him were pale, with sunken, lifeless eyes, much more like the ghosts of dark literature and horror movies.

When the lights went out, the spotlight fell on a dark, cloaked figure in a black top hat. He looked up into the crowd, his smile wide and menacing.

"Welcome to the circus... *of the dead!*" the Ringmaster announced, laughing maniacally.

The crowd cheered. Michael glanced frantically around.

I'm not dead! He tried to shout.

But he couldn't speak. He couldn't even move. In fact, it seemed that the more energetic the crowd around him grew, the weaker and more disoriented he felt.

What is happening to me?

"Ladies and gentlemen, boys and ghouls," the Ringmaster continued. "What you are about to see is an extravagant, electrifying, and enchanting performance unlike any that has ever been witnessed in this world or the next! An act so ethereal, it is not intended for mere mortals. Here, in my circus, death comes to life!"

The audience roared their approval. Michael, meanwhile, realized he was trapped. He tried to his best to figure out a way to escape. He had to get out of there. If he didn't, bad things would happen...

"I ask you now to turn your attention to the platform above, where you will meet our beautiful and daring trapeze artist, Katherine Avery!"

At the sound of her name, Michael forgot what he was doing. He followed the crowd's gaze up to a towering platform, several stories in the air. At first, it appeared empty and he breathed a heavy sigh of relief. But then, a flash of white and a shimmer of blonde hair ignited a new sense of panic within him.

Kate.

What was she doing up there? Didn't she know how dangerous it was?

He had to get her down. But how? He tried calling out to her, but the ability to speak still evaded him.

"Alright, Gorgeous! Jump!" One voice in particular stood out amongst the near-deafening cheers and catcalls of the audience. Michael glanced around to see Chance McDermott and his crew, standing a few rows back, and filming the scene unfolding before him.

"No!" Michael finally found his voice. But it didn't matter. No one was listening to him. In fact, no one even seemed to see him. It was like he wasn't even there.

That wasn't necessarily a bad thing.

Mustering up every ounce of strength and will power that he possessed, Michael was finally able to rise up from his seat in the audience. He bolted down to the center ring, where the Ringmaster was waiting for him.

"What's going on? Why are you doing this?" Michael asked.

The Ringmaster stared him down in silence before answering in a hiss-like whisper that chilled Michael to the bone, *"The show must go on."* Then, with a blank, wide-eyed smile, the Ringmaster turned his gaze up to the platform where Kate stood, ready to leap.

"Kate!" Michael yelled again.

He had to reach her. Heart racing, he ran over to the base of the platform and begin to climb the tall, dizzying ladder up into the shadowed heights of the tent. The higher he climbed, the farther away the platform, and Kate, seemed.

Time was running out. He had to get to her. But how? He'd never make it at the rate he was climbing.

Then, out of nowhere, a trapeze came swinging out of the darkness. He stretched his arm out to grab it, but it was just out of reach. When it came flying by again, Michael summoned up every ounce of courage he had and leapt. This time, the trapeze seemed to reach out for him as he grabbed the bar and swung all the way up to the top of the platform.

He landed just in time to see Kate, dressed all in white, raise her arms gracefully into the air and step one foot out and over the edge.

"Kate, no!" Michael lunged forward just in time to grab her and pull her back, away from the treacherous drop. She tumbled backwards into his arms, but she felt airy, weightless. For a moment, Michael feared that he was already too late, that she was just a ghost, an otherworldly apparition.

But then she turned bright hazel eyes up toward him, eyes so alert and lively that Michael knew, beyond the shadow of a doubt, that she was still there. She was real.

"Michael," she smiled. Then, she wrapped her arms around his neck and kissed him with so much heat and passion, he was surprised the entire circus wasn't burning down around them.

When they finally broke apart, Michael opened his eyes to a burst of beautiful but violent gray. Instead of a cascade of golden locks, dark brown hair fell around her shoulders and into those wide, terrifying eyes.

"Claire," Michael breathed. "Where is she? Where's Kate?"

Claire didn't respond. She just smiled that strange, innocent, adoring smile that never quite reached her eyes and tenderly pressed her hands against Michael's chest. Then she shoved. Michael felt himself stumbling backwards, losing balance, and toppling down, over the edge of the platform and into the black infinity below.

He gasped and bolted upright, glancing around to see the dark bedroom blissfully empty, the night air outside calm, and Kate sleeping beside him, beautiful and still and safe.

Chapter 20

The next morning, Luke awoke with a new sense of optimism and determination. He wasn't sure what it was. Maybe he'd just slept really well on the floor. Or maybe it was the golden sunlight pouring in through the window. Whatever the reason, he had a very good feeling that today was going to be their day.

Then he noticed Mikey standing alone in the dark kitchen. He wasn't moving. He was just staring at a spot on the wall. It was almost like he was in a trance.

Not wanting to wake Kate, Luke stood and shuffled silently into the kitchen. Mikey finally snapped out of it and looked up at him. Luke couldn't help but notice the dark circles under his eyes. Or the fact that he hadn't bothered to shave yet. That was weird. In all the years Luke had known him, he'd never seen Mikey unshaven.

"How long have you been awake?" Luke asked, plugging in the coffee maker.

"Few hours."

"But we've barely been asleep a few hours."

"I know," Mikey murmured through a huge yawn.

"She didn't come back, did she?" Luke asked.

"Not yet."

"Hey, like I told Kate last night, we're gonna figure this out."

"You didn't tell her why Chance McDermott thinks you deserve this, did you?"

150

"Wish I had, because that would mean I knew *why* he thinks I deserve this. But you know, I've thought about it, and maybe he's telling the truth. Maybe he didn't start that fire. I honestly don't think he's smart enough to light a match."

"Luke, I really don't care about the fire anymore. It's like the firefighters said. It was just a glitch or a spark or something."

"You don't think that. You're just tired and frustrated. I get it. I am too. But this is all connected. You'll see."

"How?" Mikey asked.

"I don't know. That's what today is all about. That and keeping you as far away from femme fatale ghosts as possible."

"Funny. How long did it take you to come up with that one?" Mikey asked with a wry grin.

"Would you believe it just came to me?" Luke asked. "Go tell your girlfriend that the coffee's almost ready. I'm going to go get dressed. In my brand new supermarket jeans and T-shirt."

"I think they're stylish," Kate called from the other room.

"Thank you, Kate. How long have you been awake?" Luke asked.

"About thirty seconds," she replied. "I smelled the coffee."

"Impressive," Luke remarked. "Alright. I'm gonna go change."

Luke grabbed the faded blue jeans and spinach green t-shirt out of the paper sack that had replaced his lost suitcase and headed for the bathroom. He'd just reached his destination when he heard a *knock knock knock* on the front door of the condo.

And just like that, the good feeling he'd had since waking up to that beautiful beam of sunlight vanished.

He emerged from the bathroom, still in his boxer shorts and undershirt. Kate and Mikey were hovering around the front door, looking wary.

"Who is it?" Luke asked them.

As if he'd heard exactly what had just been said, Chance McDermott yelled, "You know, you have to leave sometime, and

I'm just going to stand out here until you do, so you might as well open up!"

Kate, upon realizing she was still in *her* pajamas as well, ran to the bed, grabbed a sheet, and wrapped it around herself.

"Kate, you don't have to be here," Mikey told her.

"I'm not leaving you," she insisted.

"Want me to do the honors?" Luke asked.

When neither Mikey nor Kate objected, Luke marched to the front door and opened it as aggressively as he could manage. There stood McDermott, sharp, clean, and not at all looking like he'd spent the entire night running around a graveyard.

That settled it. Obviously, he'd sold his soul to Satan.

"Good morning, plebeians," Chance greeted them.

"What do you want, McDermott?" Luke asked.

"I was hoping I might have a chat with Michael if you don't mind." Chance answered.

"Why?" Kate asked, folding her arms and scowling. She was much fiercer when she hadn't had her coffee yet.

"Hey Sugar, you're still here? Good for you. I probably would have left your ghost fetishist boyfriend here once I found out... well... that he has a ghost fetish."

"We're done here," Luke announced and attempted to slam the door shut on McDermott's face.

But Chance was too quick. He stuck out a combat boot to prevent the door from closing all the way.

"Okay, okay, my bad. I can see we're still a little touchy this morning. I apologize."

"Are you serious?" Mikey deadpanned.

"What?" McDermott wondered.

"You honestly think that will make it all better? An offhanded apology?"

"What else do you want me to say?"

"How about you acknowledge that you've been hostile and provocative and sleazy since the moment you met us? That you're so desperate for fame and attention that you'll sink as low as necessary to achieve that, even when it means ruining other

152

people's lives? Why don't you admit that all you've been trying to do since day one is stir up trouble for Luke and in doing so, you went right on ahead and decided to drag me and Kate down with him? Did I leave anything out?" Mikey demanded.

"You forgot the fire," Luke muttered under his breath.

"I already told you, Rainer, I did not start that fire. And okay, maybe I haven't been particularly chummy towards the three of you. But in case you hadn't noticed, being nice gets you nowhere. I mean, look at you, Sinclair. Walking the straight and narrow all your life. And what have you got to show for it? You're unemployed. Probably close to being broke by now. Yeah, you've got a hot babe to make up for all the other crap life's thrown at you, but for the most part, you're just a loser," Chance stated matter-of-factly. "Again, not trying to offend. I just say what everyone else is thinking. I'm not afraid of a little honesty. You could be doing really well for yourself, Sinclair. Yourself and your girl. Life gave you a pretty awesome gift. You need to learn to take advantage of it. But until you do... I will."

"And what is that supposed to mean?" Mikey asked.

"Last night in that cemetery, we got *the* best footage of spiritual activity that any of us had ever seen. I'm talking EVPs, unexplained lights, you name it. All thanks to you. The only problem is it only lasts for about ten seconds before your girl on the side, Claire, drains the camera batteries completely. What we need, what *Grave Crusaders* really needs for our season finale, is more of that fantastic evidence. That's where you come in."

"So you think that after all you've done, after all the nasty things you've said, I'll just let bygones be bygones?"

"Well... Sort of, yeah," Chance admitted.

"Oh gee, how do I phrase this? No way in hell," Mikey snapped.

Yeah! Way to stand your ground, Mikey! Luke cheered silently in his head. He couldn't remember ever being more proud of his normally docile friend. Judging by the enamored look on Kate's face, she felt the same way.

"Ouch. You cut me deep, Sinclair. What will it take to convince you? Maybe a couple thousand dollars? You know, to help you out in times of need."

"Now you're trying to bribe me?"

"Yep. Is it working?"

"No."

"So you leave me no choice but to resort to blackmail."

"*Blackmail*?" Mikey sounded incredulous. Then, he did something completely unexpected. He laughed. "What could you possibly say to me that you haven't already said? You want to try to dig up something embarrassing? Go for it. I'll even make you a list. Face it, Chance. *You've got nothing.*"

"Oh, sure I do. I've got her," McDermott turned his blue, snakelike eyes on Kate.

"You think you're going to blackmail me?" she asked. "With what?"

"See, the beautiful thing about blackmail is it doesn't have to be true. It just has to be leverage. But you know, Kate, you should be flattered. First Luke uses you to get to Michael, now I'm about to do the same thing. You must feel like one special gal."

"You must be crazy to think I'd help you."

"Yeah, I don't expect you to help willingly. But Michael will do anything possible to make sure nothing happens to your or tarnishes your precious reputation. You might be the only good thing in his sad, miserable life, Kate, but you're also his downfall."

Luke had never in his life felt a keener urge to sucker-punch someone, and not just because Kate looked like she was about ready to burst into tears. It turned out that he was no better than McDermott. How many times had he used Kate to get what he wanted out of Mikey? More than he cared to admit. Kate was his friend. Mikey was his friend. How could he have been so selfish? So manipulative?

Maybe that was why he hated McDermott so much. Well, apart from all the obvious reasons. It was because in Chance

154

McDermott, Luke saw all of his worst qualities reflected back at him, and then some. And he didn't know what to do with that. Did that make him a bully? A cheat? A hypocrite?

He guessed, in a way, it did.

Meanwhile, Mikey had resorted to aggravated begging. "McDermott, I'm asking you, man to man, to leave her out of this."

"Oh, but look at her. She's so pretty. Even wrapped up in that dirty old sheet," Chance smirked. "I'm assuming your pajamas are less than flattering? If you're even wearing pajamas that is..."

"You know, McDermott, for someone with such big talk about blackmail, you have a pretty loose interpretation of sexual harassment," Luke snapped. "You heard the man. Leave her out of this."

"Or what?" Chance snickered.

"Or I will kick your ass so hard, you'll be sitting on a doughnut for the rest of your life."

At that, Chance doubled up with laughter.

"Oh Lord, you *really* need to get some better threats. A doughnut. Pitiful." Chance shook his head.

"Are you *done* yet?" Kate asked.

"Almost. Clearly we're not getting anywhere with these negotiations - "

"Negotiations?" Luke scoffed.

" - so instead, I'm going to give you an ultimatum," Chance announced. "I'm following the three of you around with cameras all day whether you like it or not."

"You can't do that. You need our consent if you want to air it on television. You'll never get that from any of us," Luke told him.

"See, that's where the blackmail would have come in handy," Chance sighed. "I technically can't use your images, but I can do my best to capture any and all paranormal activity that Sinclair happens to stir up and edit the rest of you out. Who knows? I might even prove to be a valuable ally in your quest to

155

unmask the real arsonist. I assume that's why you're still here. I mean, if I were the three of you, I would have left days ago."

"We don't need or want your help," Luke spat.

"Well, I guess in that case, my crew and I will just be following you around, making you look way more important than you actually are. That being said, I guess I should let the three of you get dressed. No offense or anything, but *none* of you are camera ready." At that, Chance finally removed his boot from the doorway and allowed the door to close.

Once they'd locked and bolted the door, Kate asked, "Are we really going to let this happen? Can't we go to Van Dalen or something? Get him off our case?"

"I don't really think Van Dalen is going to be on our side," Mikey commented.

"You know, it's not too late to pick another fight with him," Luke reminded them. "One more brawl, one more altercation, and we're all out of here."

"Luke, I know you want to get him kicked out and God knows I want to go home more than anything, but we *can't* leave until we get this ghost situation resolved," Kate said. Luke couldn't help but notice that Kate didn't call Claire by her name.

"This is such a bad idea on so many levels," Luke muttered.

"You know at this point, I'm tired of dealing with McDermott," Mikey announced. "We're obviously getting nowhere by trying to fight him. If he wants to waste a day following us around, fine. Let him. It will probably make for the most boring footage ever recorded."

"Mikey... that's *brilliant!*" Luke exclaimed. "Okay team, new plan. Today, we act as low key and boring as possible. That'll teach Chance McDermott to use other people!"

"Until she shows up again, anyway," Kate remarked, a sour expression on her pretty face.

"You sound so confident that she will," Luke said.

"She will," Mikey replied, sounding grim.

"Well, when she does, tell her to stay away from the cameras. We don't want to give McDermott anything he can use," Luke exclaimed. "Now if you'll excuse me, I'm finally going to go get dressed."

It was strange, but Luke was almost feeling enthusiastic about having Chance McDermott follow them around all day. It was like that old saying about keeping your friends close and your enemies closer. He'd be able to keep an eye on McDermott and his cronies.

And maybe, just maybe, they'd figure out this whole mess once and for all.

Chapter 21

Overall, Kate liked to think she was a pretty confident person. Most of the time, she was very forward about what she thought and what she wanted. She didn't embarrass easily. She rarely felt ill at ease or like she wanted to run and hide away from the world. But that was exactly how being followed around by Chance McDermott and his bulky cameras made her feel. Awkward. Exposed. Like she, Michael, and Luke were all on the spot, and that anything any of them said or did might prove hazardous for everyone involved.

It didn't make sense. She knew that. It wasn't like it was the first time she'd been filmed before. She'd even watched herself on television in the Stanton Hall Manor episode of *Cemetery Tours*. That had been a little awkward too, but only because she was kind of goofy on camera. It wasn't like her every move was being scrutinized by a bonafide jerk. True, McDermott was really only interested in Michael, but the way he'd talked to her, the way he'd talked about her, had left her feeling small and uncertain and guilty.

"You might be the only good thing in his sad, miserable life, Kate, but you're also his downfall."

The hurtful words echoed through her mind over and over again, like a broken record. And every time she heard them, she felt closer and closer to tears. All this time, she'd found comfort in the idea of being there for Michael; that maybe she was good for him. But if Chance McDermott was right - and she was truly beginning to fear he was - then it was just the opposite.

Before Michael had met her, he'd managed to keep the ghosts at bay. He'd been able to maintain a steady job. He was never blackmailed or manipulated, or even recognized. He'd lived a safe, normal life. Or as normal as possible, given the circumstances. Then she'd come along and the rest was history.

Maybe he really would have been better off without her.

If that were the case, then where did that leave her? She wanted what was best for Michael. But what if what was best for Michael meant letting him go? Kate didn't know if she could do that.

She couldn't remember what love had felt like when she was with Trevor, but if she'd agreed to marry him, then it had to have felt at least a little something like this. Dating was tricky. She'd never quite understood what the rules were before. How did she keep a guy interested without coming off as needy? What if a guy was more into her than she was into him? How was she supposed to know if a guy was the right guy? The proverbial "the one?"

With Michael, there were no questions. There was no doubt. They'd broken up briefly to give her time to come to terms with the revelation of her former engagement and Trevor's death, but from the moment she'd met him, Kate had known that her relationship with Michael would be different than any she'd had before. Even before she'd found out about the ghosts.

Being around him just felt so natural. She didn't have to worry about him playing games with her mind or with her heart. Her relationship with him was open, honest. Ever since they rekindled their romance back in October, she never, not once, doubted that he loved her. Nor did she doubt or question her feelings for him. Best of all, she enjoyed his company. She loved being around him. Even the lousiest day spent with him beat the best day without him. Wasn't that how love was supposed to be?

But maybe that was the problem. If they'd had a rocky relationship, then perhaps she couldn't have so easily been used against him. It was because he loved her so much that creeps like McDermott were able to get to him through her. She wondered if Michael might be thinking the same thing.

He hadn't said much of anything since entering the fairgrounds. Probably for the same reason she hadn't. He was painfully aware of the cameras pointed at his back, and when it came to Chance McDermott, anything they said or did could, and probably would, be held against them.

In fact, the only one talking was McDermott himself, but Kate hadn't been listening. Or at least, she'd been trying not to. If she'd had enough money, she would've gladly paid him to shut up.

"So, what exactly are you hoping to accomplish today? You're going to find Claire, right? Because I've got to be honest, I'm not sure if this circus is actually as haunted as Van Dalen or Rasia seems to think. Disappointing, but this is still a killer opportunity, if you'll pardon the expression. What do you think of her, Michael? Rasia?"

"Seems like a decent lady," Michael replied gruffly.

"Yeah, but you don't think she seems sort of out there? You know, a bit cuckoo?"

"Are you seriously filming this?"

"Don't worry. I'll edit it out."

"I think she's trying to make the best of her situation. Just like the rest of us."

"Forget it. You're as vague as she is. What is it with you fortune-tellers and your non-answers?"

"Fortune-teller?" Michael asked.

"What, you don't do that?"

"No."

"How about reading minds?"

"No."

"Astral projection?"

"I don't even know what that means."

"Wow," McDermott laughed. "You're the most pathetic psychic I've ever met."

"Thanks," Michael grumbled.

"So since you can't read minds, I guess you can't tell me why Van Dalen invited all of us out here in the first place?" McDermott asked.

That comment surprised Kate. She'd been certain that McDermott knew exactly why some of the world's most renowned psychics and ghost-hunters were called to assemble there in Hugo, Oklahoma.

"You mean you don't know?" Michael asked.

"Nope. All I was told was that the boys and I had been invited out here to shoot and that it might make a good opportunity for a season finale. So we took him up on it. Didn't start to get suspicious until I realized you and Rasia were out here too."

"It's for publicity. Plain and simple," Luke remarked.

"Oh? I'm sorry, what was that? Was that the sound of petty jealousy?" McDermott asked lightly.

"Yeah, you wish," Luke muttered under his breath.

"So Kate, I've got to ask. Where exactly do you fit into all this. I mean we've got Sinclair who can see the ghosts. Supposedly. Then we've got Luke, who makes a complete fool of himself looking for them. What's your story?"

"Not one that I'm willing to share while the cameras are rolling," she replied.

"Okay, okay, I can respect that. But you've got to have some sort of weird ghost connection. Otherwise, you wouldn't be giving a guy like Sinclair the time of day - "

SMACK.

It wasn't until she felt the sting in her right hand that Kate realized what had just happened. Slapping McDermott across the face hadn't been a conscious act at all. She didn't know what came over her. She hadn't thought, hadn't been able to control herself. It was like being possessed all over again.

Michael, Luke, and McDermott's thugs all stared at her with stunned expressions while McDermott himself hunched over and pressed a hand to his face.

161

"Okay," he whimpered. "I guess I deserved that."

"No. You deserve a roundhouse kick to the gut. Unfortunately, I dropped out of martial arts when I was seven," Kate spat.

"Good news for me," McDermott remarked.

"That's it!" Kate growled in frustration. "I have *had* it with your condescension and your sleazy comments. I don't understand people like you at all. You lash out and attack and belittle for absolutely no reason other than the fact that you can. What's worse, you consciously try to corrupt the lives of people you don't even know. Haven't you done enough damage to our relationship this weekend? Do you *really* have that little satisfaction in your own life that you have to tear down others? You make me *sick*."

And with that, she turned and fled. As she ran, she could hear Michael calling her name. But she didn't look back.

~*~

Michael went after her. Letting her go wasn't an option. Especially after her outburst.

In the eight months that he'd known her, he'd never seen her so upset. Sure, she had a quick temper at times and could be very emotional, but he'd never seen her lose it like that. Granted, seeing her smack McDermott had made him love her even more than he'd ever thought possible, but still, he was worried about her.

"Haven't you done enough damage to our relationship this weekend?"

What had she meant by that? She hadn't actually believed what McDermott had said last night, had she? She'd been sort of quiet, but Michael had thought that was because she was tired after a horribly long and exhausting weekend. They all were. But if she'd been hurting this whole time and he hadn't noticed...

He couldn't dwell on it. He just needed to catch up with her. Then, once they talked it all over, everything would be fine. It had to be. Kate was the best thing that had ever happened to him. She was the most important person in his life. He never wanted to see her sad or upset or hurt, especially because of him.

He finally caught up to her in the outskirts of the grounds, sitting beneath a tree and gazing at the Ferris wheel in the distance.

"May I join you?" he asked her.

"Yeah," she replied, listlessly.

Michael lowered himself to the ground and settled down next to her. They sat in silence for a few moments, watching the patrons enjoying their morning at the circus. Kids running around with balloon animals and giant stuffed animals. Families sharing popcorn and hot dogs and drinks with crazy straws. A couple waiting in line for a ride on the Ferris wheel, wrapped in each others' arms. It was only then that Michael realized that Kate was watching them, not the wheel itself.

"You okay?" he asked her.

Dumb question. Clearly, she wasn't. But he wanted - no - he *needed* her to talk to him.

"I want to go home." She sounded on the verge of tears.

"I do, too. Hopefully we can soon. Once we get this mess with Claire sorted - "

"Please." She cut him off. "Please don't say her name."

"Kate, you don't really think that I... That I would ever..."

"No, no of course not. I know you wouldn't. I'm just angry. I'm angry at her for what she's done to you, for threatening you. I'm angry at McDermott for everything. I'm angry at Van Dalen for inviting us out here in the first place. I'm angry at myself..."

"What?" That didn't make any sense. "Why would you be angry at yourself?"

"Because everything McDermott said about me was true. Maybe not the part about me being the only good thing in your life, but the fact that he's using me to get to you. Worse, he's using me against you. And I love you. I love you more than anything. I'm supposed to be there for you. I'm supposed to help you. Not this." She began to cry.

"Kate, you can't think like that."

"How can I not?" she demanded.

"Because I don't," he told her. "McDermott has been wrong about pretty much everything. We both know that. But the one thing he isn't wrong about is that you are the best part of my life. You are the reason I actually look forward to waking up every day. Before you, life was all about going through the motions, trying to get by without drawing any attention to myself. At the time, I thought I was content, but now I realize I was absolutely miserable. You changed all that."

"You almost died because of me," Kate reminded him.

"That's because for the first time, I had someone whose life mattered to me more than my own. And that's an extraordinary thing, Kate. Don't you see that?"

"But if I'm hurting you - "

"Stop. Now it's my turn to interrupt you. You could never, *ever* hurt me, Kate. The only thing in the world that could hurt me would be not being with you. I love you. I love you more than anything."

"I love you, too," Kate replied tearfully. Then she leaned over, wrapped her arms around his shoulders, and buried her face in his neck.

"We'll find a way through this. I promise," he murmured into her hair.

It was funny. Usually, Kate was the one reassuring him that everything would be alright. Michael wasn't used to being the glass-half-full kind of guy. He was normally so cynical. But he realized, as he helped her to her feet and wiped a stray tear away from her cheek, he truly believed what he had told her. Everything would be okay. It had to be.

Anything else was unthinkable.

Chapter 22

Rasia was waiting with Luke and Chance when Michael and Kate finally returned.

"Oh my dear, are you alright?" Rasia reached out comforting arms to Kate.

"I'm fine," she replied.

"Are you sure? Your aura is terribly blue, unlike the healthy red-orange you usually glow."

"Um... I'm sorry," Kate answered awkwardly.

"No, dear, nothing to apologize for. I only wish I could help you. And you, Michael. You're troubled."

"Aren't I always?" Michael remarked before he could help it.

And just like that, the cynicism was back. Thankfully, Rasia didn't seem to pick up on it. That, or the spirit world had told her that he was going to be extra snarky today so she'd been prepared to ignore it.

"We were just asking Rasia if she'd had any more visits from our friend, Claire," Luke explained.

"She has been strangely absent as of late," Rasia explained. "I thought it might be because she had found a kindred spirit in you, Michael. But it seems that something has gone terribly awry."

Michael had to bite his tongue. He appreciated the fact that Rasia was probably trying to help them. But why, for the love of God, could she not just speak in plain English? Who was she trying to impress with her fancy psychic vernacular? Seriously, she sounded like a hokey Magic Eight Ball.

Not only did her speech patterns irritate the hell out of him, but it was all because of her that Claire had sought Michael out in the first place. Why had she done that? What, was she passing the buck? *Sorry, Claire. I don't feel like dealing with you and your melodrama. Go haunt Michael Sinclair. I hear he's got nothing better going on.*

"We were actually hoping we could have yet another word with you about our friend, Claire, Rasia," Luke said. "According to you, Mikey is the only person on God's green Earth that can help guide her to the other side. But what if you're wrong? What if Mikey can't help her, and you've gone and gotten her hopes up for nothing, and now she's really, really, really pissed off that Mikey has no idea what he's doing?"

"You know what I suggest?" Chance butted in. "We call Claire in and we settle this whole mess once and for all. Or maybe stir up a bit of trouble, get some really sick footage, and then I don't care what the rest of you do."

"I'm afraid it's not that simple," Rasia told Chance.

"Sure it is. You write about it in all of your books. You sit around your little table, you play with some cards, light a few candles, and boom. Instant spiritual infestation," Chance said. "Besides, you say you've already got a connection with this girl. Surely after being scorned by Sinclair over there, she could use a little womanly advice. A little feminine comfort."

"Do you even hear yourself when you talk?" Luke snapped.

"Come on, Rasia. You already agreed to be on the show. And now you get to show your stuff in front of our millions of viewers - "

"Oh, yeah right. Millions?" Luke scoffed.

Chance ignored him.

"Who knows? The SyFy channel might like you so much, they give you your own series. *Rasia: The Genuine Oracle.* Think about it." He spoke in a low voice that Michael suspected worked well on single girls, but not so well on middle-aged mediums who looked almost insulted that he might think for even a moment that she needed his help to get her foot in the door.

"I'll have you know, young man, that I have been offered my own television series multiple times by several stations and producers. But I have turned them all down."

"Why? You appear on all those talk shows. You've written how many books? Why would you not want your own TV show?"

"Call me old-fashioned, *Charles* McDermott, but my craft is ancient and my gift, divine. I don't cater to the idea of cheapening it with a corporate label or primetime commercials. Yes, I will appear on television on the occasion that I truly believe I am called to do so, but apart from that, I keep my profession and my intentions pure."

"Okay, okay, fine. My bad," McDermott held his hands up in mock defense.

"Charles?" Luke snickered.

"Shove it, Rainer," Chance hissed. "Listen, Rasia, you know I respect you. To an extent. But we're wasting daylight here. We've only got a few hours before we all promised to be at Van Dalen's closing performance or whatnot, so I need to know. Are you going to help us or not?"

Rasia glanced over at Michael with troubled eyes and heaved a sigh.

"Yes. I will help you."

"Wonderful. Then lead the way," Chance told her.

Michael had to admit, he was taken aback. Chance - er, Charles - McDermott may have been a jerk, but he knew how to get what he wanted out of people. That didn't necessarily mean they liked him for it. More often than not, they probably didn't. He certainly didn't. But that didn't matter to McDermott. All that mattered was that he got the job done.

"Come, my dear. Why don't you walk with me?" Rasia asked, linking an arm through Michael's. Then she leaned in and whispered, "This is not the spirit talking, but I must say I will be stunned if that man's precious show lasts more than a season. Wretched, isn't he?"

And suddenly, Rasia's strange speech patterns didn't annoy Michael in the slightest.

~*~

She led them to a bohemian-looking tent, made up of red and purple fabric and adorned with gold, just like the majority of the costumes, decorations, and attractions at Cirque Somniatis. At first glance, it was so small, Michael wasn't sure they'd all fit, especially with the cameras.

But inside, the tent was deceptively spacious. In the middle of the makeshift room sat a short, rectangular, wooden table, complete with tarot cards, candles, a looking glass, and a variety of colored stones and crystals.

"What? No crystal ball?" McDermott asked.

"Crystal balls are merely a prop, Charles," Rasia explained. "A flashy, overused, overexposed prop."

"Just like McDermott," Luke remarked.

Chance crossed his arms and raised an eyebrow. "That was too easy."

Luke shrugged in response.

"Allow me just a moment to prepare, please," Rasia requested.

She proceeded to light every candle. Michael couldn't help but wonder if so many flames in such a tiny, enclosed space might be another potential fire hazard, but no one else seemed concerned. In fact, Kate was watching Rasia's ritual with a keen sense of awe and curiosity.

Once she'd finished setting up, Rasia sat down at the head of the table, took one of the stones in her hand, and closed her eyes. She took several slow, long, deep breaths. To his right, Michael could sense McDermott losing his patience. He shifted restlessly where he stood and began tapping his fingers against the back of one of the wooden chairs. Luke, meanwhile, suppressed a yawn while Kate's eyes wandered around the tent.

Michael was beginning to feel his mind drift as well when he noticed a small figure darting in and out of the flaps of the tent. It was the young ghost boy again. This time, however, he seemed completely oblivious to Michael, or anyone for that matter.

For a moment, Michael simply observed him. He hadn't gotten a decent look at him, not even that first night back in the burned down condo. He was actually a pretty cute kid, no older than six or seven, with curly auburn hair and those big, curious brown eyes. He was also, Michael noticed for the first time, wearing pajamas. More than likely, he had died at home.

So what was he doing running around a circus?

Still in her trance, Rasia didn't seem to have picked up on the boy's presence. Unsure of what to do, Michael tried to get her attention.

"Rasia," he whispered.

But Rasia held up a hand to silence him.

Michael glanced back over at the boy, who had tiptoed over to the table and was eyeing Rasia's stones and crystals with great interest. He tried to pick one up, but it didn't move. He tried again. The stone moved half a centimeter, but no one else noticed.

When he grew bored with the crystals, the boy turned his attention to one of the many candles. He leaned over and stared intently at the fire, which began to glow brighter and brighter. The wick slowly disappeared as the flame flickered and danced higher than it ever should have on such a small candle.

"Stop!" Michael cried out, startling not only the child, but everyone inside the tent, including Rasia.

"Keep your voice down," Rasia scolded. "Do you want to frighten away the spirits?"

But it was already too late for that. The boy had vanished. Michael expected Rasia to comment on the sudden lack of spiritual energy in the room, but she hadn't seemed to realize that he'd been there in the first place.

"So, is this séance going to happen today or what?" McDermott asked.

169

"Patience," Rasia replied.

"Yeah, *Charles*," Luke smirked.

"Luke, dear, that attitude will get you nowhere, spiritually speaking or otherwise," Rasia said.

"Yeah, *Luke*," McDermott sneered.

"Guys, *how* old are you?" Kate demanded.

"Not as old as Luke," McDermott quipped.

"I'm afraid that unless I get absolute silence, this is not going to work," Rasia told them.

"Why do you need silence? With Sinclair, these things just seem to kind of pop up out of nowhere. At least, that's what he claims," McDermott pressed.

"Do you want answers or do you want contact with the other world?" Rasia asked.

"Well, since you asked, I'd kind of like both."

Rasia sighed, breaking her trance.

"Michael is not a true medium. Spirits are drawn to him. He sees them. He communicates with them. But he cannot call them. He doesn't channel. He doesn't seem to have any connection with the spirit realm as most of us do. His gift is powerful, it is innate, but it is also primitive and underdeveloped. I've been trying my best to figure out how it works. The best I can determine is that his abilities, his spiritual growth, must have been stunted along the way, perhaps after years of suppression," Rasia explained.

Michael could feel all eyes shift to him as he stared curiously down at Rasia. *Was that true?* he wondered. His whole life, he'd thought of his so-called gift as a burden, and it turned out it wasn't even as strong as it could be? He didn't know whether he should feel grateful or cheated. It was a ridiculous notion, especially considering how often he lamented the day he'd been born with such an affliction, but maybe if he'd had guidance, if he'd understood it a little better at a younger age...

Maybe he could have grown up to be confident and successful like Rasia, instead of feeling like he had to hide away all those years.

Stop it, he told himself. Maybe there would come a time to reflect more on the matter, but right now, stewing wouldn't solve anything. It would just throw yet another monkey wrench into an already screwed up situation.

"So what you're saying is Sinclair is a bit of a mutant," McDermott translated.

"I'm saying his abilities are a little immature, that's all," Rasia corrected him.

"Wow. That was a much more substantial waste of my time than I thought it would be. Let's get to the ghosts."

"Did you not want an answer?" Rasia asked.

"No, I wanted you to feel pitted against Michael so you'd make with the magic and get the spirits here quicker. I didn't expect an actual lecture."

"Ask and you shall receive," Rasia replied lightly before closing her eyes once again. "Now, if you please... silence."

Michael fought against a desire to inform Rasia that it might be more difficult getting in touch with Claire than usual since she'd spent so much energy attacking him. She hadn't appeared to him since, even though he knew she was close by. He hadn't been able to shake the feeling of her watching him since the night before.

Rasia took a few more deep breaths.

"Claire. Claire. Can you hear me?" she asked in low, calm voice.

Michael looked around the tent. No sign of her.

"Claire. This is Rasia. I need to speak with you. Appear to me at this time."

"Anything?" Kate whispered in Michael's ear.

He shook his head. He didn't know whether he should feel disheartened or relieved. Perhaps a little of both.

Rasia opened her eyes. She looked confused and mildly irritated.

"It would appear Claire is not feeling cooperative this morning," she announced.

"Are you kidding?" Chance moaned. "So all this voodoo was for nothing?"

"This not voodoo, nor was it all for nothing. I am, in fact, inclined to believe that your negative energy is clouding up the atmosphere and making it difficult to connect with the other realm."

"Oh, please," Chance scoffed. "Most spirits I've encountered would give their nonexistent left foot for a chance to meet with one medium, let alone two! Not to mention a world-renowned paranormal investigator."

"Don't forget, you're here too," Luke chimed in.

"Really, Rainer?" Chance snapped. "So, what's the deal, Rasia? Are you going to get this chick in here or - "

But before he could finish, a sharp, chilling wind swept through the tent, extinguishing every candle at once. The looking glass shattered and the tarot cards began to dance around in the air, as if caught up in a whirlwind.

"She's here!" Rasia exclaimed.

"Alright! This is what I'm talking about!" Chance cheered.

But Michael barely heard him. The edges of his vision were beginning to fade as Claire materialized in front of him, her cool gray eyes cutting him directly to the core.

"Claire... No..." he whimpered.

Michael felt his knees beginning to buckle. He grasped at the air, reaching out for something, anything, that might help to stabilize him. But it was no use. With one last burst of energy, Michael felt his own body hit the ground before the world around him went black.

Chapter 23

When Michael opened his eyes, he was gazing up into a hazy, gray sky. He stood and looked around for Kate, for Luke, for a glimpse of anyone or anything he might recognize, but he couldn't seem to see anything past the thick, rolling fog surrounding him.

Then, slowly but surely, his eyes began to focus on shapes, shadows, silhouettes. Dead trees, with their crooked, knobby branches, stripped of leaves. A broken-down Ferris wheel, lonely and forgotten. The remains of tents, ripped, frayed, and shredded. It was, in its own way, a circus graveyard: a sad memorial to a once beautiful and joyful place.

What happened here? Michael wondered.

"Nothing," Claire answered, appearing beside him. "This place isn't real."

"Did - Did you just read my mind?" Michael asked.

"That's where we are, Michael. Inside your mind."

"How is that... What... Is that even possible?"

"Anything is possible when you've been dead as long as I have," she responded. "Sounds a bit cliché, doesn't it? But it's true. I have no body to inhibit me. That's how I figured out how to fly. That's how I knew how to get you here."

"But why? Why can't we just have a normal conversation, you know, in the conscious world?" It felt weird to refer to any conversation with a ghost as normal, but it would at least be more normal than whatever this was.

"Because they're all out there. Your friends. Your girlfriend. I don't think she likes me very much."

Well, you have been kind of stalking me...

"How?" Claire asked.

Dammit! He'd forgotten that she could hear his thoughts.

"Claire, I'm sorry. Maybe we got off on the wrong foot. Multiple times," Michael acknowledged. "I do want to help you. But in order for me to do that, we're going to have to work together."

"I know. That's why I brought you here."

"Where is *here* anyway? I mean, I know you said it's inside my mind but, what is all this?"

"I don't know. It's your mind."

"You mean you didn't do all this? The fog, the trees, the creepy Ferris wheel?"

"No. It does remind me of what it was like, though, after I died. At first, there was nothing. I didn't know where I was. I didn't realize what had happened. I barely even remembered my own name. Then, I heard people shouting in the distance. I tried to run and find them. By the time I reached the tent, I could hear the sirens. I knew something was wrong. So I ran inside.

"As soon as I did, I remembered I had been there. And I wondered, *Why am I not there now? I was up there, on the trapeze. How did I get here?*

"That's when I saw my friends gathered, huddled in a tight circle in the middle of the center ring. I was terrified, not for me, but for them. I was sure that it was one of them who'd been hurt. I flew down to be with them without even realizing it. That's when I saw my face."

Her words left a cold, hollow pit in the center of Michael's stomach. He'd heard plenty of after-death stories, but never, not once, had a ghost described looking down into his or her own dark, empty, dead eyes.

What was that like, to see yourself like that? To see your body unresponsive. No longer a person, no longer you, but an empty shell. A cold, inanimate *thing*. Michael recalled his brush

174

with death, but he'd never stopped to consider what it might have looked like from the outside. How it would have been to see his own lifeless corpse tied up in the middle of that field, broken beyond the point of hope, beyond the point of mortality. The very thought made him shudder.

"It's less weird than you might think," Claire continued. "I didn't look real. I looked almost like a porcelain doll, or perhaps a wax figure of myself. My neck was bent back at an odd angle, and my eyes were only partially open. But my body looked so much like a prop, that at first, I didn't realize that it really *was* me.

"But then I noticed everyone crying. Everyone trembling. And that's when it began to dawn on me. I began to panic, to tell myself that this must be some sort of mistake. I was young. I was vibrant. I was alive. This wasn't how it was supposed to be. It wasn't fair."

"They tell you all the time that life isn't fair," Michael told her. "But if there's one thing I've learned in the past twenty-eight years it's that death is even less fair. It's the one thing in the world that doesn't discriminate. It doesn't care who you are, how much money you have, what you've done in life. It can come for you any time it wants."

"Thanks. That makes me feel a lot better," Claire deadpanned.

"Okay, that probably wasn't the smartest or most uplifting thing I've ever said. But it rings true. You're not the first person to ever feel that death cheated you, and unfortunately, you won't be the last. Death never plays by the rules. And I think that's why we, as mortal beings, fear it so much. Not because it's an inevitability, but because it's so unpredictable. We all know it's coming for us. We can just never be sure exactly when."

"Well, I guess I don't have to wonder anymore." Claire sounded sad, defeated, and for reasons Michael couldn't explain, it broke his heart.

"I'm sorry, Claire," he whispered. "I wish there was something I could do to help."

175

Claire glanced up at him, a new glimmer of hope sparkling in her eyes.

"You could stay," she whispered.

"What?" Michael asked.

"You could stay here with me."

"Wait. Here? Here as in Hugo or here as in..."

"If you let go, if you don't fight it, your body will eventually give out. I can help it along if you like."

"So you want me to... *die*?" He didn't mean to say it like it was a dirty word, but that's the way it came out.

"You said that death doesn't play by the rules. Maybe if you embrace it, it will make an exception for you. Think about it. You can invite death in. You don't have to wait around for it either. And you could be with me."

Michael could feel his heart beginning to pound. He hoped that meant his body was trying to wake up and not that Claire was already attempting to wear it out.

"Claire, no. It's not right. It's not my time."

"But it was my time?!" Claire demanded.

"No! I'm not saying that it was! But I have a family, Claire. I have people waiting for me. I have Kate..."

"Kate isn't a part of this world, Michael. Don't you see that? You're alive, but you don't belong in the world of the living. And I think you know it, too."

In a way, it was true. For as long as he could remember, Michael had felt caught somewhere between the world of the living and the world of the dead. But in everything he thought and everything he did, he'd always chosen life. It wasn't always perfect. It could be cold and sad and sickening. There were times that had left him so devastated that he'd questioned whether or not life was worth it.

Then again, it was precisely those times of misery and heartache that had proved to him that life *was* worth it. If the human race had only been put on Earth to suffer, then there would be no point. But Michael had come to believe that since life existed in spite of all the trials and hardships, it had be greater,

176

more full of goodness and promises and hope than what they could ever begin to understand. Simply put, the joy of living far outweighed its sorrows.

"Claire, I know you're lonely. And I know that death wasn't fair to you, and you're still hurting because of it. But this isn't the answer. I'm sorry. I need to go back."

"No!" Claire cried out. "No, Michael. No. Please don't think this. I need you. *Please. I need you.*"

"I'm sorry." Michael felt himself beginning to pull away. The dark gray fog was lifting and he could hear Kate and Luke's muffled voices echoing somewhere in the back of his mind.

"*Tonight!*" Claire shrieked as she and the world around her faded to black. "*Tonight. In the center ring!*"

But Michael never got the chance to ask her what she meant.

~*~

Kate didn't know what to do. Luke kept pacing and asking whether or not they needed to call an ambulance. Rasia was muttering every prayer, blessing, and incantation under the sun, attempting to break him out of whatever spell had taken hold of him. Chance and his crew, however, kept right on filming and telling everyone to stay out of the shot. Kate had ignored him and dropped down to Michael's side the moment he collapsed.

She shook him and called his name. She held her ear to his mouth to make sure he was still breathing. She monitored his pulse and shed tears, begging him to wake up. What was Claire *doing* to him?

Finally, *finally*, after what seemed like a horrible, wretched eternity, Michael took a deep breath and slowly opened his eyes.

"Kate?" he whispered.

"Oh, thank God!" Kate sobbed and threw herself down on top of him, wrapping her arms around him and burying her face in his neck. "Don't do that to me!"

"I'm sorry... I'm sorry..." He whispered, clutching her back with one hand and her hair with another.

"You had us a bit spooked there, buddy. If you'll pardon the expression," Luke said.

"So, what happened? Was it Claire? Actually, no, don't answer that. I want to set the scene a little better. This looks kind of sloppy. But I think we got some great footage of the build-up to your little fainting spell or whatever that was," Chance rambled.

"Charles, let the young man breathe," Rasia scolded. "That goes for you as well, dear." She spoke gently, placing a hand on Kate's shoulder.

"I'm sorry," Kate choked, trying to get the words out.

"That's alright. You love him. But after what he's just been through, it isn't wise to smother him. He needs air. I might even have to perform a cleansing."

"What's that?" Michael asked, sounding groggy.

"A ritual in which we purify and purge you of any spiritual residue."

Spiritual residue? Kate didn't want to say anything, but that sounded kind of gross. But it really didn't matter. All that mattered was making sure Michael was going to be okay, so Rasia could cleanse him of whatever she wanted.

"It's okay. She's gone," Michael announced as he lifted himself up off the ground.

"Gone? You've seen her through to the next life?" Rasia asked.

Kate felt her heart leap. If that was true, that meant all was well. Michael was safe. They could go home!

"Well, no. Not exactly. She's just not in my head anymore," Michael explained.

"How did she get inside your head?" Luke asked.

"She's a lot more powerful than we've been giving her credit for." Briefly, he told them of his strange encounter with Claire. His description of her death was macabre enough, but the idea of her wanting him dead as well? And not because Claire's intentions were cruel or spiteful, but because she truly believed

178

that Michael would be better off dead than alive. It was crazy and creepy and it chilled Kate to the bone.

"So now what?" Luke asked. "We just wait it out, see if she comes back and tries to kill you again?"

"You know what you need? An exorcist. How far away is the local cathedral?" one of the cameramen, Robert, asked.

"We're talking about a ghost, not a demon, nimrod," Chance snapped. "And we're going to do exactly as Rainer says. We're going to stick it out and wait for her to come back."

"Stupid plan. We don't even know if she's coming back. Besides, boss, we've only got a few hours of film time left. And unless we really want to waste them on these losers, we'd better get out and get some real footage before that last show tonight," Dashiell argued.

"Dammit. I forgot about that."

"That's it," Michael said suddenly.

"What's it?" Kate asked.

"That's when she's coming back. Tonight. In the center ring. That was the last thing she said to me."

"What the hell does that even mean?" Luke asked.

"It means that every guest here is going to get the most sensational paranormal spectacle of their lives and *we're* going to get the most bitchin' season finale of any show the world has ever seen!" Chance exclaimed.

"Wait a minute, are you serious? We've got to tell someone about this!" Kate said.

"Who are you gonna tell, girlie? Van Dalen? That guy's got his head so far up in the clouds, a pink elephant could fly by and he still wouldn't think it was weird."

"That makes absolutely no sense."

"Sure it does. No one is saying anything about tonight. We'll all be there. We're all going to watch and see what happens."

"Rasia won't stand for it," Kate reminded him.

"Rasia can be bought. Isn't that right, Ras?" Chance asked her.

"No, that is *not* right," Rasia replied, her eyes narrow with contempt.

"So you agree we should tell someone," Kate translated.

"I'm afraid I cannot."

"What? Why not?" Luke asked.

"It goes against my place in the spirit world. I am not permitted to interfere," Rasia explained.

"Who the hell made that up?" Luke demanded.

"I'm sorry. I want to help you. But it goes against the natural order."

"So does talking to dead people, but you don't seem to have a problem with that!"

"Oh, Luke." Rasia shook her head, addressing him as one might a small child. "I wish that I could make you understand. I cannot interfere in what has been predestined. Whatever is to happen will happen regardless of what I say or do."

"Is that what you say to make yourself feel better? That you can't change what has been ordained by the fates so you might as well not even try?"

"You're so young, Luke Rainer."

"Oh, please. I'm not *that* young!" Luke snapped. "I think the real reason you don't want to say anything is because you're secretly in on whatever Van Dalen has planned tonight and you don't want to screw it up. Maybe you want the publicity, maybe you're being paid. I don't know. But the Rasia Leyland I know would be eager and willing to help out a soul in peril. Especially a fellow psychic."

Rasia held her chin up and looked Luke right in the eye. "I'm sorry I've disappointed you."

"Yeah. So am I," Luke muttered.

Then he turned and stormed out of the tent.

Chapter 24

Luke didn't believe in keeping secrets. He never had.

In high school, he had been voted Mr. Honesty, or as his friends had so graciously put it, Mr. Most-Likely-To-Throw-You-Under-The-Bus. But he'd never thought of honesty as ratting someone out. Truth was the most powerful thing in the world, and he sought it out above all else. Even his obsession with ghosts and the afterlife had stemmed from his quest for discovering the truth. The truth behind the paranormal. The truth behind life and death. The truth behind anything and everything that humans could never hope to explain. It existed. Luke knew it existed.

He believed in smaller truths as well, like the time he'd let it slip to Kate that Mikey could see ghosts. True, at the time, he'd also wanted something out of Mikey. But as far as he was concerned, telling the truth was so much easier and less of a burden than keeping something all to yourself. The less angst, the less drama, the better. An odd mindset for someone who'd built his career searching for dead people, but he stood by it.

That was why this whole weekend had been so frustrating. Well, part of the reason, anyway. He hated being kept in the dark. Everyone, *everyone*, had their secrets. Except McDermott, that is. He was very open about his intentions. It was all about the show for him. Luke could understand ambition. He could even appreciate it. He had plenty of ambition. But Chance McDermott wasn't interested in the noble art of connecting lost souls to their eternal destiny or in learning more about their histories. He was out for himself, plain and simple. Even if he had been a halfway decent human being, he was too hell-bent on getting the footage for their stupid season finale to even consider doing the right thing.

Luke only wished he knew what that was.

"Luke! Hey, wait up."

He turned to see Kate and Mikey running to catch up with him.

"So what now?" Mikey asked.

"I'm going to talk to Van Dalen. Unless you've got a better idea," Luke replied. He was surprised to see Kate frown and furrow her brow. "What?"

"It's just... I don't know if that will do us any good," she answered hesitantly.

"Are you kidding me?" Luke asked. "Back in the tent you were the one arguing that we needed to tell someone."

"I know, and I still think we do. I'm just not sure Van Dalen is the one we need to talk to. We've tried talking to him before and he's just... aloof. I don't know him at all, but I just get the feeling that it won't matter what we say to him. He's got his own agenda and he's going to stick to it no matter what."

"That may be so, but don't you think we should at least give him some sort of heads up? So just in case the psychotic ghost does start tearing through his circus tonight, he won't be caught off guard?" Luke asked.

"He needs to know," Mikey agreed with Luke. Then he turned his head to the right, eyes locked on a person that neither Luke nor Kate could see. "Van Dalen." Luke guessed it was Brink. Otherwise, Mikey probably wouldn't have been going out of his way to talk to him. "Claire. She's... Well, we're not exactly sure what's happening. But we think she's planning some sort of attack under the Big Top tonight."

"God, I wish I was in on both sides of this conversation," Luke muttered to Kate. "Think about it. They could be talking about anything. What if I have something up my nose and Brink is pointing it out?"

"I like to think they're a bit more mature than that," Kate replied with a wry grin.

"Oh, yeah right," Luke teased.

"Really?" Mikey sounded intrigued.

"What really?" Luke asked.

"We might have a lead," he announced. "Cindy Grout."

"Cindy Grout?" Kate wrinkled up her nose. "The condo lady?"

"Ha!" The loud and rather rude laugh was out of Luke's mouth before he could stop it. Kate glared at him. "I'm sorry, Kate. I'm sorry. It's not your fault you're such a tempting seductress."

"Hey, you're the one who burned down her condo. Let's see what she has to say about you," Kate remarked. Now it was Mikey's turn to snicker.

"Hold on, hold on. What makes Cindy Grout a lead?" Luke asked.

"Brink saw her with Van Dalen after the fire. He says that the way he talked to her, it was like he was a totally different person. He'd dropped the whole Ringmaster persona. Maybe she's one of the few people that Van Dalen trusts around here."

"She did call him Alfie," Kate remembered.

"Alright then. Let's go talk to her," Luke announced. "And Kate? If you tell her that I burned the condo down, I'm going to tell her that you spent the night not just with Mikey, but with *both* of us. And *that* actually happened."

Kate narrowed her eyes and placed both her hands on her hips, and once again, Luke couldn't help but laugh.

~*~

They all agreed that they were most likely to find Cindy back at her home-style office, so they left the circus grounds and headed back toward the makeshift neighborhood. Brink wanted to accompany them (probably because he'd gotten just as big a kick out of Cindy Grout as Luke had), but Michael asked him to go observe Van Dalen.

"And keep an eye out for Rasia and McDermott while you're at it," he added.

"Right. Because since I'm dead, I'm capable of existing in three places at once," Brink remarked. "It's not fair. Why can't I fly and control people's minds and stuff?"

"Have you ever tried?" Michael asked, sorely regretting his decision to tell Brink about his encounter with Claire and everything that she was capable of.

"No."

"That's probably why."

"But maybe I could learn! I could be like a super hero..." Brink gazed off into the distance, as though his entire life's (or death's) calling as the next member of the Justice League was playing out before him on a jumbotron.

"Just go find Van Dalen," Michael begged, trying to shake the admittedly disturbing mental image of Brink in tights.

"On it." Brink offered a valiant salute before disappearing.

When they reached Cindy Grout's office, Luke led the way inside. Mrs. Grout was sitting at her desk, knitting, and listening to what sounded like a soap opera on the radio. As soon as she saw them, she was on her feet.

"Oh. Oh, my heavens. May I just tell you how deeply sorry I am about what happened," she apologized. "I'm so, so grateful that no one was hurt."

"So are we," Luke told her. "We're sorry it happened to you, too."

"Oh Mr. Rainer, I'm just fine. I only work here. But your things, your belongings. Not to mention the emotional trauma you must have endured..." Mrs. Grout almost sounded like she was about to cry.

"Don't worry about all that. We weren't anywhere near when it happened," he assured her. "Like you said, no one was hurt."

"Where have the two of you been staying? Alfie said you'd been taken care of."

184

"Oh, uh, yeah. He helped us find another place," Michael answered. Even to his own ears, the lie sounded flimsy. He cleared his throat, thinking it might make the situation less awkward. It didn't.

"I'm glad to hear it," she smiled, looking pleased and genuinely relieved. "Now, what can I do for you?"

"We were actually hoping... That is, we were wondering..." Michael cleared his throat again. Why were Kate and Luke letting him talk? He didn't know how to talk. Especially when what he had to say was important. "Maybe if we could..."

"Mrs. Grout, do you believe in ghosts?" Luke asked, cutting directly to the chase. See? That was so painless and easy. He should have been the one talking from the get go.

"I'm sorry?" Cindy blinked, looking as though she hadn't heard him correctly.

"Ghosts. Where do you stand? Yes? No? On the fence?"

"Oh, ghosts are very real indeed. But there are ghosts and then there are demons, evil spirits who have never been human. They like to take on the likeness of those we love who have passed on, but it is not really them. You must always be very, very cautious when calling upon spirits of any kind." Mrs. Grout's reply was nothing short of passionate.

"Okay, that's great," Luke said. "But I'm pretty sure we're dealing with a legitimate ghost here. What we need to know now is what connection this ghost might have to Cirque Somniatis."

"I'm not sure I understand."

"Your boy, Alfie, invited a whole mess of mediums and ghost-hunters out to celebrate the grand opening of his circus. That wasn't an accident. It was intentional. Do you have any idea why he might have done that?"

"Mediums? Oh, young man, you shouldn't be associating with those kind of people. The living are not meant to communicate with the dead. That is a very dark calling indeed."

Michael flinched. Her words brought back rather unpleasant memories of Chastity Cannon and a dark field. He

185

hoped that Mrs. Grout wasn't the type to carry out God's will with zip ties and a silver handgun.

"Fine, yeah, we get it, but Alfie seems to believe that he needs one or two around this weekend. Can you tell us anything about him, anything at all, that might explain why he'd want them here?" Luke pressed her for answers.

"Alfie is a very private person, Mr. Rainer. He'd hate to know I was gossiping about him."

"What if I were to tell you that we think he might be in danger? That everyone who attends his show tonight might be in danger?"

"And why would you think that?"

"Call it a hunch."

"Very well, then," Mrs. Grout sighed. "Alfie has not had an easy life. He grew up very poor. Both his parents had to work two jobs just to keep food on the table. To make matters worse, when he was just a boy, the family lost their home and everything they had in a terrible flood. Alfie doesn't talk about it often. In fact, he rarely mentions it at all. I think it had much more of an impact on him than he likes to let on."

"That's so sad," Kate said.

"Yes, but at least his is a story with a happy ending. He did well in school and went on to study business in college. In the meantime, he worked hard and dedicated his life to making this circus, his lifelong dream, a reality. He's helped a lot of people see their dreams come true. He's a good man, Alfie. Highly intelligent with a heart of gold. I hold him and his entire staff in the highest esteem."

Michael had to admit he hadn't been expecting that. From the moment they'd met him, Van Dalen had seemed off-beat, to say the very least. True, he would have had to be clever to build something like Cirque Somniatis on his back like that, but clever people were often sort of out there.

There was one other possibility, however, that they hadn't explored yet.

186

"Is there any chance at all," Michael asked, "that Alfred would plan something? Like for a publicity stunt?"

"A publicity stunt?" Mrs. Grout questioned him.

"You know, would he get some famous people out here or maybe stage some sort of disaster in order to make a few headlines?" Luke translated.

"Are you suggesting that Alfie might *lie* to get a little attention?" Mrs. Grout looked positively scandalized by the mere notion.

"Well, that's putting it very mildly, but yeah. I guess we are," Luke said.

"You clearly have not spent very much time with him. If you had, you would know that Alfred Van Dalen is not capable of such deception. He is a pure, genuine soul and if you think for one minute that he might do anything to compromise his integrity or the integrity of this place, you need to think again."

"Fair enough. We really don't know him all that well," Luke admitted. "But still, he has to have some sort of reason for inviting Rasia Leyland and all the others out here. Have you heard talk about this place being haunted?"

"There are rumors and tall tales everywhere you go, Mr. Rainer."

"So there *have* been reports here."

Mrs. Grout breathed a heavy sigh.

"As I told you, you must always be cautious when dealing with troubled spirits. I'm not going to name any names, but upon learning of the death of a young girl here on these grounds several years ago, a few of the younger performers decided to try and summon her spirit. I am given to understand that it was all for a bit of fun, that none of them believed it would actually work. But nobody was there to warn them that when you open a door, when you call upon a spirit, more often than not, it will answer."

"And this one did," Kate concluded.

"There are those who will still never admit to it. But ever since that night, sightings of a ghostly young woman dressed in white have been reported around the grounds. Performers and

187

vendors alike, even those who had no knowledge of the summoning, claim to have seen her. I don't know if it's someone's idea of a joke or if she's really here. But there were a few workers who were so unnerved by the very idea of her that they resigned. Just like that," Mrs. Grout explained.

"Losing employees. That might be enough of a reason to summon a psychic or two out here. What do you think, Mikey?" Luke asked.

"It's possible," Michael answered. *A little extreme, perhaps, but possible.*

After thanking Mrs. Grout for her time and assuring her one last time that their sleeping arrangements were nothing short of wholesome, Michael, Kate, and Luke left the office and walked back out into the warm, springtime atmosphere.

"What if she's done this before?" Kate asked once the door had closed behind them.

"Who? Cindy Grout?" Luke asked.

"No. Claire. Maybe Michael isn't the first person she's tried to latch onto. He's just the first person who's been able to see her and talk to her."

"If she was making people sick, making them feel uneasy, it would make sense that Van Dalen would want her gone," Luke agreed.

"But it would also make sense that he wouldn't want anyone to know about it. So why would he bring in McDermott to film? Or a world-famous psychic like Rasia to set up a tent?" Michael asked.

"Maybe he brought all of you in, not to stir up publicity, but to keep people safe. You see her, Mikey, you can keep her away from the innocent civilians. You and Rasia were brought in as a precaution. And the *Grave Crusaders*? They might as well have called themselves the Ghostbusters. Van Dalen didn't call them in thinking they were going to investigate. He wanted them to *exterminate*. It all makes sense now!" Luke exclaimed.

Michael had to admit, it was a relief seeing Luke's spirits so elevated. He couldn't quite get used to melodramatic, pessimistic, conspiracy-theory Luke. But in the back of his mind, he couldn't help but think that if that was the case, and he'd been called to protect the crowds of circus-goers, he'd done a pretty lousy job.

In fact, all the innocent families, friends, lovers, and children may have been more at risk than they would have had he never heard of Cirque Somniatis in the first place.

Chapter 25

When Kate was twelve years old, one of her best friends received a Ouija Board for her birthday. Like most girls their age, they would sit around the board for hours, asking it questions about cute boys and school dances. Back then, they hadn't given much thought to the existence of ghosts or potentially darker spirits. They'd just thought they were having a little fun.

Once they got a little older, however, they did try summoning spirits. And it worked, too. She remembered sharing the story briefly at Stanton Hall Manor a few months earlier, but truthfully, she hadn't given it much thought until now. It had been a chilling experience, but not one that had made enough of an impact to really alter her life or her way of thinking when it came to death.

Until now, that is.

If what Mrs. Grout had said was true, and the reason that Claire was there was because a bunch of young circus performers had foolishly summoned her just for the sake of having a little fun... The idea almost made her feel sick.

To most, it probably seemed harmless enough. But as Kate imagined a lonely and confused Claire being called upon out of sheer boredom and curiosity, she found herself remembering her own near death experience. It was terrifying, not knowing where you were or how you got there. Even worse was the realization that no one could see or hear you. It was like being trapped in another dimension, one where you no longer existed. And yet, you were so very aware of it. It was enough to drive anyone to insanity.

Kate couldn't help but wonder if, by summoning Claire, those performers had given her a false sense of hope. If they'd done their research, they may have even said her name. It was probably the first time anyone had ever attempted to contact her in years, possibly decades. And yet, they reacted to her presence like she was an act in a circus show herself. Kate couldn't even begin to imagine how that had made Claire feel, and although she wouldn't have thought it possible after everything she had put them through, Kate felt sorry for her.

They decided to head back to the circus grounds and grab a bite to eat. None of them had eaten since earlier that morning, and as Kate pointed out, they really hadn't taken the time to enjoy any of the horrible-yet-delicious, artery-clogging, deep-fried goodness that was circus food.

"I'm not sure my stomach can handle that," Michael moaned.

"Oh, sure it can. This is child's play compared to what they usually fry up at the Texas State Fair," Kate said.

"I've never been to the State Fair."

"What?!" Kate exclaimed. "I'm dating a man who has never been to the State Fair?" That was appalling.

"Oh, come on, Kate. Mikey has much bigger problems than that," Luke told her. "For example, he doesn't know how to ride a bicycle, he's got the pop culture IQ of George Washington, and he weighs about as much as a baby sparrow."

"You can't grow a beard," Michael remarked.

"That is a low blow, man."

Kate laughed. It was miraculous. She felt like she hadn't laughed in ages. Tossing her hair aside, she took his hand and laced her fingers through Michael's.

"Well, this fall, you and I are going to the State Fair," she said. "We're going to eat corn dogs and we're going to ride the Texas Star Ferris wheel and you're going to win me a cheap stuffed animal and we will be the cutest thing anyone there has ever seen."

"You've got this all planned out, haven't you?" Michael grinned.

"Don't I always?"

Michael didn't respond. Instead, he turned to look at the empty air on his other side. Kate hoped and prayed that it was Brink, not Claire, who had suddenly commanded his attention. Judging by the way Michael was acting, she figured that it must be.

"So, what's the buzz, Brink?" Luke asked, having arrived at the same conclusion.

"He says that he hasn't been able to track down Van Dalen all day but he caught a really freaky contortionist show," Michael replied dryly.

And just like that, Kate had an idea.

"We should ask Brink what he thinks," she said.

"About what?" Luke asked.

"About how he would feel if he was in Claire's situation. How he would react and what he thinks we should do."

"Brink says you're going to need to elaborate a little more," Michael told her.

"We've been going around in circles all weekend. First, trying to figure out what McDermott is up to, then trying to figure out who started the fire. Now we're running around in circles again trying to understand Claire and Van Dalen and how it all fits. Of all of us, Brink is the only one who can really empathize with what Claire's been through, what she's still going through."

"That means we're going to have to start at the beginning. He's only heard bits and pieces of her story," Luke reminded them.

"Well," Michael spoke up after a brief moment of silence. "As Brink says, go right ahead. He's got nothing but time."

~*~

Michael mostly listened as Kate and Luke recounted everything Cindy Grout had told them, speaking only when Brink

192

interrupted with a comment or a question. Once they made it to the end of the story, Brink turned to Michael and asked, "Did you ever tell them about the day that we met?"

That wasn't exactly what Michael had been expecting. What did their first encounter have anything to do with what was going on with Claire?

"No. I guess I didn't," Michael replied. "But is now really the time?"

Truthfully, the day they met hadn't been all that eventful. Michael had noticed Brink around school, but at the time, he was only a freshman and he was too busy trying to figure out where all his classes were and avoid public humiliation to worry all that much about the resident ghost. But as the semester progressed and Michael began to feel a little more comfortable with his schedule and new surroundings, he began to wonder more and more about the tall, rebellious-looking ghost and why he'd decided to haunt a school. So he decided to introduce himself. The rest was history.

"Yes! Yes, it is, bro," Brink insisted. "Don't you remember? I didn't believe you at first when you told me that you could see me. You even looked me straight in the eye and asked me what my name was and I was still convinced it was a prank. Why, you may ask? Because of all the stupid kids who came before you, playing with Ouija boards, calling out to any spirits or ghosts that might be around. I thought you were just one of them. A really freaking good one, mind you. But I was so tired, by that point, of kids pretending to know that I was there that you actually made me a little angry the first time you talked to me."

"That's right." Michael had totally forgotten about that. At the time, however, he'd thought that Brink, a senior, simply had no interest in talking to a mere freshman. Fourteen-year-old logic at its finest.

"If Claire is feeling anything like what I felt after over a decade of absolutely no human contact, she's not going to trust anyone. The fact that she's opening herself up to you... It's a huge risk for her. Emotionally, that is. Physically, you know, she's got nothing to lose," Brink quipped. "And if, like you said, she's been dead since the fifties, that's more than half a century longer than I'd been dead. My guess is that she doesn't really know how to communicate, or how to interpret your interactions. What's that thing with psychiatrists? You know, when their patients think that they're in love with them but they're actually just doing a job?"

"Transference," Michael supplied.

"That's it. Sounds to me like what Claire has going on is a killer case of transference. Metaphorically, that is. I hope she doesn't actually figure out a way to kill you."

"Thanks. Me too."

"So, what does he think?" Kate asked Michael.

"It doesn't matter what he thinks," Luke said. "All I care about is figuring out a way to get her what she wants so that she leaves Mikey the hell alone and we can all go back to our lives."

"That's the issue though," Brink spoke up. "She might not know what she wants. Hell, she probably doesn't even know why she's still here. I barely know why I'm still here. You're all looking for an easy fix, a clear solution to all of her problems and unresolved ghostly issues. What does Luke call it? Unfinished business?" Michael nodded. "But from what you've told me, nothing about her situation seems simple."

"So what do we do?" Michael asked.

"If countless hours of watching daytime soaps and Lifetime movies have taught me anything, it's that sometimes there's nothing you can do. Sometimes people have to fix themselves," Brink replied.

"I get that," Michael told him. Not the part about Brink binge-watching Lifetime movies, but he understood the point that he was trying to make.

"Look, right now, I'd be less worried about getting this girl to the other side and more worried about the date she made with you tonight. If she's already that powerful on her own, imagine the kind of damage she could do thriving off the energy of a tent buzzing with warm bodies," Brink warned.

Michael felt his eyes widen. He hadn't considered that.

"We do need to go talk to Van Dalen," Michael told Kate and Luke. "The sooner, the better."

"Good luck, bro. That guy's like a panther," Brink said.

"What does that even mean?" Michael asked.

"You know. They're hard to catch."

Michael was unaware of that stereotype concerning large black cats, but before he could say anything, he was cut off by the sudden reappearance of Chance McDermott and his crew.

"Hey there, pal. Long time no see," McDermott greeted them.

Brink gaped at the trio with wide eyes and took the opportunity to vanish. Michael wished he could do the same.

"Not now, McDermott," he snapped.

"You know, you are like, the trickiest person to keep tabs on. I mean first you're here, then you're there. And you don't even have Twitter. What's up with that?"

"Do you have a point to make or are you just wasting our time?"

"Nope. No point. Just thought we'd come see what our favorite new friends were up to."

"We're going to talk to Van Dalen," Michael announced and tried to shove his way past McDermott. Unfortunately, due in a momentary lapse in judgment, he forgot that McDermott was stronger and meaner than him. He didn't even flinch.

He did, however, feign a grimace.

"See, I really wish you hadn't said that," Chance said. "And here I was so close to giving you the benefit of the doubt."

"Oh my God, what *now*?" Luke asked, sounding exasperated.

"I don't know any of you very well, and I've got to be honest with you, after this weekend, I'd like to keep it that way. But somehow, I just knew that you weren't going to be able to keep your mouths shut when it came to this whole center ring

195

thing tonight. And I just... well, I can't have that. You understand, right?"

"What did you do, McDermott?" Luke demanded.

"The only thing I could do, Luke. I went to the man first," McDermott answered. "I told him everything. Or should I say, I told him everything that I thought he needed to hear to make sure the three of you don't even set foot inside that tent tonight."

"Like *what*?" Kate asked.

"Oh, let's see. Like the fact that your boyfriend is a complete and total fraud who pretends to speak to ghosts in order to take advantage of the people around him. And that Luke is wild and aggressive with a short temper and that he'd made threats not only against my staff and myself but against his other revered guest, Rasia Leyland. Now you, Kate. It's pretty hard to say anything negative about you, but I somehow managed to work it in that you were a desperate floozy who spent her time soaking up the attention of men she thinks will make her famous and that you had made a few passes at me that made me feel terribly uncomfortable and objectified."

Michael couldn't speak. In that moment, he felt like he could barely breathe. This was what white, blinding anger felt like. It had to be. There was no room inside his mind or his body for any other emotion. It was so strong, so powerful, so all consuming, that his limbs began to shake. He didn't know what was going to happen or what he was going to say, but one thing was certain: somehow, someway, Chance McDermott was going down.

Luke, meanwhile, was having just as difficult a time stringing a sentence together.

"What the... how could... oh, you son of a - "

"Come on, Luke, it's not too bad," McDermott slapped him on the shoulder. "After all, you get what you wanted, right? You get to go home and pretend this place, these people, don't even exist. The only real catch here is that if you're not off the grounds within the next half hour, a couple of nice security guards named Theo and Maurice will be happy to escort you off the premises."

"You can't be serious!" Kate exclaimed.

"Oh, I am. And if you don't believe me, just wait around. I'm sure all my viewers at home would love watching three nitwits making a scene while security drags them out, kicking and screaming."

"I *really* thought you couldn't sink any lower," Kate hissed through gritted teeth.

Chance sniggered in response, smiling down at Kate like a hungry wolf eyeing his prey. Michael tried to shove him away, but again, his efforts proved in vain. McDermott never tore his gaze away from Kate.

"Baby, I've barely even scratched the surface."

Chapter 26

So that was it, then. This was how it ended.

Luke didn't know what he'd been expecting, but it certainly hadn't been anything like this. It was all so... *anticlimactic*. But maybe it was better this way. He, Mikey, and Kate had all had just about as much of Cirque Somniatis and its crazy cast of freak show characters as they could take. They were all tired, cranky, and homesick, not to mention the fact that he was stuck in tacky, convenient store outerwear until he could get home and into his real clothes.

Of course, once he got home, he was going to fall into bed and sleep for about ten hours, so what he was going to wear was rather low on the priority list. But still. It would be nice to not have to live out of a plastic supermarket bag.

He had never been one to concede defeat, but after almost three days of trying to tolerate Chance McDermott, he was just *done*. It was like having his energy drained by a malicious spirit. Though he couldn't recall ever encountering a spirit as vile and loathsome as McDermott.

Did this mean McDermott won? He hoped not. He tried to tell himself that word would spread soon enough about Chance McDermott and his douchebag ways. If there was any sort of justice in the world at all, viewers would end up hating McDermott as much as he did and *Grave Crusaders* would be a one-season flop.

But as far as he could see, there was nothing more to be done. Kate and Mikey seemed to be in the same boat, though Luke sensed that both were reluctant to leave. Mikey especially.

Luke had to hand it to him. Michael Sinclair was not the same person he'd been when they'd first met. Hell, that he'd been less than a year ago. That Michael had been meek, anxious, unwilling to risk anything or get involved, especially when it came to the spirit world. Now, here he was. Having to be forced out of a situation that, only a year ago, he would have given anything to avoid. Luke liked to think he may have had a little something to do with his friend's transformation, but deep down, he knew he hadn't. It wasn't even Kate. Mikey had had to find that courage, that desire to act, all by himself. And he had.

Luke was so proud.

Unfortunately, shortly after their last encounter with McDermott, they had been escorted out of the circus by security and were, in fact, banned from returning. Luke couldn't wrap his head around it. Sure, Van Dalen seemed a little loopy, and apparently he had a hell of a personal history, but Luke had thought he at least had enough common sense to see through Chance McDermott and his boldface lies.

"There's got to be a way back in," Mikey muttered, pacing around the room while Kate packed up her luggage.

"You know, maybe this is a sign," Kate sighed, tossing her nightshirt and pajama bottoms into her small suitcase.

"A sign of what?" Mikey asked.

"That we're really not supposed to be here. Maybe, in a weird way, McDermott did us a favor."

"No, he didn't. McDermott doesn't do favors. McDermott is evil," Luke reminded her.

"I know he didn't have the best intentions at heart, but we all know this weekend has been a disaster. And who knows? It may have gotten worse."

"I think it *is* going to get worse," Mikey said. "Those people going to see the show tonight... Van Dalen... None of them have any idea..."

199

"You're not making much sense there, brother," Luke told him.

"I think Claire *did* start the fire. I think she's been responsible for everything that's gone wrong. And I think she's going to try something similar tonight. I'm not saying she will but *if* she does and someone gets hurt, or God forbid, loses their life? How do we live with ourselves after that? Knowing that there was something we could have done, something we *should* have done to prevent it?" Michael asked. "This isn't just about me and Claire anymore. This is about all those innocent people out there who have no idea what they're walking into tonight."

Luke understood what Mikey was saying, and he had to admit, he agreed with him and admired him for it. Kate, on the other hand, had an undecided look about her. It was a look that Luke normally saw when someone was debating whether or not to voice an unpopular opinion.

"What are you thinking, Kate?" Luke asked.

"I don't know," she replied, crossing her arms over her chest. "I know that you want to do the right thing. And I love you for that. But I've got to be honest. I was almost relieved when McDermott said that we were getting kicked out."

"What? That doesn't make any sense. You were so angry at him," Michael reminded her.

"Yeah, for being an asshole and going behind our backs. But if this gets you out of a potentially dangerous situation... if it gives us an excuse to get home safely, and to get on with our lives... I know how selfish this sounds, but Michael, I can't lose you. And Claire wants you. I know she does. I know what she said to you. And I'm just so terrified that if you set foot in that tent tonight, then she's going to take you away from me..." And at that point, Kate broke down sobbing. Mikey rushed to her, taking her up in his arms.

"Shh, Kate. I'm sorry, I'm sorry," he whispered to her over and over again. "Nothing is going to happen to me. I promise."

"How can you promise that after what she's already done to you? After what she's put you through?" Kate asked.

200

"I... I guess I can't," Mikey conceded, stroking her hair as she continued to cry into his shoulder. "What do you want me to do? Tell me what to do and I'll do it."

"I can't," she whimpered. "I wish I could tell you to just come home with me and forget any of this ever happened. But I know how you'd feel. I know you think you're supposed to be here. And as much as I want to tell you I think you're wrong, I know you're not. I'm just so scared..."

"I know, I know," Mikey told her.

"You know Kate, if it makes you feel better, we're probably never going to find a way back inside. I mean, with this handsome face? I just stand out in the crowd. I can't help it," Luke grinned, hoping to make her feel at least a little better. Sure enough, both she and Mikey managed to crack a smile.

It wasn't a guarantee that everything was going to be okay, but at least it was something.

~*~

Once Kate had dried her tears, she stepped into the bathroom to rinse off her face and blow her nose, leaving Michael alone with Luke.

"What do you think we should do?" Michael asked him. He couldn't believe he was actually asking Luke for advice, but more often than not, he was the one getting them out of sticky situations. Granted, he also happened to be the one that usually got them there in the first place, but that wasn't the case this time.

"That's up to you, man," Luke responded. "I'm with you either way."

"I guess there really is no way in," Michael spoke his thoughts aloud.

"I know I've been telling you otherwise the entire time I've known you, but you're not responsible for every spirit still wandering this earth. You're not going to be able to help every one that you encounter. That's just life. Ironic, I know. But ghosts are always going to exist. And they're always going to want something. They were around long before you were born and they're going to be around long after you become one yourself," Luke said, placing a hand on Michael's shoulder. "This has been a hell of a weekend, and you've done the best you could in a bizarre situation."

"Thanks, Luke."

"Any time."

Michael was beginning to think that maybe Kate was right. Maybe it was time for them to bow out gracefully and head home.

But even as he thought it, he could feel eyes watching him, the hairs on the back of his neck began to stand on end. Fearing the worst, he turned, expecting to see Claire's gray eyes staring back at him. Instead, he found himself looking down into the innocent face of the young boy who'd been haunting the grounds ever since they first arrived.

As always, the boy looked up at him with a mixture of curiosity and terror. Michael knew that with any sudden movement or outburst, the boy would disappear again. He had to be there for a reason. If only Michael could get him to open up.

"Hi," Michael greeted him. "It's okay. Don't be scared."

"Are you talking to me?" Luke asked.

"We have a visitor. A new visitor," Michael explained, hoping Luke would take the hint.

"Oh. Okay. Right. Uh, why don't I go check on Kate and leave you to talk to... your friend," Luke offered.

Once he was gone, Michael knelt down onto one knee so that he was eye-level with the boy.

"Hello," he greeted the boy once again. "I'm Michael. Can you tell me your name?"

"Henry," the little boy answered, his voice small and timid.

"Henry. It's nice to meet you."

"Nice to meet you too," Henry said, staring down at his bare feet. "How come you can see me?"

"I uh... I really don't know. It's just part of who I am, I guess," Michael said. "Can I ask you a question, Henry?"

"Okay."

"What are you doing here?"

Henry thought about it for a moment before replying, "I really like the circus."

"Oh." Not exactly what Michael had meant. Then again, Henry was so young. There was a good chance he still didn't fully understand what had happened to him. "What do you like best about it?"

"The flying humans," Henry answered, his face lighting up. Michael supposed he was referring to the trapeze artists. "When I grow up, I want to be like them."

The sentiment broke Michael's heart. How do you explain to a child that they'll never grow up? That their life had ended before it really even began?

"That's neat," Michael said, hoping that his voice wouldn't betray him. "I like them too."

"Do you work at the circus?" Henry asked.

"No. I uh... I'm just here visiting."

That didn't seem to be what little Henry wanted to hear. His delighted expression faded to one of concern, sadness.

"Oh."

"Is everything okay?" Michael asked him. Henry shook his head. "What's the matter?"

"I think I'm in trouble."

"And why is that?" Henry didn't respond. Michael pressed on. "Henry, why are you in trouble?"

The boy stood stalk still, once again staring down at his feet. Then, speaking so softly that Michael could barely hear him, he whispered, "Because of the fire."

"What?" Surely Michael had misunderstood. The fire? What fire? Not the same one that had claimed Luke's condo. There was no way that little boy had started that. He was so... small.

"I'm sorry," Henry whimpered.

"No, no Henry, it's okay," Michael assured him. He tried to remain calm, but his mind was racing. Before he could sort his thoughts, however, Luke and Kate peeked out from the bathroom.

"Is everything okay?" Kate asked.

"Yeah. Um, Henry? Is it okay if my friends come out and meet you? I think you'll like them. They're really nice." The little boy simply nodded. "It's okay. You can come out," he called to his friends. He hoped they would understand what he was trying to do when he said, "Kate, Luke, this is my new friend, Henry. Henry, this is Kate and Luke."

Like a natural, Kate smiled and said, "Hello, Henry. It's nice to meet you."

Little Henry smiled up at Kate. "She's pretty," he told Michael.

"Yeah. I think so too," Michael grinned. Then he told Kate, "He thinks you're pretty."

"Aw. Thank you," Kate blushed. "How old are you, Henry?"

"Six and a half," Henry responded.

"He's six and a half," Michael translated. "Hey Henry, would it be okay if I had a grown up conversation with my friends? It will only take a few seconds." Henry nodded. "We're just going to step outside, but we'll be right back. Don't go anywhere, okay?"

Intrigued, Kate and Luke followed Michael out onto the front porch.

"What's going on?" Luke asked.

"Henry's the one who started that fire."

"What?! No way. The kid is lying to you," Luke said.

"I know. I thought so too. But he's scared to death. You know, figuratively speaking," Michael insisted. "I know it's farfetched, but if he's telling the truth - "

"It means that Claire *didn't* start the fire," Kate completed his thought.

"Which means maybe she's not as dangerous as we originally thought," Luke concluded. "So those people tonight, they should be fine, right?"

"I still don't know about that," Michael said. "I think she's still capable of some pretty monumental stuff. But maybe trying to stop her won't be as perilous an undertaking." He glanced over at Kate. "What are you thinking?"

She sighed. "Well, I do feel better know that she's not a rampaging arsonist. But what about Henry? Why did he start the fire?"

"I think it was an accident. I'd seen him before, the first night we arrived. He might not have any idea what he's capable of," Michael explained. "However..."

"What?" Kate asked.

"He's been running around the circus since we arrived. He says that he loves it here. I bet you anything he can sneak us in."

"Mikey. The kid hasn't even grown his twelve-year-old molars yet," Luke reminded him.

"I know, I know. But I bet you anything he knows the grounds."

Kate shrugged. "It's worth a shot," she said.

Michael looked at her. He knew that she was still hesitant about him running back to stop the same girl who had tried to force death on him, but he also knew she was going to support him, no matter what.

"Alright, then," Luke agreed. "Let's get this show on the road."

Chapter 27

It turned out that little Henry did know the circus grounds, or at least he claimed to. That was good enough for Michael. Still, he knew they had to be cautious, so they decided to wait until the sun began to set to venture back out.

Then, just as they were preparing to walk out the door, Brink appeared.

"Dude!" he exclaimed. "What the hell is going on? Where have you been? I finally tracked down Van Dalen, but when I went back to find y'all, you were gone."

"Sorry, Brink. It's a long story. We - "

"Then I thought that maybe you'd gone ahead and found him yourselves, so I went back to Van Dalen to see if you were with him, and you weren't there but Rasia was. And that's when Van Dalen said something about you being booted out of the circus for being an impostor? I mean, how does that even work?"

"Brink, I - "

"So then, I decided to eavesdrop a bit further, and it turns out that Rasia is totally in on it! She kept going on and on about how McDermott was right about you and how she'd felt since the moment she met you that you didn't actually possess 'The Gift' or whatever, but she hadn't thought it her place to speak out against you. I mean, what kind of crap is that?"

"Brink, will you let me - "

"So then, of course, I tried to set the record straight. You know, she's supposed to be this world famous psychic medium or whatnot. But she didn't hear a word I said. I don't think she even knew I was there. Some medium. Then Van Dalen started talking about what a shame it was that you turned out to be such a fraud since he really thought you seemed like a decent guy and that he really thought you'd enjoy the performance tonight and - "

"Wait, what?" Michael asked.

"You know, that grand opening weekend, last performance, whatever thing he has going on tonight."

"No. Not that. Rasia. You don't think she could see you?" Michael asked.

"*What*?!" Kate and Luke both gasped.

"No. I mean, maybe she has to be 'in the zone' or something, but she definitely can't see or hear me the way you can," Brink replied.

Michael turned, stunned, to Kate and Luke.

"Is that possible?" He asked them. "Guys, do you think it's possible that... That Rasia - "

"Is a big, fat fake?" Luke asked.

"But what about everything she said? The thing about the ghosts and Luke's fear and you being in grave danger?" Kate asked.

"Anyone can make vague predictions and watch them come true. It's called self-fulfilling prophecy," Luke told her.

"What about her books? Her guest appearances where she does all those readings for people?" Kate asked.

"Trust me, all those so-called psychics have their ways. She's either very good at people reading, or she's got a bug somewhere in the audience. I once heard a story about this psychic who had a guy who went out and interviewed people before the beginning of those shows. He was hooked up to a tiny microphone and therefore was able to communicate all their personal information, including details about their deceased loved ones, straight to the psychic's ear."

"Yeah, that's probably why she wanted you out of here so bad," Brink remarked.

"What do you mean?" Michael asked him.

"If Luke is right and this lady is a phony, the last thing she's going to want is having you around, exposing her for what she is. You were never in any danger. She probably just made that up to get you to leave."

And suddenly, everything became clear. What Brink said made absolute sense. If Rasia thought, even for a moment, that Michael might discover that Rasia wasn't who she'd claimed to be all those years, she would want to do everything in her power to get him to leave.

"It was all a lie," Michael said.

"You mean... ?" Kate trailed off.

"The prophecies. Her talks with Claire. The supposed danger. She just made all of it up to get us out of here." He suddenly remembered what Claire had said to him. *"She doesn't see me the way you do."* Did that mean that Rasia had just been speaking to empty air in the hopes that Claire might hear her? And what? Paint her as a credible psychic?

Kate, however, didn't seem altogether convinced.

"But what about Luke's greatest fear?" Kate asked.

"She could have known McDermott was around," Luke remarked dryly. "That'd be enough to scare anybody."

"And what about me? My unresolved ghostly love?" Kate pressed.

"If she had access to Google, she had access to your personal life. Remember last year when all those articles were written about Mikey and what happened with Chastity Cannon and the field? You know at least one or two must have mentioned you. And Trevor," Luke explained.

"Okay, that explains why she wants us gone. It doesn't explain why she wouldn't want to tell Van Dalen about a potential attack," Kate argued.

"Unless she thinks she can stop it," Luke said.

"What does that mean?" Kate asked.

"Hear me out. For once, Rasia has something that she's never had before, and that is an actual medium talking to ghosts for her and telling her what they're planning. If something happens tonight, and she stops it, or takes credit for predicting it in some way, she legitimizes her claim as psychic extraordinaire."

"But hasn't she already done that? Why would she need to take credit for this?" Kate wondered.

"McDermott," Michael spoke up. He wasn't sure how, but he knew it was true. "They probably made some kind of deal. He gets it on film, she takes the credit."

"So all that fussing back and forth at each other was probably an act too," Luke said. "Seriously, that sanctimonious speech she gave about being on TV? Did anyone actually believe that?"

"I kinda did," Michael admitted. Although Rasia was a bit outlandish and had a propensity for scaring the daylights out of people, he'd kind of reached the conclusion that she was okay. She really seemed to believe that she was doing some good in the world, making a difference. He couldn't fault her for that.

Unless that had all been an act as well.

"That's because you're innocent and trusting," Luke sighed, making Michael sound like a lost cause.

"Regardless, we really need to get going if we're going to infiltrate the circus by sundown," Kate advised.

Michael agreed with her. Their six-year-old guide was getting antsy. Clearly, Henry had no interest in corrupt psychics or the reality television personalities who enabled them.

"You're right," Michael said. "Let's get going."

~*~

They followed Henry through the woods, all the way around the perimeter of the circus grounds, bypassing all entrances and dodging the one security guard making a routine patrol. It was another gorgeous evening. Kate wished that she was spending it atop the Ferris wheel with Michael, gazing out at the tree tops, watching the sky changing colors. She kept telling herself that once all this was over, those were exactly the kind of moments she had to look forward to with him. They were also, she realized, the moments that she so often took for granted.

No more, she told herself. From now on, she was going to appreciate every day for what it was. Especially if those days were nice and normal and mundane. One where her biggest concern was another failed attempt at learning to make oatmeal, or having to run to the grocery store because they were out of toilet paper. What she wouldn't give for one of those days.

"Henry says we're getting close," Michael informed them in a hushed voice.

Kate figured as much. She could hear the chatter and laughter of patrons, exhausted from a full and exciting day at the circus, yet eagerly anticipating the closing show inside the center ring.

They finally made it to the backside of the Big Top, where a much smaller tent and three trailers sat pitched and parked behind the main tent. One must belong to Van Dalen. Kate couldn't help but wonder what someone might find if they were to go searching through his belongings. It was a strange thought, but it crossed her mind nevertheless.

Of course, their mission tonight had little to do with Van Dalen and everything to do with the very ghost he may have been hoping to banish from the grounds. If Claire did, in fact, show up tonight, there was no telling what she might do or how she might be stopped. They were quite literally winging it.

Fortunately, they all had a bit of experience in that department.

"Okay," Michael whispered when they'd made it to the edge of the woods. They were crouched behind a couple of trees, mere meters away from the closest trailer. "I think I should go on alone."

"What?" Kate asked.

"No way!" Luke exclaimed. "Make that no way in hell. We're coming with you."

"Yeah, I get that you think you should, but if we're going to sneak into the backstage area of a very large tent with dozens of performers, then I think the fewer of us sneaking in, the less likely we are to get caught."

"Or if all three of us go and we do get caught, then we split up and make it more difficult to catch us. Kate and I would be your diversion."

"That's great, but I don't want to put either of you in any sort of danger, spiritual or otherwise," Michael said, looking Kate directly in the eye. "If we get caught and Van Dalen isn't willing to listen, he could have us arrested for trespassing."

"Then I guess we'll go home with a heck of a story, won't we?" Kate asked. "We're going with you. And I know it's silly to think that I can protect you from her. She's made that abundantly clear. But I still feel like if I'm there, as long as I can see you, then nothing bad will happen. I know it makes absolutely no sense. But I'm not letting you walk in there alone."

"Neither am I. But you know, minus all that mushy stuff," Luke said.

"Thanks guys," Michael said. He sounded like he meant it. "Alright. Let's go."

As stealthily as possible, the three crept through the shadows of falling night and hid behind the closest trailer. They watched as performers and acrobats dressed in an array of costumes flitted back and forth inside the small tent, preparing for the show.

Looking around at the trinkets and props stashed around the backstage area, Kate almost felt like she was on the set of a Vaudeville movie. In fact, watching the performers in their dazzling attire, witnessing the behind-the-scenes magic in action, she forgot for a split second why they were really there.

"Brink. Step inside and let us know when the show starts. When the coast is clear, we'll sneak in and keep an eye on things from the sidelines," Michael instructed.

"Wouldn't it be great if this was all for nothing? And we just got to see a great show, and - hey, some of these show girls are awfully cute..." Luke remarked as his eyes wandered after a couple of blondes dressed in sequined leotards.

"Luke. Focus," Kate hissed.

"Right. Sorry. But you know, maybe this will be a good night after all. If I can help out in any way and be seen as a hero, that would really impress that pretty brunette over there - "

"*Luke!*" Michael and Kate both snapped simultaneously.

"Again, sorry. Waiting for Brink's cue. That's what we're doing."

Kate rolled her eyes, but grinned nevertheless. She had to admit, she was thankful for Luke and his quirky ability to keep the mood light, even in the face of ghosts and grief and death. He really was a breath of fresh air.

Just then, the backstage area went dark and a chorus of cheers and applause erupted from somewhere off in the distance. Kate caught herself holding her breath.

It wouldn't be long now.

Chapter 28

Once Brink returned and informed Michael that the show had begun, he led them into the smaller tent, through the dressing corridor, alight with the faint glow of a dozen old-fashioned vanity mirrors, and into the backstage area, where a dozen show girls were waiting to go on.

Michael, Kate, and Luke ducked back behind a curtain and waited for the girls to file out into the center ring. While they stood by, they listened to Van Dalen's booming voice echo through the tent and into the night.

"I want to thank all of you for an opening weekend like no other. For sharing this monumental event in my life and in the lives of those who worked alongside me to turn this little Circus of Dreams into a reality. It has been a pleasure to have you here with us. The show that we have planned for you this evening is a once in a lifetime opportunity. It is the only time we will be putting on this particular performance, at least for the foreseeable future. I would ask that you please turn off all cell phones and any other electronic gadgets that might interfere with what we're hoping to accomplish here tonight."

Van Dalen's words struck Michael as odd. They had been to that first show a few days earlier and he hadn't said a word about making sure all electrical gear had been turned off. So what was so special about tonight's show?

"Oh, no..." Luke murmured.

"What is it?" Kate whispered.

"I think... and I might be wrong, but we all know how unlikely that is... but I think this is a casting out."

"A what?" Michael asked.

"You know, like an exorcism. But instead of some spooky séance or Ouija experience, he's turning it into some flashy song and dance routine."

"Who's he casting out? Claire?" Kate asked.

"Exactly, but in order to cast her out, he's going to need to summon her first."

"Wait a minute, where's Henry?" Michael asked, suddenly. *Dumb question.* He realized. Neither Kate nor Luke could see him. But one swift glance toward the open curtain revealed the little boy watching the show in wonder from the sidelines.

"You lost the kid?" Luke asked.

"No, he just wanted a better view," Michael answered.

"Well, you might want to tell him to get back unless he wants to be cast out, too," Luke told him. "That goes for Brink also."

"Can that actually happen? Can you just force a spirit to move on like that?" Kate asked.

"There are those who claim they can," Luke said.

"That sounds so barbaric," Kate shuddered. Michael had to agree.

"Well, the good news is the only person around here who might make such a claim is none other than our paranormal impostor, Rasia Leyland. I doubt any spirits will be cast out under her watch," Luke commented.

He had a point, and Michael had to admit, he was grateful. Kate was right. The whole idea of casting out was brutal and unfair. Death didn't dehumanize these spirits. Centuries of superstitions and rituals and ghost stories had done that, turning innocent souls into monsters in the minds of the living.

"I implore you, keep your eyes, your ears, and especially your minds open." Van Dalen seemed to be wrapping up his introductory speech. "Now... let us begin."

The entire tent descended into complete darkness and the audience began to buzz with anticipation. As his eyes adjusted to the light, or lack thereof, Michael glanced over at the girls, each of whom appeared to be holding something.

Moments later, the tent lit up again, but the glow was dull and the shadows cast upon the curtains danced and flickered. Someone had lit a candle, the only source of light inside the enormous Big Top tent. It was eerie, but oddly hypnotic and soothing.

Then came the music. A haunting and ethereal flute melody drifted through the air. At first, it was the lone instrument, but soon clarinets and what sounded to be a harpsichord began to join in the serenade. If this was a casting out, it was a strangely beautiful one.

It was only then that Michael realized that the object in each of the girls' hands was a candle. In an almost prayer-like ritual, they lit the candles by passing the flames back amongst themselves. Then, after each candle had been lit, they began to slowly file out into the center ring, reminding Michael of a church processional.

As though she had read his mind, Kate commented, "Call me crazy, but this seems more like a memorial service than a casting out."

Once the last show girl was gone, Michael, Kate and Luke crept over to watch the show from a more open angle. Henry barely even noticed their presence.

Brink, on the other hand, glanced over Michael's shoulder and asked, "Any sign of your crazy ghost girlfriend yet?"

"No," Michael whispered.

He was trying his best to keep an eye out for Claire, but the performance inside the center ring was mesmerizing. Van Dalen stood atop a tall platform, like a makeshift stage, dressed in his usual dark attire, while the girls danced around him with the candles. Two trapeze artists, dressed in glittering silver sequins, leapt and tumbled through the air, the light from the candles reflecting off their sparkling outfits like thousands of tiny, glimmering diamonds. Other acrobats appeared, balancing on balls and juggling silver rings. Still, it wasn't your typical high-energy, colorful circus scene. Like Kate observed, it seemed more like a funeral.

When the opening act ended, Van Dalen raised his hands in the air.

"We dedicate this night to those we cannot see, to those who've vanished into death's dark shadow. We do believe in that which we cannot explain, in the most ancient of mysteries, and in the realm that lies beyond. Tonight is our way of reaching out and honoring those who did not live to see their dreams fulfilled. We hope that if you're here with us, whoever you may be, you make your presence known. We invite you in. Please, accept."

"Does he not realize how dangerous his phrasing is?" Luke asked. "With all the candles, the weird voodoo atmosphere, not to mention all the energy... This guy is literally asking for it!"

"For what?" Kate wondered.

"For whatever dark, creepy, or demented spirit that happens to be out there to come make themselves at home," Luke answered.

Michael glanced over at Brink.

"Does this kind of thing really work on ghosts?"

"I guess it all depends," Brink shrugged.

"On what?"

"How deluded they are."

Before Michael could ask whether "they" meant the ghosts or the people summoning them, a flash of white caught his eye.

Claire had appeared at the edge of the ring, gazing in awe at the dancers, acrobats, and jugglers. Then, she caught sight of Van Dalen and, with a hopeful look, flew up to the stage with him. Michael knew what she was thinking. That Van Dalen had arranged all this for her. That he was her new hope.

That he could see her, too.

Michael knew how it would all play out before Claire even realized that Alfred Van Dalen was yet another disappointment. Claire would try to speak to him, to get his attention. After all, he had called upon her. He was inviting her in. But he would ignore her, just like all the others.

And that's just what happened.

Although he couldn't hear her voice above the roar of applause and the beginnings of a new act full of new music, Michael could see that Claire was distressed. Her smile had vanished as she yelled and screamed, trying to get Van Dalen's attention. But it was no use.

Desperate, frustrated, and ultimately betrayed, Claire turned to look out at the audience. Michael watched as her hands balled into fists, her beautiful face contorted into an odd mixture of rage and sadness. Then, she closed her eyes.

Michael felt the effects almost immediately. It began as a sensation of mild vertigo and developed into a sickening feeling of being overly medicated. Michael couldn't think straight. His head felt heavy and muddled. He was beginning to worry that he might fall over when all of a sudden, Kate clasped a hand to her head and dropped down to her knees.

"No... Kate..." Michael tried to call out to her, but he could only muster a whisper.

Not her, he pleaded silently.

Only Luke seemed unaffected by it all.

"What's going on?" he asked, kneeling down next to Kate.

"It's beginning," Michael grimaced. "Don't open yourself up, okay?"

He glanced back out to see if anyone else was displaying similar symptoms. A few of the show girls looked paler, weaker, but they were doing their best to keep up with their fellow dancers. The low lighting in the audience, however, made it impossible to make out faces of the hundreds of men, women, and children seated there. But if Michael had to guess, he would be willing to bet that at least half of them were feeling exactly the same spiritual force draining them of their energy.

Then, just like that, it stopped. Michael still felt woozy, weak, and disoriented, but the attack itself was over.

Until it wasn't.

A burst of white, blinding light began exploded forth from Claire, so intense that Michael had to shield his eyes.

Too bright, too bright. Others had to be seeing this. He couldn't be the only one. How could the others not see that light?

And then, a collective gasp from every single one of the tent's occupants.

"Oh, my God!" Kate exclaimed. "Oh, my God! I saw her! She was there!"

"What?" Michael asked her.

"Claire! She was there on the platform, next to Van Dalen. I only saw her for a moment... But oh, my God! It worked!"

Michael looked back toward the platform. Claire was still there, but the light surrounding her had faded. She stared out into the audience, a determined gleam in her narrowed, gray eyes. She knew she had their attention, and she wasn't about to let it go.

It was only then that she turned toward Van Dalen himself. He too had seen her in that brief moment, but it was apparent that she was once again invisible to him. With one fierce look, Claire extinguished the candle that he was holding. Again, the audience gasped. Van Dalen, on the other hand, seemed apprehensive. This wasn't at all what he'd been expecting, Michael realized.

Just then, the makeshift stage began to tremble beneath Van Dalen's feet. He looked down, terrified. The performers around him stopped what they were doing and began to back away. This definitely wasn't part of the act.

Claire meanwhile, kept her gaze fixed and focused on Van Dalen.

Michael had to do something. Someone was going to get hurt.

Without thinking, he bolted out from behind the backstage curtain and into the dizzying, open space of the center ring.

"Claire! Stop!" he yelled out.

He knew she heard him, but it was too late. With a loud, ugly *creeeeeak*, the pillars supporting the platform gave way, and the stage and Van Dalen tumbled to the ground in an explosion of dust and splinters.

In the back of his mind, Michael heard the audience screaming, but he tried to tune them out. Instead, he raced toward the mess of shattered wood and rubble that covered Alfred Van Dalen.

He found the Ringmaster lying in the heap of what had been his platform, blood oozing from fresh cuts on his face, his right arm bent at a sickening angle.

"Are you okay? Can you hear me?" Michael asked.

Van Dalen groaned, but before he could offer a real answer, Michael was struck by a crippling headache, so severe that he saw stars and heard a high-pitched ringing in his ears.

"This is *your* fault!" Claire hissed. "Why couldn't you stay with me? Why did you leave me?"

"I didn't leave you, Claire," Michael insisted. "I just... couldn't stay."

"Why not?"

"Because I want to live. I want to stay alive."

"I wanted to stay alive, too!" Claire cried.

"I know. I know you did," Michael said, trying his best to empathize and to calm her down. "What happened to you isn't fair. I know that. But taking your frustration out on innocent people isn't fair either."

Claire didn't appreciate the lecture. Michael's headache intensified and he found himself balancing on the edge of consciousness.

Stop it. Focus. Focus...

But try as he might, Michael knew that he was losing.

It was only after he heard a new voice calling out to Claire that the pain finally began to subside.

"Claire! Claire, stop!" Luke yelled. Michael glanced up to see his friend barreling out into the ring. Claire looked over to him as well. When he was close enough, he stopped and held his hands up. "Claire, my name is Luke Rainer. I have a proposition for you...."

With Claire momentarily distracted, Michael took the opportunity to catch his breath and to crawl back over to Van Dalen. His eyes were open, but his breathing was rough and labored.

"Alfred? Can you hear me?" Michael asked him again.

Suddenly, an older woman from the audience appeared and dropped down onto her knees next to them.

"I'm a doctor. You're going to be just fine. Help is on the way," she assured Van Dalen.

"Why is he breathing like that?" Michael asked.

"I don't know for sure, but after a fall like that, I'm guessing he has several broken ribs, maybe even a punctured lung," she answered.

Oh God. That sounded horrible. Much worse than anything Michael had ever endured at the mercy of a spirit.

Glancing back around, he saw that Luke was still talking to Claire. She looked oddly calm, intrigued even.

"Hey Mikey. Come over here," Luke called out to him. Hesitant yet wildly curious, Michael stood and walked over to Luke and Claire. "As I was telling Claire, since all of the equipment I brought was destroyed in the fire, I really can't hear what she has to say, so I was wondering if you might translate for us."

"Um... sure..." Michael responded.

"So, Claire. What do you think?" Luke asked.

"Yes," Claire answered.

"She says yes," Michael told Luke.

"Perfect. I was hoping you'd say that," Luke grinned. "You're going to make a great addition to the team."

The team? What team? Surely not the *Cemetery Tours* crew...

But just as Michael was about to ask, the now-familiar sound of sirens rang through the air and a team of paramedics came rushing into the tent. The doctor waved them down to the floor where Alfred Van Dalen still lay on the pile of wood and splinters.

Meanwhile, Claire looked back at Luke, an adoring smile on her beautiful face.

"I'll see you soon, Luke Rainer."

And then she was gone.

Chapter 29

"How is it we always end up in a hospital?" Kate wanted to know. It was well past midnight and she, Michael, and Luke were all waiting in the lobby of Choctaw Memorial Hospital for word on Van Dalen's condition. The room was dimly lit and silent and Kate couldn't shake the heavy feeling that they were being watched. "I mean, first it was Gavin and his broken elbow. Then it was you and the gunshot wound."

"Don't forget your stitches, courtesy of Sterling Hall," Luke said.

"Well, I don't actually remember that trip," Kate told him.

"You don't want to," Luke remarked.

"And now we're here," Kate concluded.

"That's the paranormal business for you."

"And you still wonder why I try to avoid it," Michael commented, sipping hospital coffee out of a Styrofoam cup.

"Come on, Mikey. Admit it. You can't stay away. You *ran* out into the center ring in front of hundreds of people to confront Claire," Luke grinned.

"To try to help Van Dalen," Michael corrected him. "And speaking of Claire, just what exactly was it that you got her to agree to back there?"

"Well, we determined that what she really wanted was recognition, for someone to really see and hear her, and to help her come to terms with her death and why she's still here. So I made a deal with her," Luke explained. "I told her that I had the means and equipment to record her voice, maybe even capture her on film. That, if she agreed, my team could not only talk to her and see her, but we would do our best to help her through whatever she's feeling. The only condition was that she had to leave you alone."

"You really think you can handle her?" Kate asked.

Luke cast her a sidelong glance. "Please."

"I'm sorry. I forgot who I was dealing with."

"Besides, unlike Mikey, I rather like the idea of having a ghost girlfriend," Luke teased.

The idea was so absurd, yet so typically Luke, that Kate couldn't help but laugh. As she tried to silence her snickers, the doors to the hospital opened and a most unwelcome figure appeared in the lobby.

"Well, well, well. I thought I might find the three of you here," Chance McDermott smirked down at them.

"Ah. We meet again," Michael deadpanned.

"Funny how that keeps happening, isn't it?" McDermott grinned. "I just thought I'd stop by and see how the whack job is doing. And to tell you, Sinclair... that I'm impressed."

"Excuse me?" Michael asked.

Kate was just as stunned as he was. That was the last thing she'd been expecting to hear from the man who'd gone out of his way to make their lives a living hell for the past three days.

"You heard me." Apparently, McDermott was unwilling to restate his compliment. "I did my best to get rid of you, but you're a lot more resilient than I thought. And that performance in the ring tonight? Outstanding. We got some killer footage. You know, we could use a man like you in the *Grave Crusaders*."

"What?"

"Are you serious?" Michael and Luke asked simultaneously.

"You're damn right I am. Can you imagine the kind of ratings we'd get with a guy like you? Especially after tonight's story goes viral?"

"Thanks, Chance, but no thank you," Michael told him.

"Oh, come on," Chance scoffed. "Don't sit there and tell me you'd prefer toiling away in the daily grind to life as a TV star. I don't believe it for a second."

"Believe it," Luke muttered.

"I know he's been turning *you* down for years, Rainer, but you know, I thought that was because, well, it's *you*."

"Yeah, okay, what is your deal with him?" Kate asked. Chance, Luke, and Michael all looked at her. "I'm sorry, but I've got to know. What did he do to you?"

Chance laughed and crossed his arms over his chest.

"You really want to know?"

"Yes," Kate, Michael, and Luke responded as one.

"Can't believe you haven't figured it out by now." McDermott was clearly enjoying the power play he had going on. "This dim-witted Neanderthal stole my girlfriend."

"I *what*?!" Luke demanded, rising to his feet. "Who? When did this happen?"

"Oh, about five or six years ago. She'd come home just gushing about you, how smart and talented you were and how you were going to change the world with your paranormal insights. And then she left me. For you."

"McDermott, I don't know what you're on, but I have never stolen another man's girlfriend. Not intentionally, anyway," Luke insisted.

"Oh yes you did. In fact, you've still got her."

"Wait a minute... Are you talking about Gail?" Luke asked.

"Gail?" Kate asked. "Gail Marsh? As in the Gail who all but threw herself at Gavin during their excursion to Stanton Hall Manor? *That* Gail?"

"The one and only. Don't tell me she never mentioned me to you. I was the guy she was dating when you offered her a spot on your stupid ghost-hunting team. Or should I say, the guy she dumped when you offered her a spot on your stupid ghost-hunting team."

"Look McDermott, no offense to Gail, she's a great friend, but the way she goes through men, I don't even bother to learn their names anymore. No way am I going to remember a flame that fizzled out before we even really got to know each other," Luke told him. "So that's really want this whole rivalry is about? Gail?"

"Well, no. I guess it started with Gail. Now, I just really kind of hate you and I want to take you down," McDermott admitted. "But not this weekend. I'll let the ratings speak for themselves."

"You do that," Luke told him.

"Well, I guess I'd better be off. The boys and I have an early morning flight, have to be at the airport in about five hours," McDermott shoved his hands into his pockets. "By the way, Sinclair, even if you don't want to be on television, you ought to at least capitalize on your talent somehow. Write a book or something."

"A book?" Michael asked. "I don't think so."

"Why not?"

"I wouldn't even know where to begin. Besides, my stories really aren't that remarkable."

"Hey, Rasia Leyland makes a fortune off hers and she's not even a real psychic," McDermott quipped.

"You knew?" Kate asked.

"Oh jeez, you are just a pretty face, aren't you? Everyone knows. The woman's a joke," McDermott said.

"If you knew she was a fake, then why did you want her on your show?" Michael asked.

"Ratings." McDermott shrugged. "And on that note, I really need to jet. Take care of yourselves. Except you, Rainer."

Once he was gone, Kate asked, "Think that's the last we've seen of him?"

"No," Michael muttered.

"Oh, I really hope you're wrong," Luke told Michael. Then, he yawned and rose up out of his seat. "Okay, I've got to go stretch my legs. Might go try and find a vending machine. Either of you want anything?"

Kate and Michael both declined and Luke disappeared down the hall. Kate, meanwhile, looked at Michael and kissed his cheek and then his lips. He, in turn, took her hand in his, closed his eyes, and rested his head on her shoulder. Kate was beginning to doze herself when a young doctor approached them.

"Are you with Jeremy Byrd?" she asked.

"Who?" Kate wondered.

"Um, no. Sorry," Michael said, wiping the sleep away from his eyes.

"Are you Michael Sinclair?" the doctor asked.

"Yes..."

"Well, he's asking to see you."

Michael and Kate exchanged confused glances. It was possible that word had spread through the hospital that he was there. Maybe Jeremy Byrd was a patient seeking comfort.

"You go," Kate told Michael. "I'll stay here and wait for Luke."

"Okay," Michael agreed.

The young doctor smiled at him.

"Follow me."

~*~

The doctor led Michael back past a nurse's station and down a dimly lit corridor and to a small room. As they walked, she explained Jeremy Byrd's condition.

"He was pretty banged up when they brought him in. Three cracked ribs, a punctured lung, and a severely broken arm. He also has a concussion. All things considered, he's doing remarkably well," she informed him, opening the door to a room at the end of the hallway. "He does need his rest though, so you might not stay too long."

"Thank you," Michael told her.

He stepped inside the room. The young man lying on the bed appeared to be sleeping. His arm was cast and set and his face was covered in superficial cuts and bruises. Without his top hat and circus attire, Michael almost didn't recognize him, but after a moment's observation, there was no doubt: Jeremy Byrd was in fact Alfred Van Dalen.

He opened his eyes when he sensed Michael approaching.

"Hi," Michael greeted him.

"You're still here." Van Dalen offered a weak grin.

"Yeah. Kate and Luke and I... We just wanted to make sure you were okay."

"I appreciate it. Truly. And I also appreciate what you did for me back in the center ring. I don't think I shall ever be able to thank you enough."

Michael wanted to tell him the truth, that it was only because of him that Claire attacked that evening. But Van Dalen - or Jeremy - had already been through so much that night. He wasn't altogether certain that confessing everything would be doing him any favors.

And yet, Michael couldn't help but feel that the young man deserved to know.

"Actually, I kind of knew that Claire would be there tonight..." he began. Soon, it all came tumbling out. Rasia and her false prophecies, Claire and her misplaced infatuation, even McDermott and his grudge against Luke. "I'm sorry. I tried to find you so that I could warn you, but - "

"But Rasia Leyland and Chance McDermott got to me first," Van Dalen concluded. "In that case, I believe I owe *you* an apology, for taking their word and not making the effort to consult with you personally. I guess you could say I was preoccupied, making sure that everything was in place and ready for this evening."

"That's understandable," Michael assured him. "I'm sorry that things didn't go as planned."

Van Dalen breathed a heavy sigh.

"It was a long shot anyway," he murmured, closing his eyes. Michael almost thought he'd fallen asleep when suddenly he asked. "So, how did you get in?"

"What?" Michael asked, wondering if maybe he was slipping into a drug-induced stupor.

"How did you get back inside the circus? I thought my security was pretty top-notch."

"Oh, that. There's another ghost who's been running around. A young boy named Henry."

At that, Van Dalen's eyes opened and he sat up. Or he did his best to sit up, anyway.

"What did you say?" he asked.

"There's a young boy who haunts the grounds. He's six years old. His name is Henry. He says that he really loves the circus.... that he wants to work there when he grows up. He showed us a back way in through the woods." It was only then that Michael noticed the tears trickling down Van Dalen's bruised and battered face, and he thought that maybe he'd said too much. "I'm sorry," he quickly apologized. "Maybe I should go."

"No! No, please," Van Dalen reached out for Michael with his god arm. "Henry... He's the reason I did all of this."

"He is?"

And then, as though he'd been summoned by the sound of his name, Henry appeared in the corner of Van Dalen's hospital room.

"There's a reason I invented a new name for myself, why I didn't tell any of you why I really invited you out here this weekend. I even forged a family history so none of you would know. I wanted to be sure that what you told me was genuine." By now, Van Dalen was laughing through his tears. "Henry is my little brother."

And just like that, everything made sense. It was so easy to tell grieving loved ones exactly what they wanted to hear and then capitalize on it, by means of both notoriety and monetary gain. Van Dalen wanted to know, really know, that his brother was still there with him.

Michael finally looked over at Henry, looking small, timid, and confused in his pajamas and bare feet.

"He's not my brother," the little boy piped up. "Jeremy is ten."

"No, Henry. No he's not. Not anymore," Michael told him. "It's been a long time. Jeremy's grown up now."

"Wait," Van Dalen said. "He's here?"

"Yeah. Standing over by the window."

228

"Henry?" Van Dalen asked.

"Jeremy?" the little boy responded, taking a few apprehensive steps closer to the bed. Then, when he finally realized that he was, in fact, looking at his brother, Henry threw himself down on top of Van Dalen's blankets. "Jeremy, I'm sorry. Please don't be mad at me."

"He's saying that he's sorry. He's worried that you're mad at him," Michael translated.

"Why? Why would I be mad at you?" Van Dalen asked.

"Because of the fire. The fire. It was my fault," Henry wept.

"He um, he thinks that the fire was his fault," Michael said.

Van Dalen closed his eyes and took a deep breath. Then, speaking with a kind of passion Michael had never heard before, he said, "Henry, you listen to me. That fire was not your fault. It was nobody's fault. Don't you think for one minute..." But Van Dalen choked up in the middle of his sentence. "*I'm* the one who's sorry. I tried to get you out. I'm sorry I wasn't strong enough to save you. I'm sorry. I'm so, so sorry." And with that, he broke down sobbing.

Michael suddenly knew that Cindy Grout had been wrong, or at least misinformed, about Alfred Van Dalen and his tragic past. It hadn't been a flood that had destroyed everything that his family had once held dear. It had been a fire. A fire that little Henry believed had been his fault when in fact, no one was to blame. If that were the case, then he would have carried that guilt with him for at least the past twenty years. It would make sense, then, that his spirit would be curiously drawn to fire, as he had been earlier that afternoon in Rasia's tent. It might even make sense that the little boy had no idea how to control or contain his abilities and that fire might be an outlet for fear or stress.

Case in point, the fire at the condo.

Michael then turned his attention back to the brothers, both of whom had a look of peace about them.

"I love you, Jeremy," Henry said. Michael repeated the sentiments.

"I love you too, Henry," Van Dalen whispered. "If you need to leave now, it's okay. I understand. Just... look in on me from time to time. Okay?"

Henry nodded. Then he took one last look at his brother's face, smiled, and disappeared in a shimmering flash of white and gold light.

Chapter 30

In the days that followed their trip to Hugo, Oklahoma and the self-professed Circus of Dreams, Michael found himself feeling uncharacteristically optimistic. About life. About Kate. Even about himself. He couldn't explain or describe it, but something was different.

Luke had gone back to his home in L.A., and he had, in fact, taken Claire with him. Michael wasn't sure how serious Luke had been with that whole ghost girlfriend remark, but honestly, he wouldn't put it past him. After all, Luke had never seemed all that eager to pursue romantic relationships with the living.

Still, he was fairly certain his friend had been joking.

A few days after Luke left, Michael received a letter from an unfamiliar address in Florida.

Dear Mr. Sinclair,

I am so sorry that I did not get to bid you a proper farewell after our weekend together at Cirque Somniatis. I was in attendance that last night and witnessed Mr. Van Dalen's dreadful performance. I wanted to tell you that you behaved quite admirably. I also want you to know that I was not aware of Mr. Van Dalen's intentions. Had I been, I of course would have discouraged him from attempting to perform a summoning, especially for show. As you and I well know, the spirit world is not intended or designed for amateurs and can be very, very dangerous.

I also thought you might like to know that Claire has finally moved on to the next world. After Sunday night's catastrophe, I approached her distraught spirit and I am quite pleased to inform you that her transition was peaceful and she will no longer be wreaking havoc on you or anyone else who hopes to enjoy a weekend at the circus.

My best wishes to you and Kate. I foresee a bright future for you both.

Most Sincerely,
Rasia Leyland

Not really sure what to make of the letter, Michael gave it to Kate to read after work. She settled down on his couch with a glass of wine and tried her best not to laugh, especially when she got to the paragraph about Claire's supposed transition.

"Well, at least she got that last prediction right," she remarked.

"You think?" Michael asked, wrapping his arm around her shoulders and smiling.

"I might not be psychic, but I know a good thing when I see it," she told him. Then she took his face in her hands, leaned in, and kissed him, effectively ending their conversation.

A week later, another letter arrived, this time from Hugo, Oklahoma.

Michael,

I just wanted to thank you once again for everything you did for me and for my family. I told them about the experience the same day I was released from the hospital. I never told you this, but after Henry died, my relationship with my parents became strained. They insisted that they didn't blame me for what had happened. After all, Henry and I were alone the night of the fire and I was supposed to be the responsible party. But I couldn't help but feel that a part of them never forgave me for letting their youngest child die. Perhaps more significantly, I was never able to forgive myself for what happened to my little brother. He was my responsibility. And I failed him.

232

Thanks to you, however, I have reconnected with my parents and made the first steps in rebuilding our family. It won't be an easy road by any means, but I know it's what Henry would want. I wish he could be here with us, but I find comfort in knowing that he does live, just not in his Earthly body.

My little brother lives. How extraordinary a thought that is. I've been yearning to believe it for the past sixteen years, and it's because of you that I finally do. Words will never be able to adequately express my gratitude.

I wish all the best for you, Michael. Please know that the gates of Cirque Somniatis will always be open to you and your lovely Kate.

Best wishes,

Jeremy Byrd

By the time Michael put down the letter, a lump had formed in his throat. He knew what it was like to lose a brother. He knew how much comfort it would bring to his mother to know that Jonathan was still with them and that his spirit was at peace, especially after his long and hard-fought battle with mental illness. He wished he could give her that comfort. He wished that same comfort for himself. But Jonathan's ghost had never contacted him in any way. He had no hope to offer his own family.

He did, however, have it within his power to bring that sense of hope and peace to other families. Even if the ghost in question didn't always believe it to be a good idea.

The next day, Michael told Brink that he had errands to run, but that he could really use some company and was wondering if Brink might like to tag along.

"Sure thing! Where are we headed?" the young ghost wondered.

"Just around town," Michael replied. "I really need to run to the grocery store. And I might stop by the library to pick up a few books. Of course, I haven't been back there since I was let go, so it might be a bit awkward..."

"So in other words, it will be just like every other day of your life," Brink quipped.

"Fair enough."

Michael knew that if he was too chatty or upbeat, Brink would know that something was up and he would hop out of the car or disappear. Instead of engaging in conversations that would give him away, Michael turned up the radio in his car and indulged in some morning NPR.

Thankfully, Brink didn't seem to catch on, even though they drove right past Michael's usual supermarket and two more after that. In fact, he didn't say anything at all until they turned left into a modest neighborhood of two-story houses, flower beds, and several sedans.

"Michael," Brink asked in a tone that Michael had never heard before. "Where are we?"

Michael didn't know how to answer, so he remained silent until he pulled up to a white brick house with blue shutters. He turned off the engine and looked at his friend. But Brink wasn't looking back. His eyes were fixed and locked out the house.

"Are you okay?" Michael asked him. For once, Brink seemed at a loss for words. "You don't have to go with me. I just thought that you should know that I decided to reach out to them. And I hoped that maybe seeing this place, seeing them, might be good for you, too."

Still, Brink said nothing.

Michael took that as a no.

With a deep breath, Michael climbed out of the car, locked it, and made the short trek up the sidewalk to Mr. and Mrs. Brinkley's front door. Heart racing, he rang the doorbell and shoved his hands into his pockets. While he waited for them to answer, he turned and took one last look at Brink, who had left the car, but hadn't found it in him to move more than a few inches up the walkway.

Finally, the door opened, and Michael found himself face to face with a couple much older than he'd been expecting. He quickly realized it was because in all of Brink's stories, they'd been young. Of course they would have aged since Brink had last seen them. It had been more than twenty years.

"Mr. and Mrs. Brinkley?" Michael asked.

"Yes," Brink's mother answered. "Who are you?"

"My name is Michael Sinclair. I, um... " He was never quite certain how to introduce himself to total strangers. *Hi, I'm Michael and I see ghosts. Can I come into your house?*

"Michael Sinclair? I've heard about you," Mr. Brinkley spoke up. He was wearing a red polo shirt and a baseball cap, though Michael didn't recognize the logo. Probably something to do with sports. "You're that kid who talks to dead people."

"Yes, Sir. That's me," Michael confirmed.

"Well, come in! Please! It's not every day that we have a celebrity come knocking on our door."

"Thank you."

Stepping into Brink's childhood home was strange. For as long as Michael had known him, Brink had been a cool, carefree teenager. And a ghost. It was unnerving to see the place where Brink had spent his childhood, his short life; the house in which Brink had been alive.

Brink had once been alive. And now he was dead. Even though Michael could still see and hear him, his best friend was dead. How could that have never fully hit him until now? Perhaps he hadn't wanted to acknowledge what had happened. Or perhaps Brink hadn't wanted him to. Either way, the experience was taking a much more substantial emotional toll than Michael had anticipated.

It wasn't until Michael noticed the pictures of Brink lining a shelf in the living room that he began to fight back the tears. Mrs. Brinkley noticed.

"Are you okay? Would you like some water?" she asked, visibly concerned.

"I'm fine, thank you," Michael replied, wiping his eyes with the back of his arm. "You've got a lovely house."

"Thank you. It's a good home. It holds a lot of good memories," Mr. Brinkley told him.

"I can imagine," Michael said. "In fact... that's why I came here to talk to you today."

"Oh my goodness." Mrs. Brinkley clapped a hand over her mouth and dropped down onto the sofa. "It's Eugene, isn't it? You've found him. I knew he was here. I could feel him."

"Yes," Michael answered her. "Brink - uh, Eugene - is here."

And he was. He still hadn't spoken, but Brink had made it into the house. He stood in the doorway separating the entry hall and the living room, watching his mother while she sobbed.

"I knew it. I knew it," she wept.

"How did he find you?" Mr. Brinkley, who seemed to be in a bit of shock and possibly operating on auto-pilot.

"This might sound crazy, but he's actually been my best friend for years. We're kind of roommates," Michael told them.

"Have you tried contacting us before?" Mrs. Brinkley asked.

"No, actually. And that's all my doing. I went through a pretty long phase of self-denial. I didn't want anything to do with ghosts or grieving loved ones. It was selfish of me, and I'm sorry. I should have tried to find you a long time ago."

"No, no, please don't apologize. You being here today... I just can't tell you what this means to us." Mrs. Brinkley began to cry again. "I knew I would see my boy again. I knew he was still here with me. I knew it."

"Michael?" Brink finally spoke.

"Yeah?" Michael asked, turning to look at him.

"Would you give them a message from me?"

"Of course."

"Would you just tell them that I love them and that I miss them? And tell my mom... I'm sorry I didn't wear my helmet."

"Is he talking to you?" Mrs. Brinkley asked.

"Yeah, he is," Michael answered. "He says he loves you and he misses you. And... and he's sorry that he didn't wear his helmet."

"Oh, baby," Mrs. Brinkley cried. "It's okay. It's okay."

By that point, Mr. Brinkley had sunk down onto the couch, next to his wife. He'd buried his face in his hands and his shoulders were shaking. For a brief moment, Michael worried that this hadn't been a good idea after all, but as soon as Mrs. Brinkley wrapped her arms around his husband and he returned her embrace, he knew he'd made the right decision.

"We just..." Mr. Brinkley finally spoke. "We just have so many questions for you."

"I know," Michael replied. "And I'll do my best to answer all of them. Or Brink will answer and I'll translate."

"Brink," Mr. Brinkley laughed. "That's what he used to call himself. He hated the name Eugene so much."

"Trust me, he still does," Michael informed them.

"Oh, but it's such a lovely name. His grandfather was named Eugene, you know. That's who we named him for," Mrs. Brinkley said.

"Yeah, he told me," Michael grinned.

"He did?" Tears shimmered in the woman's eyes. "What else has he told you?"

"Everything," Michael replied. He recited several of the stories that Brink had told him over the years, like how he'd gotten his first skateboard for his seventh birthday and how he'd run straight out into the pouring rain to learn how to ride it. Then there was the story of the night they'd found their dog, Jacques, who was still running around the house, despite the fact that he'd probably died at least a decade earlier. Then there were Brink's favorite stories: the ones about his brother and sister. The nights they were born, watching them grow up, countless hours spent teaching them to ride bikes and playing with them on the playground. All three of the Brinkley siblings loved being outside.

Finally, Michael told them about the day that their son died, how Brink had been with them that day, and everything he'd seen. Michael didn't know how he made it through that particular story without crying, but somehow, with Brink there with him, he managed to maintain his composure.

The same couldn't be said for Mr. and Mrs. Brinkley. For several moments thereafter, they simply held one another and wept. Since Michael didn't know what to say, he thought it better if perhaps he just didn't say anything. Brink remained silent as well.

Once his tears had subsided, Mr. Brinkley looked up at Michael and simply said, "Thank you. Thank you."

Michael could only nod.

They talked for a short while after. Michael told the Brinkleys about himself, about Kate. He left out all the misadventures concerning ghosts, though he did mention that if the Brinkleys were interested in the paranormal, they might enjoy a little show called *Cemetery Tours*.

After promising to stay in touch and to visit again, Michael bid the Brinkleys farewell. He didn't ask if Brink was coming with him or if he wanted to stay. He didn't know how.

As it turned out, he didn't need to ask. The moment the Brinkleys shut the front door, Brink appeared on the porch next to Michael.

"It was so good to see them again," he spoke softly.

"I'm glad you came," Michael told him.

"So, is this it then?" Brink asked. "Am I ready to move on?"

"I don't know. Do you feel ready?"

"What is it supposed to feel like?"

"I don't know. I've never been there before. But I think it's supposed to be peaceful, natural. I also think that you're supposed to want to move on." Michael explained it as best he could. "I know it's not my place to decide what happens, or to tell you whether to stay or go... but I'm not ready for you to move on."

"I don't think I am either," Brink smiled. "There's too much fun to be had at your expense."

"I'm *so* happy you feel that way," Michael remarked dryly. Still, he couldn't help but return his friend's smile as together, they walked down the sidewalk and back to the car.

"So what happens next?" Brink asked once they were on the road. "Are you going to start working with the local law enforcement to help bring murderers to justice? Open up a ghost counseling center?" He paused, a mischievous glimmer in his eye. "Get married?"

Michael laughed. Those first two sounded a little too farfetched to actually consider, but he supposed that anything was possible. As for the third... That one might not be too far out of reach. At the right time, of course. There was no rush. If Michael had learned anything over the last year it was to appreciate every moment for what it was, and not to pressure or try to hurry things along. It would all happen as it was meant to happen.

"Actually," he finally answered, "I was thinking I might write a book."

Acknowledgements

As always, thank you to my Lord and Savior for this life and for everything that You have given me. Words will never be enough, but they are all that I have.

I'd also like to thank...

My delightfully weird and charming parents, Susan and David, for always being themselves and inspiring and encouraging my sister and me to do the same. You accept us as we are and we accept you as you are. I love y'all. Please never change.

My sister, KJ. You are the Niles to my Frasier. You know this. The world knows this. I love you forever. And yes, the next BOY BAND will be out soon. I promise.

Nancy Lamb, once again, you go above and beyond for me, as you have my entire life. Thank you for your wisdom and grace and for being a second mother to me. I love you and your beautiful talents.

Hannah Alvarez, I miss you so much. I can't thank you enough for being one of the absolute best friends in the world, even though we remain miles apart. Thank you for your snarky comments and constant friendship.

Kathleen Farmer, you are an absolute gem. I am so fortunate, not only to call you my editor, but one of my very best friends. Thank you for correcting my text messages as well as my manuscripts. Girls' night with wine and Mario Kart soon!

Thank you also to all the amazing librarians, book reviewers, volunteers, reading advocates, independent publishers, book store owners, and fellow authors whom I have met and befriended over the past two years. I cannot begin to tell you how greatly you've impacted my life and my career, and I will be eternally grateful for all of you.

Finally, to my beloved readers, thank you. Thank you, thank you, thank you. For taking a chance on a relatively new author, for leaving reviews, for loving my characters as much as I do, thank you. I always hope to give you the kind of books you deserve. Until next time.

© 2014 by Kaylynn Krieg Photography
http://www.kaylynnkrieg.com/

JACQUELINE E. SMITH is the author of the CEMETERY
TOURS series and BOY BAND. She is also featured in the
horror anthology, LURKING IN THE DEEP. A longtime
lover of words, stories, and characters, Jacqueline earned her
Master's Degree in Humanities from the University of Texas
at Dallas in 2012. She lives and writes in Dallas, Texas.

Made in the USA
Charleston, SC
04 February 2016